The Last Perfect Summer

Karla Stover

Print ISBNs
Amazon print 9780228638278
Ingram Spark 9780228638285
Barnes & Noble 9780228638292
BWL Print 9780228638308

BWL Publishing Inc.

Books we love to write ...
Authors around the world.

http://bwlpublishing.ca

Copyright 2026 by Karla Stover
Editorial Supervisor JD Shipton
Editor Nancy M. Bell
Cover artist Michelle Lee

Table of Contents

Chapter 1

Even during the day, walking in parts of Wright Park was difficult. Not all the old growth trees: firs, cedar, and big leaf maples, had been harvested and they towered over the ground blocking sunlight. Under them, moist loam provided natural environment for sword ferns, oak ferns, and wood ferns, some of which local tribal elders occasionally came to harvest and used to treat wounds. The ferns knit deceptive blankets through Oregon Grape and Salal, climbed rotting trunks, and entwined and encased broken limbs and boulders. Where the trees had been cut, their stumps attracted both soft moss and thorny berry vines. In those places, the park still resembled an ancient forest, and the smell of pitch and fir needles and rotting foliage filled the air. Roots protruded through piles of broken tree limbs, twigs, and decaying leaves, and Louise Tanquist took care not to trip. She wanted to be hidden before dawn broke, but the unwieldly bundle of canvas tarp she carried was heavy and Louise had to stop several times to shift it from one arm to another. She realized that dawn wasn't far off when first one rooster and then another began to crow. The sounds seem to usher in a pearly light on the horizon behind Mount Rainier which was partially obscured by an opaque haze, the result of smoke from distant forest fires. When City Hall's clock began to sound the hour, doors in the area opened and slammed as men left for work. With a frantic look around, and just in time, she found the remains of several downed trees and dropped onto the fragrant but damp sawdust. There she hunkered down and covered herself with the tarp.

Through a small hole she watched as legs in a variety of pants, mostly dungarees and Carhartts, and an assortment of boots passed by: footwear belonging to loggers, fishermen, boat builders, dock laborers, railroad employees, and brewery workers. For several minutes their voices rose and fell, sometimes talking seriously, other times laughing: Tacoma's work staff hurrying to the streetcar lines. In the brief quiet that followed Louise shifted around trying to find a soft spot, wishing she was kneeling on moss instead of sawdust. Then the new Central School's bell rang a warning. Having gone to the first Central School, she knew the final bell would ring fifteen minutes later and woe be until the child who was late without a good excuse. She was remembering her own school days when, through the hole, Louise saw groups of boys taking the park path to Eighth Street. Tacoma's fast-growing population, both white and ethnic, meant they wore a variety of clothes: short pants, knickers, hand-me-down overalls with rolled up cuffs, belts, suspenders, button-down shirts or threadbare flannel, and jackets, many known as working-man's style. Some of the boys had on laced-up oxfords, others high-tops or boots. Most wore socks which poked out of the tops but some didn't, exposing an inch or two of bare legs. They ran and shouted, kicked leaves, and punched each other in the arm, but the little girls who followed behind, often walking arm in arm, were much quieter. Louise's mother, Nell Tanquist, was a renowned dressmaker with a *couture* in downtown Tacoma and Louise had learned a lot about styles when helping there. Now she saw how the shortages of fabric, which some blamed on the war in Europe, had changed clothing styles even for little girls. Unlike when Louise was in school, these girls wore loose-waisted dresses or skirts, both of which ended near the knee. Smock dresses with pinafores, skirts with middy blouses, prints and ginghams in bright colors, paired with knee or ankle socks. Watching the schoolgirls Louise thought they were very lucky that their hems were so much shorter than when she had been in school.

"The mills are so busy making cloth for uniforms they don't have time to make fabrics for civilians," Nell had said.

"Does that mean you won't be going to San Francisco this year to look for fabrics?"

"It's not likely."

Louise sighed. Except for the year she'd been adopted, the year Nell had gone into Mexico, had been gone for over four months, and returned with some beautiful embroideries, she generally spent a month shopping for both fabrics and trims in San Francisco. Louise knew she devoting hours at O'Connor, Moffat and Company, The City of Paris, and the Salon de Couture making notes of the newest styles; going to Fownes to look at leather and fur, and ending with trips to The Emporium, the Sing Chong Importing Company, the Sing Fat Company and the Nan Fook Who Company, all in Chinatown, where she placed bulk orders for silk and embroidered Mandarin coats, kimonos, and skirts. "A feast for the eyes and a joy for the body," Nell said when her orders began arriving and she and Louise unpacked the crates. The previous year, she'd promised to take Louise with her the next time she went south, and Louise had two reasons for wanting to go: one was that she hoped to find information about her birth family and the other was that since she was a photographer, she wanted to take pictures of all the different things she'd see there. Now, hunkered under the smelly tarp and thinking about the trip postponed until the war was over, she tried not to moan. *When I'm an old lady I'll likely still be waiting for something interesting, like a trip to California, to happen.* She was getting ready to leave the park when two boys came running, obviously late for school.

"Hurry up, Billy. We're gunna be late," the boy in the lead shouted.

"I can't run faster, Joe. My shoe's come untied," Billy shouted back.

"For crying out loud. Why didn't you tie your shoes before we left the house?"

"Ma practically pushed me out the door before I had time."

The boys stopped and Joe said, "Sit on that log there and fix your shoe and shake a leg or that ole Mrs. Guenther Greene be all over us and we'll be kept in at recess.

Billy hobbled over to what he thought was a log and sat down, only to have someone yell as the log seemed to collapse.

"Gee whiz, now what?" said Joe as Billy disappeared. He ran to investigate and saw his brother and Louise fighting their way out of a large piece of stained canvas.

Louise sat back and laughed at the amazement she saw on their faces. "It's a camouflage log," she said.

"What's that?" Joe asked, adding, "Billie, tie your vazey shoe."

"If it's a vazey shoe it's because it used to be yours," Billie muttered but he sat on the ground and pulled on the laces.

"'Camouflage' is something that hides things in plain sight." Louise said. When it was apparent that the boys hadn't a clue what she meant, Louise added, "Like you thought this was a log but it's just an old piece of canvas I painted to look like a log, and came here to see if it works. It's for the war, for the soldiers, so they can hide and creep up on the enemy. I didn't want to paint anymore if it didn't work but since it fooled you, I guess it does." As she finished speaking, they all heard the final school bell.

"Well, dash it, now we've had it," said Joe."

Louise felt in her pocket for a piece of paper and the nub of a pencil and wrote The Women's Reserve Camouflage Corp. "Here," she handed the paper to Joe. "Show this to your teacher and tell her the Corp was experimenting on hiding in plain sight in the park and you stayed to learn about the war effort so you could write a paper on it."

Joe grinned and pocketed the paper. "Thanks, lady. Come on, Billie."

They took off running and satisfied that her painted tarp worked, Louise folded the canvas up and hurried out of the park intending to cut across Tacoma Avenue and over to 9th Street. Unfortunately, most of the vacant lots that used to be there and that she hoped to cut through had recently been built on and a group of firemen had Tacoma Avenue blocked.

"Here, Miss," one of them shouted. "Mind the hose."

"Golly." Louise stopped and tried to shift the tarp into a more comfortable bundle. She looked up and gave a start. "What happened?"

"Geeze, lady, can't you smell?" someone in the crowd of onlookers shouted and those around him laughed.

"Here now, you," one of the firemen rounded on him. "We'll have none of that. Mind your manners." He turned back to Louise. "Garbage hauler lost control of his team of horses, and the mayor detailed us with cleaning up the mess."

"Goodness." Louise watched as two men wielding a hose maneuvered the scattered trash into a watery pile, while off to the side, another tried to calm the fidgeting team of horses, one of which emptied its bowels on the street, adding to the smell. The assorted odors had begun to attract crows and gulls which circled overhead, filling the air with screams as they competed over food scraps. Louise wondered how they knew about the accident. She had no idea if birds had noses like the dogs that had appeared from various yards and the feral cats that seemed to come from nowhere. Mice and rats came and went, too, and the air was a cacophony of noise. Turning a beaming smile on one of the firemen Louise said, "This would have made a wonderful picture for the paper." Then, looking at the small, time piece pinned to her bodice she said, "Oh, dear, I must dash. Goodbye, sir."

Trying not to run, she saw that traffic on 9th Street was picking up but that horse drawn wagons and buggies no longer predominated. Automobiles had taken over. They weren't the most practical mode of transportation, however. Downtown Tacoma sat in a bowl and the gravity-fed engines meant people had to back up the hills to get out of town. Nevertheless, Louise was already saving to buy her own automobile.

As she burst through the kitchen door and dropped the tarp, she let behind a frisky breeze that was whipping up small eddies in the dirt, attracting small birds that pecked hopefully.

"There's no time for coffee," said Annie, a long-time friend who made up the house's trio of women. "I've ironed your black skirt and white shirtwaist. They're in the parlor."

"You're a dream, Annie. Thank you." Louise hurried to change, leaving the door open so she and Annie could talk. "First I got caught up with some schoolboys and then there was a garbage spill blocking things."

"What are you photographing today?" Annie asked.

"The Pure Food Show is having a series of contests," Louise said. "Today it's pie-eating and babies."

Annie laughed and shut the icebox door. "There's variety for you."

"Both guaranteed to include chaos of some kind or another," Louise said. She hurried up to the bathroom, filled the sink with water and began washing her face and neck. Next, she opened a small jar and rubbed something under her arms.

"I've been meaning to ask you what that is," said Annie who'd followed her upstairs with a pile of clean towels.

"It's called deodorant." Louise examined herself in the mirror. Her new skirt had a hem which ended at her ankles, and she smiled knowing it would no longer drag in the dirt. "It's supposed to take care of smells coming from under the arms."

"Does it work?"

Louise laughed. "I can't tell, only those around me can." She pinned on a black bicorne hat with a tall feather and hurried down the stairs. "Will you be here when I get home?"

"No, Dovie asked if I could be there. She hasn't been feeling well."

"Well, don't work too hard."

At the end of the road, Louise joined others waiting for the streetcar and was soon joined by the one woman among the crowd of neighbors who she least liked: Mrs. Doris White. "I saw your cousin Dovie Bacom with that Chinese man the other day," Mrs. White said.

"Dovie isn't my cousin."

For a minute Mrs. White looked nonplussed, then she ignored the comment

saying, "They had a picnic basket and some poles and caught the Spanaway car."

"Oh?" Louise checked her lapel watch for the time. Unless she encountered trouble, she had plenty of time.

"Yes. Seemed to me like they planned to be gone all day, what with a blanket and a picnic basket and all."

"That must have been the day they went fishing out at Clover Creek," Louise said. "They supplied all of us with some fine, fat trout."

"She and that Chinaman are thick as thieves, aren't they?" There was no doubt Mrs. White's inference was salacious, and Louise scowled. Nell, she knew, would have put the woman in her place with a few carefully chosen words but Louise was aware that she lacked that particular ability. She pursed her lips for a moment before saying, "Chong has been with Bacoms since Dovie was a baby. She thinks of him as a second brother."

"Well, they looked very happy, heads bent together and all."

Louise scrambled for an appropriately scathing response and failed. Thankfully, the streetcar appeared and she nodded at Mrs. White then moved to the end of the boarding line. *Better to stand than to have to share a seat with her,* she thought. *Odious woman.* Starting up the short flight of stairs, Louise saw an unfamiliar man at the wheel.

"Where's Mr. Jacks?" She asked the conductor while giving him her money.

"Hospital." He handed over her change and nodded to the driver.

"Oh, dear." Louise held on to the back of his seat. "It's not serious, I hope."

The driver snorted and muttered something beneath his breath, and realizing she wasn't going to get an answer, Louise dropped onto the pew facing the aisle. A copy of the *Tacoma Times* folded to "Letters to the Editor" had been left on the seat next to her and she picked it up and put her camera bag there. With no place to put the paper, she looked at what the person who left it behind had been reading. It was a complaint about Louis Bean, manager of the street cars. *How fortuitous*, she thought with a grin. It had been written by someone identified only as W.J. and Louise wondered if it was a man or a woman since women often felt compelled to use initials. Either way, W. J. had wasted no words in expressing an opinion.

I wish to state a few facts, concerning the working conditions of the men who operate our street cars under the management of the Hon. Mr. Louis Bean, W.J. had written. *Mr. Bean has always treated the trainmen the same way he had treated the public in general, very generous, as he considers it.* Louise huffed a noise. Mr. Bean, she knew, was trying to raise rates. *I do wish the said same Mr. Bean would go and try putting in the same number of hours and mingle with the public and learn their wants instead of putting his time at golf. Mr. Louis Bean has a standard for a modern streetcar man, and here are some of the requirements: A man has to report at 4:40 and 4:55 a.m. and work 'til 9 a.m. and then from 1 p.m. to about 3 p.m. and from 4 p.m. to 9 p.m. and 10 p.m.; that is what he classes as a run. Then if this same crew, who only had a few hours' sleep with irregular meals, had an accident, the officials generally hold an investigation and lay the whole blame on the crew for the same. Now who should be held to account for the accident, the crew or the officials who force the men to work without rest or sleep? I wish the question would be considered. Mr. Bean has also given orders for his men not to go to meetings. I think he better go to Mexico where the country is not free, where he could use an iron hand to dictate to his subjects, or back to Everett where he came from.* Confusing grammar aside, she decided, the letter was blunt and to the point.

Putting the paper under her camera, she looked out the window. The streetcar turned north on C Street and, as usual, the road was crowded, more so with the additional street cleaners the city had hired. "The streets are dirtier than ever before," one commissioner had said, "and blame lies with the merchants who let their janitors sweep store debris out their doors right onto the roads and into the gutters." Louise wondered if any of the merchants would have to help pay for the cleanup.

The streetcar swayed on its tracks and Louise's gaze shifted back and forth between the people and the buildings, catching a brief glimpse of the old Hosmer House on the 9th Street hill. *Not a particularly attractive home,* she thought, but then it was over 30 years old. Dovie Bacom, who had come to Tacoma in the 1870s, was collecting stories about Tacoma's early years for a book she planned to write. She said the house had been built in 1875 for use by officers of the Northern Pacific Railroad. After they no longer needed it, the manager of the Tacoma Land Company used some of the rooms and leased others to several attorneys. "I'm still researching to find out how it got the name Mills House," she told Louise who liked to hear Dovie talk about the old days in Tacoma. "But in 1905 when William R. Rust bought it, that was what it was called." *And now it's the Exley Apartments*, Louise thought. *I guess it has earned the right to be unattractive.*

The streetcar stopped in front of Rhodes Brothers Department Store where more people got on than off. Louise picked up her camera bag and just as she did, the car started with a jerk and a man half fell into the empty seat next to her.

"I beg your pardon," he said while straightening his hat.

"That's Jake."

"Sorry?"

Louise turned away from the window. "It means, 'that's fine.' The streetcar always jerks at that particular corner. Locals prepare themselves. That means you must be from out of town."

"Yes, ma'am."

Louise nodded at her companion, ready to give a perfunctory smile but he smiled first, an action which completely changed his looks. Before he'd put his hat back on, she'd caught a glimpse of thick, curly dark hair. Below a very straight nose, he had a full lower lip and above his mouth, his eyes were as black as his hair. It was an average face, neither handsome nor plain until he smiled, which caused his eyes to crinkle almost shut and sent laugh lines fanning out. *It's almost a gypsy face*, she thought and realized she was staring when he asked if something was wrong.

"I'm sorry," she said before bringing out an excuse she'd used before. "It's just that I'm a photographer, you see, and tend to look at things as if I was going to photograph them."

The man's eyes dropped to her bag. "Is that a camera you're holding? I sometimes used photographs in my medical studies."

"You're a doctor, then?"

"Newly qualified."

Feeling more comfortable now that the presence of her camera seemed to have put them on familiar ground, Louise said, "Yes, it's a Kodak Camera No. 2 Model A, Box Camera. Brand new off the assembly line. Here, hold the bag and I'll show you." She put the bag on his lap and opened it. "See, the wooden frame has a metal film carriage. It uses a 130-roll film."

"How do you open it?"

Louise returned the camera to the bag. "You twist and pull out on the film advance handle here, the one here on the side that looks like a T. Then you unhook the top and side latches. I'd show you but it's loaded for use because I'm going to take photographs at the Manufacturer's Food and Industrial Exposition." She laughed. "That's a mouthful, isn't it?"

Her companion grinned. "That's where I'm headed, too." He pursed his lips. "I don't mean to sound bold, but would it be possible for us to go together?" When Louise looked startled, he continued, pushing the words out as if in a rush. "I'm going there because my uncle wants me to get to know Tacoma before starting work for him. His name is James Altamont."

"The doctor?"

"Yes, I'm his nephew; my name is Matthew Altamont. Uncle James has asked me to join his practice.

"You look too young to be a doctor," Louise said without thinking.

Matthew grinned. "And here I've been thinking that I've never met a lady photographer before."

By this time, the streetcar was turning up Sixth Avenue then slowing to a stop across the street from the Gipsy Smith Tabernacle, a newly-constructed building put up in a hurry to accommodate the evangelist. Over the previous weeks Louise had read a number of newspaper articles about the Tabernacle but its size surprised her.

"What will you be photographing, exactly?" Matthew asked as he helped out of the streetcar and Louise wished there was a reason for him to keep holding her hand.

"There are two contests I'm here for," she said as they crossed Sixth Avenue and joined the line, "the Prettiest Baby Contest and the children's Biscuits and Jam Eating Contest. My employer, Mr. Aldrich, doesn't like photographing children and decided to cover the installation of the Elks Club's new clock." As they passed through the door and joined a milling crowd she added, "Every night at 11:00 it plays *Auld Lang Syne*."

Matthew laughed. "The wives will always know when their husbands are due home, won't they?"

"Goodness, I wonder if the Elk men . . . ah, that doesn't sound right, does it? Anyway, I wonder if they thought about that when they decided on a new clock." Louise looked around and spotted a sign with an arrow pointing toward the opposite end of the room and bearing the words, "Boy's Biscuits and Jam Eating Contest."

Matthew paused and picked up a flyer touting the local car races known as the Montamara Festo.

"You probably don't want to hang around while I take photographs," Louise said as they passed a display case of postcards for sale.

"Uncle Altamont doesn't believe in my having leisure time until folks know that I'm his partner in the practice," Matthew said. "He sent me here to introduce myself to people."

"Well, I'm people," Louise said with a laugh, "but probably not the right kind." She didn't elaborate and he didn't ask.

"I'll mingle for a while and then I'll catch up with you." Matthew bumped into a man and apologized.

"Golly, I didn't expect so many people," he said before disappearing in the crowd.

With much apologizing on her own part, Louise squeezed her way through milling clusters of mostly women with children, feeling both sad and glad that she was alone to do her job. Sad because she liked the way Matthew Altamont's presence made her feel inside, but glad because she had work to do and he was a definitely a distraction.

The single-story, Gipsy Smith Tabernacle had been built in a hurry because the city fathers weren't sure how soon the evangelist would arrive. It covered 9-square lots but was built to take advantage of the land's natural slope which allowed for tiers of wooden benches to accommodate 6,000 people. The elevated pulpit-turned-podium where the contests were to be held was at the far south end. When Louise reached it, she that sawhorses on the stage held a fifteen-foot-long plank lined with chairs facing the audience. Men were walking back and forth moving things and then putting them back while boys ran among them pushing, shoving and occasionally punching each other. The noise was ear splitting. Louise set her bag down and pulled out her camera. Taking photographs required her holding it at her waist and looking down into a small square aperture. The lens was below and on the camera's front. She quickly realized she needed three places to stand: on a box facing the stage, plus additional places either side of the stage high enough to so she had a good view of the biscuit eaters. That meant standing on the benches, so she took several placards reading, "Reserved for the Photographer" out of her bag, set them in the appropriate places, then flagged down a man to find a box. As the contest's starting time drew near, Louise had to raise an eyebrow and shake her head at more than one person who tried to do away with the placards. Then former Tacoma mayor William Seymour took the stage and blew a wooden whistle. From where she sat, Louise saw that it was carved with a stylized face, and that the whole piece was stained in colors which were beginning to fade. There had been controversy over his ownership of the whistle because the previous owner had been Peter Stanup, a preacher and spokesman for the Puyallup Tribe whose wife had sold all his possessions claiming he'd left her destitute. When Mr. Seymour put the whistle to his lips to blow it again, Louise snapped a clear picture of his hand and face in profile. *Later,* she thought, *I'll develop it to emphasize the artifact.*

"Ladies and gentlemen, boys and girls," Mr. Seymour began, "welcome to the Manufacturers' Food, Household and Automobile Exposition. As you know, today is Children's Day and first thing on the agenda is the Biscuits and Jam Eating Contest, being sponsored by the Allen Motor Company whose general manager, William O. Allen, likes to remind us, that though you can't buy happiness, you can buy a quality automobile, and quality never goes out of style." A generous applause followed his words and a young woman sitting next to Louise snorted and whispered, "Mr. Allen told my brother that his wife can't drive him crazy if he doesn't give her the keys."

Louise burst into laughter which she tried to turn into a cough. She recognized the voice as belonging to Jean Ford, a friend from school. Jean's quick wit often got her into trouble, and her winning smile generally got her out of it. Louise liked her and wished they could be better friends, but Jean worked long hours at the Tacoma Hotel as well as on the Ford family's hops farm near Roy. Seeing who had laughed, Jean nudged her and they exchanged grins. Meanwhile, Mr. Seymour continued. "Of course, with an event such as this, it's all hands on deck and that includes the Puyallup and Sumner Fruit Growers' Association which, courtesy of Mr. William H. Paulhamus, donated all the jam and would like to remind us that the new plant devoted to raspberry jam just received an order from Kansas City for 5 carloads of jam and one of jelly. And to you mothers I say, "Jam is like Happiness, you can't spread even a little without getting some on yourself" and your boys will not only be well-fed, they will just as likely be messy."

Louise could tell from its wiggling that the audience was getting restive and when Mr. Seymour spoke next, it was to lukewarm applause. "And finally, I say to you, 'If something is missing from your life, it might just be a biscuit.' Not to worry, William P. Matthaei and the Matthaei Bread Company have made sure our boys won't go without." *Good grief, that's a lot of men named William*, Louise thought as Mr. Seymour said, "Now, boys, come on up."

Twenty boys chosen from a write-in campaign charged the stage grabbing chairs from each other and waving to their family and friends.

"Here, now, settle down." Mr. Seymour blew his whistle. "Quiet!"

Chairs thumped the wooden stage before the boys became relatively quiet but resorted to kicking each other under the make-shift table.

"Girls," Mr. Seymour continued, "bring on the biscuits and jam."

Six self-important-looking girls wearing identical checked, gingham aprons over their dresses climbed the steps to the stage carrying platters which they set in front of the boys. Then they left the stage and returned with a cup for each contestant and several buckets. "Now, boys," Mr. Seymour's energy seemed to be flagging. "Each biscuit has a marble on top. When you pick up a biscuit, put the marble in your cup. When the final whistle blows, you stop eating and we will count the marbles. He who has the most wins. And," he paused and used a handkerchief to wipe his forehead, "do not, I repeat, do not hesitate to use the buckets if you need to. Now, napkins in place? Good. Here we go." He blew the whistle and retreated to an empty chair at the rear of the stage. As he did, the boys started grabbing at the biscuits and Louise began moving around the area snapping pictures. Soon the ping of marbles falling into cups filled the air. The box to stand on was invaluable; the height from the second-tier pews a necessity, and Louise forgot about everything except looking for good shots and advancing the film.

The piles of biscuits shrank and the audience called out encouragement. After the first flurry of shoving the pastry in their mouths, eating fell into a sort of routine. Ten minutes in, the first boy threw up into a bucket. He stumbled up from his chair and staggered off the stage amidst the clapping of those who appreciated his effort. Louise managed to capture a snapshot of his mother, one arm around his shoulder the other hand wiping his face as she led him away. Twenty minutes in, the majority of the boys were leaning back in their chairs, groaning. Bits of jam dropped off their chins and had become smeared in their hair. The tabernacle's doors were opened to let in much-needed fresh air and a couple of stray dogs. One ran onto the stage and tipped over a bucket. Louise took a picture of the dog, the bucket, and its contents, including two men trying to get the animal off the stage. It was down to five boys, then three, then two still gamely eating until one of them threw up in his napkin and called it quits. He stood and offered a jam-encrusted hand to the winner.

"Ladies and gentlemen," Mr. Seymour returned to the front of the stage, taking care to avoid sticky messes on the floor. "It looks like we don't have to count the marbles in the cups. It was a hard-fought battle but a no-contest ending." He turned to the winner. "What's your name, son?" The boy muttered something. "Speak up, there, young fella. . ." He'd barely finished when a woman in the audience stood up and shouted, "That's my son, Walter Raymond." When the crowd burst into laughter, she sat down looking much embarrassed. "Well, young Walter, what do you have to say for yourself?" Mr. Seymour asked.

With a cheeky grin Walter stood up and shouted, "What's for dinner, Ma?"

The spectators stomped their feet and hooted and someone handed Mr. Seymour a parcel which he presented to Walter.

Walter took the package and ripped off the paper. "It's a model Sturtz 1916 Fokker D.11 Biplane," Mr. Seymour told the spectators, "Courtesy of Rhodes Brothers Department Store. Hold it up so people can see it, Walter." Walter, with a big grin, held it up, not noticing the glances exchanged.

"I don't think people want to be reminded about the war," Jean said as Louise returned to her seat on the pew.

"When the neighbor boy came home from school a couple of weeks back sick and with a high fever, his mother thought he might have Liberty Measles," Louise said.

Jean snorted. "'Liberty Measles!' Oh, good grief. And at the Tacoma Hotel some people want to change the menus to offer Liberty Cabbage instead of sauerkraut and Liberty Sausages and all kinds of other 'Liberty' things. Anyway, if people are so anti Germans, you'd think they wanted to keep the name German measles so as to insult the enemy."

Louise sighed. "Nell wants me to read the war news every day. I think the new flamethrowers are about the worst thing ever invented."

Around them, men were swabbing the stage and wiping off the make-shift table, setting up for the Beautiful Baby contest. Mothers and their boys were leaving, replaced by mothers with their babies. Louise watched feeling unexpectedly dull.

"Seems like the war is all the men at the hotel talk about," Jean was saying.

"I went to see *A Modern Enoch Arden* last week at the Apollo. Have you seen it? The Keystone Kops are so funny, but then there was a newsreel of the Somme, and we left practically in tears."

Jean nodded. "I know, my brother Albert went and he told me all about it. He wants to go to Canada and enlist but he's only 17 and Pa says, 'No.'"

"Lord Kitchner wants us to get involved."

Jean sighed and wrung her hands. "And all President Wilson has done is to say to Germany, 'Please stop your submarines from sinking all ships in enemy waters without, at least, a warning.' But why should they if that's all he's going to do?" She shook her head.

"Well, that's not all he's done." Louise paused to create a dramatic effect. "He brought a herd of sheep to keep the White House grass cut."

Jean laughed. "He did do that."

Up on the stage men had finished cleaning up the remains of the biscuits and jelly and were returning the chairs to the table. The banner announcing the Biscuit and Jam contest came down, and men hoisted up one reading, 'The Better Babies Contest.'

Jean nodded toward the camera. "More pictures?"

"Yes." Louise stroked the case.

"I hope I get to see them sometime." Jean stood and looked around. "I get enough baby stuff at home," she said, "and I better get going. This is a rare morning off for me." She stooped and gave Louise an awkward hug. "It's good to see you."

"You, too. Take care."

Jean disappeared into a crowd of women toting babies as they looked for empty seats. And Louise took one of the flyers a boy was handing out.

The Manufacturers' Food and Industrial Exposition Presents:

A Better Babies Contest

Based on Criteria Developed by:

Mary deGarmo, Educator, State-wide Organizer of the National Congress of Mothers, and Originator of the Better Babies Contests. Measurements and observations as follows:

Height:

Weight:

Symmetry:
Quality of skin, fat, and bones:
Length and Shape of head:
Size of ears, lips, forehead, and nose:
Disposition, energy, facial and ocular expression, and attention.

We will use the categories of the scorecard and the typical measurements for normal boys and girls. Across the country, physicians have served as judges, examining babies in order to score and rank them, often differentiating between boys and girls, and urban and rural children.

Louise made a derisive noise. *How ridiculous,* she thought. *Quality of bones? I want to see how they figure that one out.*

This time it was a different type of person who took the stage to introduce the contest. Louise recognized the white dress covered by a white bibbed apron that nurses from Tacoma General Hospital wore. There were eleven women in all, and each sat at the table while the extra chairs were removed. A girl put pencils and piles of paper in front of them as a man walked to the front of the rostrum.

"Ladies and gentlemen," he said, "welcome to the Better Babies Contest. I am Morley Jackson, Chairman of the Board of Directors for Tacoma General Hospital and, as you probably have guessed by now, behind me sitting at the table are hospital nurses. They've generously volunteered their time to be part of the event." Applause followed and Mr. Jackson beamed. "And, if you didn't know, Mrs. deGarmo, herself, will be participating in a similar event at the Puyallup Fair; this is a precursor, a chance to have your child evaluated by professionals so that you can do what is necessary to make improvements to your baby."

"Like change the shape of his head," Louise muttered. "How's that going to happen?" She wished Jean was still there to help her poke fun at some of the categories.

The Tabernacle had multiple doors on either side and with all of them now open the air was becoming relatively cool. After her exertions, though, Louise was warm, slightly winded from climbing up and down on the benches, and happy to sit quietly, though she did wish she had a couple of the leftover biscuits. Seeing a man carrying a box and leaving the area, she jumped up.

"If there's an uneaten biscuit or two in that box, I sure could eat a couple," she said giving him her most winsome smile.

Though he didn't return the smile, the man set the box on the stage and lifted the lid. "The Charity Commissioner left word to take any leftovers to the Associated Charities office down on Commerce, but I don't suppose they'll miss a couple," he said. "Wait a minute and I'll find something to use as a napkin."

He turned to go but Louise already had a handkerchief out. "No need to trouble yourself, I have a handkerchief I've not used today." She helped herself to two biscuits, licking the jam off her fingers as it oozed out and returned to her seat. "Thank you so much. Golly, I was hungrier than I realized."

"My pleasure, Miss." The man disappeared into the crowd, eventually leaving through a side door and Louise returned to her seat trying not to wolf the food down. *Annie was right*, she thought, *she's been telling me I need to start carrying something to eat.* She had just finished the biscuits and was trying to get the jam off her fingers when someone poked her in the back.

"Piney," she said, turning around and recognizing the woman. Years ago, when Nell was riding on the prairie, her horse threw her and she was knocked out. Piney found her and got her to where the Puyallup Indians were having a potlatch. She and her mother, Mary, treated Nell's wounds, fed her and, using a canoe, paddled across the bay taking her back to Tacoma. Nell never forgot and visited Piney and Mary often.

"How's your mother?"

Piney laughed and shifted the bundle in her arms. "She says Joey is perfect as he is and doesn't need to go to a Better Babies Contest." As if to agree, the baby beamed at his mother showing a deep dimple in each cheek.

Louise smiled and ran a finger down one cheek. From what she'd seen so far, he was certainly the cutest baby there but, being Indian, she knew he wouldn't win any of the ribbons. However, she'd seen them piled in a box at the back of the stage. Waiting until Piney joined the line of mothers, she snuck over and swiped one.

The contest wasn't nearly as interesting or enjoyable as the earlier one had been. Doctor Yokum, a man Louise recognized because he treated injured union workers, of which her uncle Ike was one, introduced the proceedings, after which each woman was given a scoring sheet where she wrote her name and that of her child. She then climbed the stairs to the stage and gave it to the first nurse. The nurse made whatever examination was within her purview, jotted something on the paper, and handed it and the baby to the next evaluator. Within minutes, most of the infants were screaming in rage, and making copious use of their diapers. Trying not to breath, Louise did her best to take some decent photographs, but she doubted whether many mothers would want to buy one.

Eventually, a short, stalky and slightly balding man took the stage and beamed at the crowd. "Ladies and gentlemen," he said, "My name is George Smith, not the New York Giants pitcher," he chuckled. "I'm Nurse George Smith, and I had the pleasure of being the first graduate of what was then the Fannie C. Paddock Memorial Hospital School of Nursing and of being Washington State's first male nurse. That was in 1895, and I think it's safe to say that we've come a long way since then." He beamed, seemingly oblivious, at the fidgeting audience and continued. "It is said that in

England one out of every four men wanting to enlist and fight for their country is rejected as being unfit. In the United States, it's one out of every five. And according to Dr. C. W. Saleeby, contributor to *The Children's Encyclopedia*, the trouble begins with the babies." The audience had grown quieter; many of the infants having cried themselves out, and Nurse Smith knew that until the results were announced, he had a captive audience. "From ages 1 to 5 the neglected child is a weak child. Yes, we do some things better here in the United States, but more can be done. There is now a nationwide attempt to improve our child-rearing methods and to instruct parents in the best ways to raise their children. And currently, more than 400 communities are planning to get involved in the Better Babies Movement."

"Well, quit grousing like some two-bit hawkshaw and get on with it," a man shouted. "Some 'a us gotta get a meal."

"Ah, yes, quite." Nurse Smith waved the tally sheets. "I have the results right here." He took a pair of spectacles out of his pocket, put them on, and began reading the names of the winners in various categories. As the names were announced, each woman took her tally sheet and accepted her ribbon. When the box of ribbons was empty, Nurse Smith looked around. "I could a'sworn there was one more."

Louise stood and approached the stage. "Yes, there is. I found it." She moved to stand below him in the middle of the room. "If you'll allow me." Without waiting she smiled at the audience. "The last ribbon goes to Piney Satiacum, mother of the baby with the cutest dimples, and to baby Joey, of course."

Some of the mothers looked at each other as Piney walked up and accepted the ribbon. When Louise held the baby up and tickled him, he giggled making the other mothers laugh. "Well, he surely is a cutie," one woman said and well-pleased, Louise handed the baby

back to Piney and left the building through the nearest
door.

Chapter 2

Outside Louise took a deep breath of air that didn't smell of too many people crowded into one place, and of way too many dirty diapers. For the space of twenty or so feet the noise followed her until at last it faded away. Louise wished she could walk home but she needed to beat Mr. Aldrich back to the photography studio. Ever since his arrest for taking an illegal picture of the labor federation in front of the Capitol building in Olympia, he'd been a nervous wreck.

"It's ridiculous that the only photographers allowed to take photographs in Olympia have to have their offices there," he said loud and often.

"Tacoma might have done the same thing if the capitol had been moved here," Louise pointed out.

"The capitol should be available to everyone," he said and recognizing his tone of voice, Louise was quick to agree.

The streetcar back to town was just stopping as she left the Tabernacle and Louise hurried across the road, dodging traffic to catch it. Not for the first time, it occurred to her that the traffic was almost all automobiles. *I miss the horses*, she thought. *They were so much quieter. They may have left dung on the roads, but the automobiles make the air smell bad, and they're noisy.* Staring out the window Louise wondered what happened to Matthew Altamont. *I thought he liked me, but I guess not.* With a sigh she turned her thoughts to the photographs she'd taken. *With luck I'll get in the darkroom before Mr. Aldrich gets back from the Elks Club. He's such a fussy little man.* But then Louise remembered that he was the only photographer in town willing to hire her and reminded herself to be grateful.

Aldrich Fine Arts was located in a two-story, brick building on Pacific Avenue, sandwiched between the National Realty Building and the Palace Theater, just down the street from Feeny's Cafe. Within days of her employment Louise was quick to realize that all the street traffic meant business could be better.

"We should be attracting more walk-ins," she said to Mr. Aldrich not long after he hired her.

Louise's employer was more than a bit of a fuddy duddy. He was so old fashioned that he'd only hired a her, a female, the day she'd walked in asking for a job, because he'd injured his right hand and needed help. When she'd said that, he immediately looked suspicious. "What do you mean?"

"Oh, I don't know," said Louise, realizing she was walking on thin ice. "You do such fine work, why not enlarge some of your best photographs and display them in the window?"

"The building owner probably hung those blinds on the windows for a reason."

"Maybe he just hung them there to encourage renters. Just think," Louise clasped her hands together and tried to look cajoling, "how wonderful the picture you took and enlarged of Mount Tacoma at dawn would look front and center. Why, everyone going up and down Pacific Avenue would stop and look."

Louise wanted to know how to enlarge photographs and, with Mr. Aldrich looking gratified by her praise, he finally showed her how. She wasn't just flattering him, though. He had captured the mountain on a cold winter morning when the pink sunrise cast color on a heavy fall of snow. Louise asked Reuben Bacom, a member of her extended family, to make a frame and planned to put a display in the window over the end of the week when her boss would be at a convention in Portland. She only had three-and-a-half days to fix the window and wondered if there would be time to paint the trim.

Eventually, the streetcar reached Pacific Avenue, she got off and hurried to the studio. The locked door told her she'd beat Mr. Aldrich, and once inside, she shed her lightweight sweater-coat and headed for the darkroom. From the first day of her employment, Mr. Aldrich insisted that the items needed to develop film—measuring cups, reels to put the film on, containers of fixer chemicals, and film clips, etc. had to be returned to the proper shelves near the developing tank and water spigot when she was done. Louise tied on a bib apron to protect her clothes and began transferring the camera film to reels. She was agitating it in the developing fluid when she heard Mr. Aldrich.

"I'm just getting ready to rinse out the tank and put in the finisher," she called through the door. "If you want, I'll develop your film when I'm done."

"Thank you, that would be nice," he surprised her by saying. "My arm is aching." She heard him put something outside the darkroom door and then heard the creaking desk chair.

When all the firm was developed and the negatives were hanging up to dry, he walked slowly down the line making comments. As he did, Louise made notes in a small commonplace book she kept just for that purpose. She nearly always agreed with what he had to say but wasn't afraid to question something. "You've taught me so much," she said as they prepared to close shop for the day. "Have you ever thought of opening a photography school? I think lots of people would want to come."

"Well, that's nice to hear but I'm afraid Mr. Jackson has that market cornered."

Louise sniffed. "Mr. Jackson does so much retouching on his photographs they all look the same."

As she spoke, their clock's hands clicked over to five; time to close for the day. Mr. Aldrich locked the door and gave it a little shake and Louise hid her smile;

it was something he always did. Then they parted ways, him to the Feeny Cafe and Louise to walk home. Pacific Avenue to C Street was level, but from there clear up to K Street, several blocks above where she lived, it was straight up hill. She checked her pockets for change and found enough to pay the passenger car on 11th Street. *Downtown is getting too ritzy to be interesting,* she thought, while hurrying down the street, *at least to a photographer. Someday when I have time, I want to go up to K Street and take photographs. I wish Nell didn't think it was unsafe up there. Nell and I are just opposites about some things, I guess.* One thing they did agree on, however, was the idea that downtown was getting very expensive. High-rent downtown was home to the big department stores, fancy restaurants, haberdasheries, and fashionable dress shops, none of which were particularly appealing to a photographer. K Street, on the other hand, sold furniture, ethnic specialties, hardware, appliances and had appliance repairmen. There were also barbers and even a Marcel Shop. Louise had never been in a place that did things to women's hair. It was the boulevard of shopkeepers, candy makers, bread companies and merchants, many of whom had emigrated and barely spoke English. They provided for their own, many items that were hard to find elsewhere. Sometimes, when the wind was just right, unfamiliar smells drifted down the hill and Louise thought K Street must be very exotic.

She caught the passenger car, picked up a magazine left on a seat near the door, and dropped into it as the car pulled away. *Why do people buy these things then leave them on streetcars,* she thought. In spite of the chatter, the low rumbling sound of the wheels and cables from the underground system was easy to hear and Louise wondered if it was something she could photograph. She'd been told it was like a massive clockwork that K Street merchants set their clocks by it. Louise got out her photography-notes ledger and using the magazine as ballast to support it, turned to the back and added it to the list of places she thought would be interesting. The car started up 11th Street, its sway bar twisting, shifting the weight back and forth. Accustomed to the movement, Louise looked at the discarded periodical: a copy of *The Boys Magazine* which was free with a one-year subscription to *The Tacoma Times*. In addition to adventure stories, the cover boasted articles by the well-known athlete— *well-known to the boys, anyway* she thought—Walter Camp. Also included were helpful hints on any number of things such as carpentry, stamp collecting, and photography. *Photography.* In her bedroom Louise had a small portfolio of pictures she'd taken. *Golly, too bad there's nothing in it that would interest a boy*, she thought. *And, anyway, I'm just a beginner and probably don't have any advice. I'd better stick to taking some interesting photographs.* Deep in thought, she almost missed her stop.

Chapter 3

Prominently displayed in the foyer of Louise's home was a sampler on which, as a child, she had embroidered the proverb, 'East, west, Home's best'. Walking down D Street to her house, Louise was thinking about how much she agreed with the words. Unfortunately, that evening being home was going to have to wait. Nell met her at the door saying, "I was afraid you'd forgotten."

Louise looked blank. "Forgotten what?"

"Forgotten about the first meeting of the Camouflage Corps."

"Oh, golly. I did." Louise hung her hat on the hall tree, looked at the clock and sighed. "I'm starving but I'll barely have time to wolf something down."

"Well, you're on your own. John is taking me to dinner and to the Plulomathean Literary Society's annual meeting at the College of Puget Sound. The society is putting on a Scottish program."

"Oh, golly," said Louise again. She and Nell exchanged looks and burst into laughter.

"Shame on us," Nell said. "John didn't have much of a childhood and he's finding comfort in anything Scottish."

"I know; I know," Louise paused, "it's just that a meeting of the Plulo—Plulo—I can't even say it, sounds deadly dull."

"I agree, but I'm sure he finds many of the things I drag him to, equally dull. Just, please, when you see him next, be sure and ask him about it. He's awfully good to you and it's the least you can do."

33

"I know he is, and I will. He bought me my bicycle and my lovely camera, after all." Louise said as she followed the smell of stew to the kitchen. She was happy to find the Dutch oven full of meat and potatoes, and a loaf of fresh baked bread cooling on the counter. "I'd almost rather stay home than go to the meeting," she said to her cat, Princess. Louise filled a bowl with stew and buttered a thick slice of bread. Princess jumped onto the table, showing an interest in the food while, mindful of the time, Louise ate as fast as she could. When she was done, she pushed the half-empty bowl over to the cat. Finding it to her liking, Princess began licking and Louise grinned. "For goodness sakes, don't let anyone catch you doing this," she said, "or we'll both be in trouble." She hurried to her room and gave herself a quick sponge bath before putting on a navy blue, high-waisted bicycle skirt, and a red, white and blue blouse. At the front door, she grabbed her straw boater off the hall tree and pinned it on. Then, picking up the camouflage canvas she'd tested at the park, Louise left the house and hurried to the lean-to where she kept her bicycle, John's gift from her on her last birthday.

She wheeled the bike, a Raleigh Lady's Roadster, out to the road. After her camera, it was Louise's most prized possession. She put the tarp in a basket mounted on the handlebars, checked the street, and hopped on the seat. Just last week a bull escaped while men tried to load it onto a railroad car and had run rampant in her neighborhood. It leaped a fence and charged at a pair of red flannel underwear hanging on Mrs. George Johnson's clothesline and then stormed her front porch. "It held me hostage in my own home," she told a *Tacoma Times* reporter. After a lengthy pursuit, the bull was rounded up but the whole thing left many people, mainly pedestrians, more than a little leery. Then, the following afternoon, the brakes slipped on a Ford Model T delivery truck parked on 10th Street sending the empty vehicle careening down the hill.

Letters to the editor in *Tacoma Daily Ledger* had been full of indignation, ranting about danger to life and limb, however, Louise was sorry she'd missed the excitement. "But then," she'd said after reading the letters, "there was generally something to see on the roads, not to mention things to be careful of." *Case in point*, she thought as she approached the Cow Butter Store on Jefferson Street. So many boxes and barrels crowded the sidewalk, they'd turned it into a maze, and she applied the bicycle's brakes and coasted to a stop. She dismounted and wheeled her bike through them and past a horse-drawn delivery wagon which had been backed up to the curb with the horse filling half the road. Once past the horse, she found it nearly impossible to speed up again. Drivers cut corners, drove on the wrong side of the road, swerved around pedestrians, buggies, and other vehicles. The city was in the midst of planking sidewalks and when the workers quit for the day, they left piles of wood where they'd been working. And those grocers who had celebrated when sidewalks were installed, had cluttered them with crates of freshly picked fruit delivered from the Puyallup Valley.

With an exasperated sigh and mindful of the time, Louise turned off Broadway and peddled back up to D Street. *It supposed to be part of the Red-Light District,* she thought, *but at least the only clutter is the women, themselves.* Two blocks later, she turned back onto C Street, a neighborhood of large homes set back from the road under canopies of equally large trees. There, both the sidewalk and street were planked, except where streetcar tracks ran up the middle. Hoping her hat was safe and whistling a song called, *I Am a Poor Wayfaring Stranger*, Louise peddled up the gentle grade, watching for rotten and broken wood. Before reaching her destination, she passed the modest Wilkeson house and St. Luke's Episcopal Church on one side and the massive Queen Anne home belonging to the Nelson Bennett on the other. The two-and-a-half story home belonging to John Baker and his new wife, Florence, was near the top and had an unobstructed view of the bay. "The Wilkeson place might not be as extravagant," she muttered, "but at least it's fenced and has fewer stairs." She hefted her bicycle up fifteen stairs, leaned it against the side of the porch, climbed several more steps, and arrived out of breath at the door before remembering she'd left her canvas in the bicycle basket. When she returned, panting to the door a second time, it opened before she knocked.

"Good evening, Miss," said a young woman. "They're waiting for you."

"Yes, I can hear them," Louise said dryly. "Am I awfully late?"

"Only five minutes." The maid stepped back. "This way, please."

Feeling hot and sticky, and at a distinct disadvantage, Louise was prepared to dislike most of what she saw and was, therefore, not disappointed.

"The walls were papered in gold, burgundy and green damask," she told Annie later, "and there were several wingback chairs, a tufted sofa and too many footstools, in my opinion. The windows had drapes and shears, and the tables were absolutely covered with bibelots."

"It sounds lovely," Annie had said to which Louise snorted. Louise generally found it difficult to get rid of a bad mood.

When she entered the room, conversations stopped, and all eyes turned in her direction.

"You must be Louise Tanquist," said a slender blonde coming forward while in the background someone muttered, "about time." The blonde smiled, either in greeting or at the remark. "I'm Florence Baker." She looked around the room and back at Louise. "You appear to be warm; I'll have Penner bring you something to drink and then we can get started. I'm afraid you'll have to sit on an ottoman, though."

Unfortunately, the one Louise chose was overly soft and her knees came up practically to her chin. She re-pinned her hat, conversation resumed, and the maid, *Penner, evidently*, came in with a sympathetic look and a glass of lemonade.

"Ladies," Mrs. Baker looked around the room and smiled, "now that we're all here it's time to get to the business at hand. As you know, Mrs. Nelson Bennett has been visiting family in New York. I'm going to read part of a clipping from the *New York Tribune* that she sent me." She cleared her throat.

"Imagine taking a quiet stroll through the expansive wilderness of Van Cortlandt Park in Bronx, New York. You're surrounded by a forest of oak trees, stony ridges, and a tranquil lake—completely isolated and alone in nature. But recently, visitors to the 1,146-acre park were unaware that they were in the company of a group of women hiding among the rocks, trees, and grass. Weird shapes, the color of the rocks and earth, moved here and there, and from the tops of trees came loud halloos and catcalls from other shapeless objects. I stumbled over a hump of grass, which squealed when I stepped on it, and rose before me,"

Mrs. Baker stopped, some of the women chuckled. "That would certainly give the body the flesh creep," said one.

Louise nudged her tarp with her foot and muttered, *"New York Tribune*, bosh. What a goop. At least my tarp fooled people here not back in New York."

"Miss Tanquist?" Louise jumped. "You look as if you want to say something." Mrs. Baker raised her eyebrows.

She probably thinks I won't say anything, Louise thought, *but I'll take her at her word.* "Yes, Mrs. Baker, thank you." Louise looked around the room and smiled. "I had a similar experience at Wright Park that I thought you'd find amusing."

Some of the women sat up a little straighter as if in anticipation but Mrs. Baker immediately squashed the idea saying, "Since you'll want to expound and I'm sure we'll all enjoy hearing about it, perhaps a little later. Right now, I think we owe it to Mrs. Bennett to hear the rest of the clipping she sent, don't you? Now then,"

"women disguised in special (and fairly creepy) dried grass or 'rock suits' were student military camouflage artists, or camoufleurs, of the Women's Reserve Camouflage Corps, a division of the National League for Women's Service."

She folded the paper and returned it to its envelope. "And as you all know, that is why we have gathered here today, to form a local chapter of the camouflage corp."

"But it's a European war, isn't it, that is being fought?" one woman asked. "Who would we be making camouflage items for?"

Mrs. Baker sighed and sat in the chair behind her. "Yes, well, as you know, Pierce County men recently voted to give the government seventy thousand acres of land for a military base out on the prairie just south of Tacoma. I've just learned that Captain David L. Stone and his staff arrived some time ago and are already overseeing construction. It seems both possible and impossible that we will, sooner rather than later, be in the war."

Louise already knew of Captain Stone' 's arrival courtesy of the gossipy women at Nell's couture and she also knew something Mrs. Baker didn't. "The War Department is calling it Camp Lewis after Meriweather Lewis."

Mrs. Baker gave a start. "Are you sure? I hadn't heard that."

"So I've been told."

"Well," Mrs. Baker sounded peeved, "all the more reason to push on with our own camouflage corps." She picked up another sheet of paper. "In 1917, a British artist named Norman Wilkinson submitted a proposal to the royal navy, there, for a design of optical illusions known as dazzle camouflage to be painted on the hulls of ships to help disguise them from enemy submarines. And, our very own Foundation Boat Building Company, which is building ships for France, has to have the hulls razzle dazzled before they ship out." She gave a slight chuckle. "And, ladies, beginning next week we'll be meeting in a room set aside for us by Samuel Perkins in his building." She beamed and looked around the room. "Oh, yes, Miss Tanquist, you were going to do a little show-and-tell, weren't you?"

Golly, she really doesn't like me. I wonder why. Louise ignored the rudeness, related her experience in the park with the schoolboys, and dropped to the floor covering herself with the tarp. Several comments reached her ears:

"I could paint something like that."

"No wonder the boys were fooled. It's very realistic, isn't it?"

"It certainly was a brave thing to do, wasn't it?"

Louise was laughing and pulling off the tarp when she heard her hostess saying, "Hello, Mildred. Doctor Altamont. Back so soon?" And looking up, she saw a slender blonde with her hair piled in a Gibson Girl pompadour dressed almost completely in pink. Standing next to her was Matthew Altamont. Louise's smile froze and she immediately became aware of how she must look. Her eyes met those of the young doctor and Louise saw his mouth twitch and his eyes crinkle in a smile.

"Miss Tanquist, how nice to see you again."

"Likewise, Doctor Altamont." Conscious of one of Nell's favorite sayings, "Always remember to rise to the occasion," Louise sat back on the ottoman, tidied her hair, and re-pinned her hat.

"Let me help you," Mildred unexpectedly said. "I can fold the tarp." She smiled and set to it and Louise found herself smiling back. *Oh, dear, now I'll have to like her,* she thought.

The room was gradually emptying as the women thanked their hostess and left chattering among themselves. Mildred was called away, and Matthew approached Louise. "Can I drive you home?"

Outside, it was halfway between daylight and dusk, and Louise knew she'd have to hurry to beat the dark. Regretfully, she said, "It would have been lovely, but I came on my bike."

"No worries." Matthew smiled. "It should fit in the back of the car." He tucked the tarp under one arm and helped her to stand. Then, with him holding her elbow, she thanked Mrs. Baker for letting them use her home as a meeting place. After which he ushered out the door followed by Mildred who leaned over the porch railing to thank Matthew for the ride and say to Louise that she hoped to see her at the workshop.

"She's lovely, isn't she?" Louise led Matthew to her bike.

"Her fiancé thinks so," Matthew said. He started wheeling the bike to his car while Louise skipped to catch up. With the bike in the backseat and Matthew and Louise in the front, he turned to her. "Where to?"

"I beg your pardon?"

"Your address."

"Oh, yes." She explained how to get to D. Street and relaxed against the seat. "This is lovely. It's been a long day."

"How did the photography work go? Do you know yet?"

"Oh, I think really well. Mr. Aldrich was very pleased. He's taught me so much and I tried to put it all to good use. I developed the film as soon as I got back to the studio."

"And then came home and rode your bike here?"

"Yes."

"And that all came after testing a tarp at the park?"

"Yes."

Matthew laughed. "Well, you have certainly disproved the proverb about All Work and no Play. It definitely hasn't made you dull."

"Maybe not but definitely hungry and tired. Best to turn down here and then left onto D Street."

D Street was in an older section of town and most of the houses showed it. However, not where Louise lived. Her home and those on either side of it and directly across the street were lovingly maintained with fresh paint and fenced yards full of flowers and trees. Matthew slowed down to give a cat the right-of-way and the action roused Louise.

"Golly, I must have dozed off. I beg your pardon. How terribly rude of me."

Matthew grinned. "As a man, it is a bit insulting, but as a doctor, I'd say you needed it." She pointed out her house, and he stopped and opened the car door. "I'll just get your bike, and you can show me where it goes."

"That's not necessary. I can put it away." A shiver went up her back when she met his eyes, and she was pleased to hear him say, "I want to."

They walked through the garden, listening to a few birds settling in the trees for the night, and smelling the sweet peas. Once the bicycle was back in the lean-to, Matthew walked Louise to the front door where she thanked him for the ride. "I'd like to see the pictures you took this morning," he said.

"Then you must come down to the studio. And, after all, my boss, Mr. Aldrich is a pillar of the community." Matthew grinned, his eyes crinkled, and they both laughed.

"I will."

Inside, Louise hung her jacket and hat on the hall tree and hearing her uncle Ike's voice followed it to the kitchen. Nell looked up and smiled. She came around the table and gave Louise a hug. "My goodness, you've had a day."

Before Louise could answer, Ike half-scowled. "Who brought you home?"

"Don't worry, Uncle Ike." Louise put some bread on a toasting fork and held it in front of the stove. "It was Doctor Altamont's nephew. You know the doctor, don't you?"

"Huh. Tacoma's biggest high-hat if there ever was one. Always looking down his nose at people."

"Matthew is nice. He was bringing the Baker's niece, Mildred, home from some dinner and offered me a ride." Ever the protective uncle, Ike raised an eyebrow and asked why. "Because it was getting dark and I'd ridden my bike to the meeting." Louise spread a thick coat of butter on her toast, poured a glass of milk, and sat at the table. "Where's Annie?"

"She went to bed with a sick headache."

"Oh, dear. She should see a doctor." Annie had lived with the Tanquists ever since she was a little girl, moving into Nell's house to act as a proper chaperone when Nell bought it. Annie's sick headaches occurred about every three months, sending her to lay down with a cold compress and small amount of laudanum in a dark room. "Should I take up something?"

"Best to let her sleep."

Fearful that the conversation would turn into something female-related, Ike cleared his throat. "Frieda Faye's bible study group is at the house," he said, and Louise and Nell exchanged grins. "Do you remember my telling you that Mike Pete broke one of Jack Hartford's ribs at the boxing match last week?" Without waiting for an answer, he continued, "Well, a week later, when Hartford met Walter Porsch at the Glide Rink, he had the left rib taped using that adhesive stuff Stone and Fisher carries, and what with the injury and all, folks just naturally assumed Porsch would win their match and bet accordingly." Ike laughed and took a long swallow of the beer Nell kept around just for him. "His pal Eddie Bates told me it was a trick to keep Porsch aiming for the left, which he did, then, when he was getting tired, Hartford brought him down with a strong left hook. The broken rib was on the right side." Ike laughed. "Now Porsch is getting rid of his upright piano because he needs money to pay off his gambling debt and he's willing to make a deal. I aim to use my winnings to buy it for Frieda Faye." Ike laughed again and finished his beer. "Shouldn't 'a bet it all on hisself."

Ike and Nell continued talking and Louise half listened as she studied the photographs in *Street Incidents*, a secondhand book of photographs John bought her. She had reviewed the book before taking pictures at the Gypsy Smith tabernacle. And knowing she would be responsible for displaying the photos, she'd purchased some of the adhesive tape Ike had mentioned with the idea of sticking the best ones on the studio's front window. After a yawn so big it made her eyes water, she said good night, picked up Princess, and carried her up to bed.

***

The following morning, well before her boss would arrive, Louise caught an early streetcar and reached the studio carrying the frame for the Mount Rainier photograph, a bag of cleaning supplies, and a tin of the adhesive tape her uncle had mentioned.

On the desk she found a list of the negatives Mr. Aldrich wanted made up first and went to work. When he came in, she greeted him from the darkroom. "I've developed the negatives you chose and I'm ready to begin mounting them," she said, taking off her coverall. Coming out of the dark room, she saw her boss picking things up and putting them down, clearly uncomfortable about something.

"How nice you look." Louise plucked a carnation from a vase of flowers on the desk and attached it to his lapel. "I know you're nervous about going away but I don't want you to worry. I promise everything here will be fine. If something comes up that I can't take care of, I'll just set it aside until you return. Please try and relax and have a good time. This is a wonderful opportunity to hear about new developments in photography." When her boss smiled, she laughed. "Goodness, I didn't intend to make such a silly pun."

Outside, a vehicle stopped in front of the studio and Mr. Aldrich quit fiddling. He took a deep breath which ended in a heavy sigh and straightened his shoulders. "I'm sure you will do just fine, Miss Tanquist." Picking up his bag, he turned toward the door. For a moment he hesitated, then went out and got in the waiting car. Behind him, Louise walked to a window and watched as the car pulled into traffic. *He should be a little excited*, she thought, *but he only looks apprehensive and sad. No doubt a wife would have made him feel comfortable. I wonder why he never married.* Feeling as if some of the bloom had gone off the day, she filled a pail of water, tied a scarf around her hair, and took a box outside to stand on while washing the bowed windows. For a few minutes, she heard their neighbor, Olof Bull, tuning instruments, knowing that when school was over for the day, a stream of students would converge on his atelier to take music lessons. The previous week she'd delivered a photograph he took from the top of Mount Rainier and was amazed to see the shelves, tables and piano covered with piles of sheet music, portraits of some of his former students and, as in the case of the Mount Rainier photograph, pictures, and newspaper clippings of things he found particularly interesting. "I haf no voman to keep it tidy," he explained. Louise liked the elderly man but wondered if his students were able to understand his thick Swedish accent.

As she worked, the street filled with milk wagons beginning to make deliveries, and then by farm carts full of produce rolling in from outlying areas: vegetables that had been buried in straw and kept in root cellars all winter, and the first of the season's strawberries. Nell said that before they were driven out of town, the Chinese always brought in the season's produce ahead of everyone else.

Through reflections in the glass, Louise spotted a few coal peddlers, and for a brief period, before automobiles appeared, the air was fresh and birds foraged for food mostly uninterrupted. A man passing by stopped and offered to wash the places at the top she couldn't reach and when he was done, Louise made short shrift of cleaning the glass on the inside and unjamming the resonator, so the door chime worked. She also polished the brass street numbers until they gleamed. *Now for the fun stuff,* she thought, setting Mr. Aldrich's easel in one of the windows and heading for the storage closet. A photographer's studio, she'd quickly learned, was full of chairs, rugs, small tables, potted plants, and any number of things necessary to create a setting. Louise found several baskets and an old buffalo hide rug and arranged them around the easel. The Mt. Rainier photograph fit perfectly in the frame she asked Reuben to make. Going back outside to stand on the sidewalk, Louise was pleased with the display. Mr. Turrell, who owned a nearby shoe store, joined her.

"Nice photograph."

"I think so. Mr. Aldrich is terribly talented."

At that moment Vic Malstom's clock began to chime and as if on cue they both laughed. "Looks like Vic got his clock fixed," Mr. Turrell said.

"I guess the complaint in the *Times* did the trick."

The shoe salesman consulted his pocket watch. "It's running fast, though."

Louise nodded. "Jane Austin said she wouldn't be dictated to by a watch because they were always too fast or too slow."

"Hmm." Mr. Turrell returned his watch to his vest pocket. "I feel sure Mrs. Turrell would agree." He gave the mountain picture a last look, nodded to Louise, and continued down the sidewalk to his store, stepping into the street to avoid the shoeshine man. Mike had been a fixture on Pacific Avenue for as long as anyone could remember and was well known for touting his favorite causes. Louise watched as he hoisted signs in support of Camp Lewis and heard him say to a passerby, "I'll boost anything that makes more shoes." Sighing, she went back inside. Several times recently she'd heard young men singing, war songs, most often, *Keep the Home Fires Burning*, which brought tears to her eyes. *And then there's that odious man, Henry Ford,* she thought. *Went to Europe on a peace mission and came back home all excited about Russia's needing tractors.* The window glass shook when she slammed the door.

The previous evening Mr. Aldrich had chosen the Better Baby photographs he felt were the best and Louise spread them out on the counter and went in search of mattes. What she found was a motley collection made from wood pulp paper or cotton rags, all of them either dark gray or black. "Lord, love us," she muttered.

For the next half an hour she did her best to make them presentable and shifted the pictures and mattes around until she finally decided on what looked the best with what she had. Using the adhesive, she hung one of the Beautiful Babies contest's advertising posters on the left side of the empty window and positioned the best of the photographs around it in a circular pattern. Then she did the same with the Biscuits and Jam eaters. However, here she'd had some fun on several of the pictures inserting shadowy ghost images of disapproving women looking over the boys' shoulders. It was only when she started outside to see how the window looked that Louise realized how cold it had gotten. Looking up, she saw ominous, charcoal-colored clouds pressing down. The stores across the street were no longer visible. A serious rainstorm was hunkering down over the city. The few earlier raindrops changed to a downpour and Pacific Avenue was rapidly filling with puddles. She took one quick look and ran back inside only to discover that the room had grown very cold. Mr. Aldrich was paying off a stove called the Merit Heater which he'd purchased from the Stone Fisher Company.

"You can burn either wood or coal," he told Louise, "But let's not be overly extravagant."

Remembering his caution, Louise put on a moth-eaten sweater she'd found hanging on the back of the darkroom door and placed two pieces of coal and a single log in the stove. She was pumping a pair of bellows to encourage the flame when a thump on the door caught her attention. Thinking it might be a bird, she opened it and saw a small, thin, and very wet dog trying to find a place out of the storm. *Oh, dear, you are a sad looking thing.* She stood aside, and the animal made a beeline or the stove. "Well," she laughed, "As Lady MacBeth said, 'Stand not upon the order of your going,' or in this case, coming in." She shut the door, took off the sweater and made a bed near the stove. "You're lucky I'm such a softy, but lately, there's been someone killing dogs and tossing them in Gallagher Gulch and you're too cute for that to happen." She gave the dog half-a-sandwich from her lunch and ate the other half.

It had always seemed to her as if when people couldn't be outside, they took to the phone and, sure enough, it began to ring. Louise sat at the desk with a pad and pencil answering questions, taking inquiries, and passing on information. Two men and a woman who had been in town earlier called about the Mount Rainier photograph, four people wanted to know if she'd taken a picture of their baby at the contest, and a man from the *Tacoma Times* asked her to mail one with a biscuit eating boy and ghost image. Nell called to say she'd be working late with Annie helping her. Louise had just hung up the phone when the door flew open and ricocheted off the wall. She gasped and jumped up, and the dog stood and growled. A man almost completely covered in an oilcloth cape burst into the room.

"Sorry," said a familiar voice. "It got away from me." He pulled off the oilskin, shook it outside, and shut the door. "Did I startle you?"

"Well, yes, but, good grief, Matthew, what are you doing out in this weather?"

"You invited me to come by to see your work?"

"Invited? I believe I merely suggested." Louise tried to sound frosty, but she raised her eyebrows and half smiled.

"A man acts on suggestions when he understands their aim."

"Oh, really." Louise sat back down and rested her chin on her hand. "And what, exactly, was my aim, do you think?"

"Uh?"

Louise had surprised herself with the easy banter, but Matthew clearly wasn't prepared to flirt. *Did he even know how handsome he was?* she wondered. *Hadn't other women found him so? And told him?* Almost immediately, he regained his poise. "Anyway, besides seeing the pictures, I came to see if you can help me with something." He walked to the stove and held his hands out to catch some heat. "This the best you could do?"

"I didn't want to use a lot of Mr. Aldrich's fuel. I have no idea what he can afford. His business seems a bit slow, at least it has been since I've been working here. Anyway, what do you need my help with?"

Matthew squatted down and stroked the dog's head. "Yours?"

"A stray. He came to the door and asked for shelter."

"She."

"Pardon?"

"The dog. It's a female." He stood and sighed. "I have to check up on two boys living in a shack down on the tide flats. Their mother was just put in the sanitarium, and they've been alone ever since. The Juvenile Morals Officer learned about them and came to us. My uncle had a meeting to attend and sent me to pick the boys up. He found them a temporary home."

"Your uncle or the Officer?" At that moment the phone rang. When Louise answered, the caller was her boss, and the conversation was brief. She hung up after a few yesses and noes. "Mr. Aldrich heard about the storm and is sending me home."

"Good. Then you can come with me first. The dog, too. Boys usually like dogs. Where's your coat?"

"Hey! Don't you think you're presuming upon yourself just a little?"

"Yes. They teach us that in medical school."

Louise snorted but she tidied the desk and addressed an envelope to the *Times* for the requested photograph and left it for the postman to pick up. Then Matthew helped her with her coat. "I'm afraid this won't be very warm," he said, "Wait here and I'll get a blanket from the car." Louise, feeling his breath on the side of her face, tried not to tremble. *What is wrong with me,* she thought, *I barely know this man.* While he was out, she shut down the stove and put a fire guard in front of it to stop any stray sparks, then turned off the lights. He returned with a blanket for her and one to wrap the dog in and the three dashed to the car.

"Goodness, what weather." Louise wiggled to find a comfortable position and cuddled the dog. "Where are we going?"

"Just beyond the Puyallup River Bridge to Lincoln Avenue. They live in a hovel their mother pieced together on some upright timbers sunk into the mud."

"Oh, my."

"'Oh, my' is right. According to the Officer, the boys have a small windowless room in the back. The tide brings water up almost to the floor."

After that, the noise of a rumbling streetcar and the sound of rain hitting the car put an end to their conversation. While Matthew concentrated on keeping the car from slipping on the wet road, Louise hugged the dog and looked out the window at empty sidewalks and some of the still well-lit businesses: People's Store, the Union Suit House for Men and Young Men, and Commercial Auto; but the Moose Confectionary and the Imperial Cafeteria were dark. Pewter-colored clouds hunkered down over the city, and Louise poked the dog under blankets to help keep both of them warm. After a few minutes, they passed the Northern Pacific Building and the massive Tacoma Hotel and started down the 80-foot-wide wharf road to the waterfront. "Did you know this is called the Magnificent Drive?" she said. Matthew mumbled something. He kept a tight grip on the wheel as the car slid on quagmires of mud and lurched in and out of unseen holes. At the bottom, he flexed his hands and exhaled in relief. "'Magnificent, my er—never mind." He made a sharp right, turning south. Barely visible in the water-saturated air hovering over the city were the tall shapes belonging to the Northwestern Wooden Ware Company, and the Eureka Dock's shorter ones. An undeveloped piece of land separated them from the Tacoma Gas and Fuel. Any lights that happened to be on made an eerie glow in the murkiness.

Driving carefully, Matthew crossed a narrow, questionably safe plank bridge over the Puyallup River / Commencement Bay estuary and headed toward Lincoln Avenue where he stopped.

"Wait here until I get out some lanterns." He rooted in the back and soon handed one to Louise plus a length of rope. "For the dog."

Matthew led the way over couple of boards, half submerged in mud, to the door which he knocked then opened. Inside, Louise saw a table, planks laid across logs for a seating bench, and a rusty stove. In one corner, a low chair hovered above a hole in the floor. *Good Lord, it's an indoor outhouse,* she thought as the smell reached her. On the back wall was a second door which opened into a lean-to where the boys huddled in a bed. The room was dark, damp and smelled of sewage and low tide.

"I told you I'd be back," Matthew said cheerfully. He handed his lantern to Louise. "And first things first, I brought you some food." Putting a basket on the foot of the bed, he began unloading it, bringing out sandwiches, milk, and a lid-covered pail with soup in it. "Boys, this is my friend, Miss Tanquist. She's a photographer. Louise, this young man," he handed the older boy a sandwich, "is Howard." Smelling food, the dog jumped on the bed and the younger of the two laughed weakly before breaking into a hacking cough. Louise's heart constricted when, before eating himself, he broke off a piece of the sandwich and gave it to the dog. "And this fellow feeding the dog when he should be eating himself is Gene."

"Hello boys." There was no place to sit so Louise hunkered down on the floor. "Yikes, this is cold."

Matthew continued chatting while the boys ate and Louise took flannel shirts, jackets, and pants out of the basket. She smiled when Gene asked if she was going to take their picture. "Do you want me to?"

"No," said Howard. "Not until we're cleaned up. Then you can and we can give it to Ma. Matthew, will we be seeing her when we leave?"

"Not right away. She's been resting and trying to get well. But when she's a little more up-and-at-'em you will."

It didn't take long for the food to disappear. Matthew gave them a few minutes to rest then handed shirts to each of them. "Unless you want your old clothes, we'll just leave them here. That way someone can find them and use them. Okay?"

"Nobody'd want these old rags."

"Hm, well, you might be right."

"Gene laughed and coughed. "You made a poem."

"Well, so I did. Now, when you're done, Miss Tanquist will close her eyes while you put on the pants."

Louise put the uneaten food and the pail back in the basket. It seemed to her that the boys hadn't eaten much. From the bay a foghorn blew long and low and, near the shack, a rat screeched and she jumped. "We have an owl what catches them," Gene said between coughs. "Say," he paused to catch his breath, "What's the dog's name?"

"She doesn't have one yet. I just got her this afternoon." Louise said. She wasn't used to talking to children, so she responded as if he was an adult. Helping him sit up and pull off his shirt she thought, *I may just need a fine-tooth comb after this,* and was torn between being ashamed for passing judgement and merely facing facts. "You see, it's been raining something awful, and she came to the door of the studio where I work and asked to come in, so of course I said 'yes' and gave her an old sweater to lay on and she snuggled right down in front of the stove to dry off and take a nap."

"But she has to have a name." Gene scooched over to the edge of the bed and began pulling on the pants. "Say, these are nice and warm, aren't they?"

"That's because they're lined with flannel," Matthew said. "And they're yours to keep."

"I think we should call her Queenie." Howard said.

"That's a good name." Louise helped Gene stand and rolled up his cuffs. "I have a cat named Princess and the names match, don't they?" When he began coughing, she handed him her handkerchief. "Cough into this."

With Howard taking Gene's hand and Louise holding onto the dog's lead and carrying the basket, they followed the lanterns Matthew held outside. The rain had stopped but moisture still hung heavy in the sullen sky. "Once, when it rained real hard," Gene began, but stopped to catch his breath, "and water was coming through the floor, Ma got on our bed, and we pretended we were on a ship. We didn't have a lot to eat but Ma said that was like being at sea and that sailors had to fish for their food. She told us stories about being sailors."

They squelched through the mud to the car where the boys got in the back and huddled under a blanket and Louise, holding Queenie, shivered in the front. She sniffed and whipped her nose on her cuff and Matthew handed her his handkerchief.

"I'm going to drop Miss Tanquist off first," he told the boys, "then I'll take you to your new home."

"I want to see Ma," Gene said, his trembling voice barely audible over the grinding gears. And Louise and Matthew exchanged looks.

"If she's well enough for company, I'll take you to see her tomorrow."

"Why wouldn't she be well enough?"

"Well, she was pretty sick when she went to Mountain View." Matthew fiddled with a lever and a blade came up and cleaned off the windshield. "But that was a month ago and likely she's much better now. Okay, everybody be quiet so I can focus on driving."

It took much longer to get back to town than it had to reach the waterfront. Thanks to road conditions, the wharf road had been closed, and Matthew was forced to drive to Old Tacoma and creep up Star Street toward Stadium Way. Once there, though, it was a fairly easy drive to D Street. "I hear the street name is being changed to Market Street," he said.

"Yes," Louise shifted Queenie off her left arm which was going to sleep. "The mayor thinks the name change will make it more respectable."

"How's that?"

"There's a lot of prostitution on D down closer to Eleventh Street, but I just can't imagine hearing any of the ladies of the night saying, 'Well, I can't stay here on a street called Market. It sounds too respectable.'"

Matthew laughed. "I agree." He pulled over to the side of the road. "Here we are."

"You remembered where I live."

"Of course. And your—uh."

"Nell is my adopted mother. She was on a trip to San Francisco and that's where she found me. She's the best I could have ever wanted, but someday I want to go to San Francisco and find my real mother. It feels funny to not know who you are." Suddenly, the emotion of the day caught up with her, and she didn't wait for him to come around and help her out. "Keep me posted on the boys, I have a vested interest."

"I will and thank you. Children always do better when there is a woman around and the dog was a bonus."

"Don't forget about our picture," said Howard.

"I won't. You can come to the studio, or I can come to where you're living. Just let me know. Bye boys, bye Matthew. Drive carefully." Louise shut the door and hurried up the sidewalk. "I'm taking the hottest bath I can stand," she said to the dog, and then I'm putting you in the tub." She unlocked the door, adding, "And don't pick on the cat."

Chapter 4

Of all the rooms in the house, next only to her bedroom, Louise loved the bathroom the most. Nell had spared no expense on the porcelain, hex-tiled floor, white tile wainscotting, and deep, free-standing bathtub. The room was on the second floor so she had the tub placed where bathers could look out the window. Louise turned on the hot water, added rose scented, Bathodora bath salts, and peeled off her clothes. "The one time a corset would have kept me warmer than this backless brassiere," she said to Queenie who was watching her from the doorway. She tossed her clothes into the laundry basket and climbed into the tub. Scented steam filled the bathroom as she sunk down into the hot water. Outside the sky was slowly clearing and a few brave birds were leaving the protection tall trees provided. As she watched, crows, gulls, and a robin passed the window. "I think I'll call Nell and see if she needs anymore help," she told the dog. "I'll leave you in my room." However, Nell arrived home while she was toweling off Queenie and before she could make the call.

"I bought home dinner from Chong Wa's restaurant," Nell said. "Lordy, what a day. Get the dishes out, will you." She filled a coffee pot with water, added grounds, and put it on stove. Turning around she gave a start. "What's a dog doing here?"

"The poor thing came to the studio door absolutely drenched from the rain and I had to let her in. Her name is Queenie."

"How do you know?"

"Because I named her."

"And you plan to keep her?"

"Yes, ma'am. I couldn't put her out now."

"What does Princess think about this?"

55

Louise grinned "She's already let Queenie know she's the boss. Cats always do, don't they."

Nell sighed, but she remembered bringing a dog home when she was about Louise's age, one that lived to a ripe old age, and broke her heart when he died. She sat at the table saying, "Mrs. Altamont was in. She was telling me about a party she and the doctor gave to introduce their nephew, Matthew, to society."

"Society." Louise made a rude noise which Nell ignored.

"She said you're a friend of her nephew."

Louise put down plates and silverware. "Where's Annie?"

"She grabbed something to eat from a street vendor and went with some friends to see *The Immigrant.*"

They began spooning rice and chicken on their plates and Louise said, "Yes, I met Matthew on the streetcar. He wanted to know if it was the right car to get to the Tabernacle. Then today I helped him with a couple of sick boys. He's a doctor, too."

"Yes, Mrs. Altamont said he's joining her husband's practice."

"That's what he said. Umm, this is yummy."

They ate in silence for a few minutes before Nell put her fork down. "We should be using chopsticks." She closed her eyes and rubbed her forehead. "I think I'll have my eyes checked."

"Can I get you a cold compress. Would you like a BC Powder."

"No to the powder but yes to the compress. I'll build a fire in the parlor and sit there, and it would be lovely if you could bring me a cold compress." She smiled at Louise. "You mentioned helping the young doctor with some boys and I want to hear about it."

"I'll just clean this up and be right with you." Louise began clearing the uneaten food away, feeding some to her pets. When the kitchen was clean, she filled a basin with water, found a scrap of towel and joined Nell.

Soon all four were sitting in the dimly lit room, Nell with a small glass of whiskey in one hand, a purring cat on her lap, and a cold compress over her eyes. A madrona wood fire burned quietly, sending out heat and a pleasant aroma reminiscent of honey. "The Murrays were arrested for selling alcohol," she said, breaking the silence, then added, "again."

Louise laughed and cuddled Queenie. "Pete Marinoff and the Murrays will figure out a way to keep the city fathers supplied."

Nell sighed. "You're too young to know about these things." She sipped her drink. "Tell me about your day." Listening to Louise's voice, which was a particularly pleasing contralto, and knowing how the girl's dark eyes sparkle as she talked helped her relax. "Well, you had quite a day," Nell said when Louise wound down, "and Matthew sounds like a nice young man."

"I think he is, and probably all the women he meets through his aunt and uncle will, too." She pulled the tie off her hair and re-tied it. "I think I should get my hair cut. It's so fine I just can't control it."

Nell moved the cat off her lap, put her empty glass on an end table, and stood up. "I'm too tired to talk about that now. We can discuss it later." She kissed Louise on the cheek. "'night, love. Don't forget the fire screen."

Louise put it in place, took the empty glass to the kitchen to wash, and then went to her own room. Princess jumped onto the window ledge and Queenie hopped on the bed, burrowing under the blankets. Five minutes later, they were all asleep.

Overnight, the storm blew itself out. In their yard, warm sun began drying the land, much to the distress of worm-seeking robins. Louise caught the streetcar to work and sat near a window to finish an article on Irene Castle she'd begun reading at breakfast. A young woman seated next to her glanced over saying, "I just read that article. Have you seen the picture of her new haircut? It's on the last page." Louise flipped to the end and grinned. Here was just what she wanted. "It's called 'a bob,'" the woman continued. "It's French."

Louise breathed a happy sigh and the two exchanged smiles. "I love it."

"Me, too."

When she arrived at the studio the phone was ringing and continued doing so for most of the morning. The *Times* used the photograph she'd sent, and people wanted to know if she had a similar picture of their son. While explaining to an umpteenth caller that she didn't know the boys, but that people were welcome to come in and look at the photographs, she was hard-pressed to find time to make a pot of coffee, something her boss liked as much as she did. Then, between phone calls, a middle-aged woman, severely dressed in black, arrived wanting a picture of her twin boys that she could use in an advertising poster. With an actual customer to take care of, Louise shut the phone in a desk drawer.

"I'm Mrs. Merritt," the woman said.

"It's nice to meet you." Louise held out her hand, and the surprised woman took it before she had time to think. Then Louise looked pointedly at the boys who were teasing Queenie.

Mrs. Merrit said, "Harold, Eugene, leave the dog alone and come here where I can keep my eye on you. Now," she pulled a bag out from under her coat, "they are pugilists; perhaps you've read about them. Both the *Times* and the *Ledger* have been following their career, and I'd like a photograph showing them boxing."

"John L. Sullivan, himself taught us," one of the boys said.

"My goodness." Louise tried to show the proper reverence. She knew the name but not much else. Looking at the pair, she said, "do you have any ideas about how you want to appear in the picture?"

"Show me knocking Eugene out." Harold danced around his brother jabbing him at intervals. Eugene immediately retaliated and their mother grabbed a handful of hair from each of them.

"Ow, ow." They both wiggled around, trying to pull loose.

"Do you have a background that would be appropriate?" Mrs. Merritt released her grip, and the boys rubbed their heads.

Louise knew they didn't but was loath to say so. "Let's me see, what do you have in the bag? Okay, three pairs of boxing gloves" She pounced on the extra pair. "What if we hang these on the wall." She unrolled a newspaper with an article from one of their fights. "And this. Boys, are you going to change your clothes?" With Mrs. Merritt watching and Queenie hiding under the desk, she hung the paper and gloves on a wall, stretched a piece of rope between two old curtain rods and once the boys had changed, told them to start posing as if they were boxing. The doorbell rang when a couple of women came in to look at pictures of the biscuit eating contest and then stayed to watch and comment. With their mother calling out instructions, the boys played to the audience and Louise took several pictures. "There," she said, "I think we have some good shots from which to choose."

"Harold, Eugene, change your clothes, and quit fiddling with things." Mrs. Merritt took the paper and gloves off the wall. "When will they be ready?"

"I'll have the negatives ready tomorrow, and you can choose what you want."

"That will be fine." She shoved the twins' boxing attire back in the bag. "I'll be here early."

The three left and Louise turned to the women. "Ladies, thank you for waiting. Did you see your son's pictures on the window?"

"I didn't," said one.

"I did," said the other. "Can you make it like the one in the paper?"

"Would you like your photograph as a ghostly figure?"

59

"Can you do that?"

"Yes, certainly. It's a matter of overlaying negatives. Now," Louise shuffled a few things around before asking the woman to stand against a wall facing the window. She fussed a bit to make the process appear more complicated than it was and took more pictures than necessary. In answer as to when the picture would be ready, she said in two days.

"Well, lucky you," said her companion somewhat peevishly.

"I can always create one for you," Louise smiled. "You can make an appointment right now and bring your son in and I can replicate a photograph and have it ready by the end of the week."

"I'll think about it," she said. "Come on, Evie or we'll miss the sale."

The lucky woman paid for her picture and the two left, but other people came in, and Louise was busy selling photographs from the window and taping up replacements. The clock was striking two-thirty when she refreshed her coffee, sat out of sight of the window with her feet up, and started eating lunch. Pedestrians, their shoes echoing on the wooden sidewalk, stopped to look at the new displays. Some laughed, some didn't, but all of them seemed to approve of the framed Mount Rainier. The post office motorcycle man pulled up, and Louise walked out to the road to get the mail. Streetcars came and went. Store awnings snapped in a slight breeze, and automobiles either pulled into the first parking place available or pulled out. The only horses Louise saw was a pair pulling the Tacoma Laundry wagon. A little girl rode on the back of one, her skinny legs sticking out on either side, and Louise ran to get her camera. When the wagon stopped, she waved at the girl and took several pictures. Then Queenie barked, looking as if she wanted to charge the horses, and Louise pulled her back inside. "Time to do some work in the darkroom," she said to the dog. Mrs. Merritt had left a sizeable deposit and Louise locked it in the desk with other money. She took the phone off the hook and hurried to the darkroom. "In or out," she said to the dog and Queenie sighed and stretched out. She'd already taken a dislike to the room.

With the safelight on, Louise carefully wound her film onto a spool and put it in the developing tank. In her opinion, seeing what she'd captured was like opening a Christmas gift. She'd just finished rinsing off the fixing fluid when the doorbell sounded, and Queenie barked.

"I'll be out in a minute," she shouted while hanging up the negatives.

Leaving the darkroom, she found the dog glaring at a policeman. Her first thought was that Nell had been in an accident. Seeing her alarm, the officer was quick to reassure her.

"I, that is we, Detectives Wiley and Moudahl and me, I'm Detective Moudahl, by the way, need a photographer, a female—for a female—for a crime. Not for something she did but something that was done to her." He fidgeted looking uncomfortable. "You came recommended." Louise poured him a cup of coffee and invited him to sit down.

"Really? Golly. Well, take your time and tell me what this is all about." She sat at the desk with her own coffee and waited.

The detective sighed and ran finger under his collar. "We're investigating the attack of a young woman. It's similar to one that happened a year ago. At that time a girl walked to a gulch about a mile from her house and was sitting on a log reading a magazine when someone beat her."

"Oh, how awful. The poor thing. Is she alright? What a horrible thing to do."

"Yes, ma'am, I agree. We got a hobo camp near Seventeenth Street, and a boy was murdered there, and another girl was attacked and hurt pretty bad. A man came up from behind and struck her with a club. He tied her hands and stole her jewelry and some cash. We never caught him and now another young woman has been attacked." He took a gulp of his coffee before continuing. "Her name is Irene Carmel. She got sick while at work and asked to go home. She works at Carstens Packing Company which isn't far from her house, so she generally walks to and from. She lives on East Thirty Fourth and usually takes a trail in a local gulch. Her brother found her when he was walking home from work. She was able to tell us that two men accosted her. One aimed a revolver at her head, and the other began beating her on the head and shoulders with a piece of wood. She began to stagger and could barely stand, and they gagged her, and tied her wrists behind her with some rusty bailing wire at which time she fainted. Her brother found her four hours later."

"Golly." Louise was at a loss for words and thankful when the phone rang. After taking care of the call, she asked Detective Moudahl why he had come to the studio.

"We need photographs of the injuries," he said. "And naturally a lady photographer is more appropriate than a male."

Louise pursed her lips. "I'd like to help you but I'm new to photography. Surely you want a woman with more experience."

"The doctor recommended you; he thinks a young woman would be better than an older one."

"Matthew Altamont?"

"Yes, ma'am. That's the one. Look, Miss Tanquist," the detective stood up and put his cup on the desk. "I need to know if you'll do it or not. If you won't I'll have to find someone else."

"Of course, I will." Louise looked at the clock. "The studio closes in forty-five minutes. Give me the address and I'll take a cab. Does she know a photographer will be coming and will the doctor be there?"

The detective smiled, looking relieved. "No need to pay for a cab, I'll send a car for you. The driver will wait and take you home."

"Does an officer have to be present while I take the pictures?"

"No, just you and the doctor."

"Fine. Now, if you'll excuse me, I'd better collect what I need. Oh," she stood and looked at him, "Who should we bill?"

"The police department will pay." He opened the door letting in fresh air and street noise. "Thank you, Miss Tanquist."

Forty-five minutes later, a partially enclosed patrol wagon stopped in front of the studio and a policeman got out leaving the vehicle running. He opened a door to the back seat door saying, "It's a hand crank, ma'am and easier to leave running."

"That's all right." Louise lifted a reluctant Queenie onto the seat and blocked her with the photography bag. She smiled at the officer. "I'm Louise Tanquist."

"John Doyle." The weather-worn looking man in a rumpled uniform helped her in and shut the door.

"I haven't seen many police cars on the streets."

"No, ma'am." He did something with the gears, made a U-turn, and merged into the traffic going south. "This is a 1908 Stoddard-Dayton."

"My goodness," Louise said, for lack of an appropriate comment.

"Yes, ma'am. It doubles as an ambulance."

"Well, that seems a good use of city dollars."

"Yeah, maybe, but I got a brother-in-law works in Akron and the police car he drives has electric lights and gong and has a stretcher. "A 'course this one can go up to fifty miles an hour and his can only reach sixteen miles an hour. But a paddy wagon shouldn't be toting sick folks to the hospital."

Thinking that a motorized vehicle of any kind was probably the best way to get people to the help they needed, Louise decided to change the subject. "Where are we going?" She pitched her voice so it could carry over the sounds of the engine.

"The Carmels live on East Thirty-fourth. He turned onto Puyallup Avenue saying, "Fewer hills this way."

Puyallup Avenue's poor condition put an end to all conversation. Louise held onto a shaking Queenie with one arm and her camera bag with the other while the car juddered about on the pitted dirt road. They passed Gentell's soft drink parlor and offices for the Tacoma Railway and Power Company. When they had to slow down approaching a tall building at the corner of Fourth Street, several women waved at them out the window and as soon as he could Detective Moudahl increased the car's speed.

Louise grinned. "Look," she said," next door is the Puget Sound Homesteaders Ladies Reading Club. Do you think the ladies who waved at us are club members?"

The officer was quiet for so long Louise wasn't sure he heard her. "When he finally spoke, it was as if he'd given a lot of thought to the question. "I've arrested a lot of bad girls in my time and they're generally good girls who fell in with the wrong man, one who just happened to say the right things. But I don't remember any of them professing to love books."

"Oh, dear," Louise said. "Now I feel ashamed of being flippant."

"Not to worry, Miss." Officer Doyle turned south off Puyallup Avenue. "I've lived a lot longer than you and I try to remember to forgive others as I want to be forgiven. Now, here we are." He stopped and set the brake in front of a modest, one-and-a-half story house. Thirty-fourth Street was a hill, and Louise had to climb a short slope and then six steps to reach the porch. She knocked on the door, and it was opened almost immediately by a middle-aged woman whose ashen face showed the strain she was under.

"Photographer?" She kept the screen door closed.

"Yes, ma'am. My name is Louise Tanquist and this is Queenie." Louise gestured to the dog. "Can she come in?"

The woman lifted the latch and stepped aside. "Irene wants all the doors kept locked; she's that nervous, but she likes dogs. Hers died a while back and I been meaning to get her another but, what with one thing or another, I haven't gotten around to it. Follow me, she's there in the parlor."

Louise followed the sound of voices and found herself in a surprisingly large room where all the lamps were lit, and a gentle fire in a brick fireplace cast dancing shadows about. Matthew sat on a loveseat and Irene Carmel on a chair in a corner. Setting her bag down, Louise went immediately to the fireplace followed by Queenie. "This is lovely. I didn't realize how cold I was. I hope you don't mind Queenie. Your mother tells me you like dogs." While the dog plopped down, Louise held her hands to the heat.

"Mine died."

"Yes, she said that. I don't know if it's a good thing or a bad thing that there are always plenty of dogs needing a home. I've only had Queenie for a few days. She was a stray caught in that terrible rainstorm we had." Louise laughed. "I think she's about the laziest thing I've ever seen."

Pictures and figurines a filled a mantle above the hearth and Louise leaned in to look. Half-turning, she smiled at a young woman who'd shifted her chair as far as possible from the street-facing window. "Who's this with you?"

"My brother."

When she was comfortably warm, Louise sat in the chair nearest Irene. "The brother who rescued you?"

"The only one I got."

"You're lucky. There's just me at home. I was adopted." She took a deep breath. "It smells good in here."

"I've been feeling puckish since—. Anyway, Ma's roasting a chicken."

"I guess you know why I'm here."

"Yes." Irene's voice was no more than a monotone, but her eyes darted around the room and her fingers plucked at her lap blanket.

Louise beckoned to Queenie who left the hearth and walked over. "Queenie loves to have her ears rubbed," she said. Irene stroked the dog, and Louise got a good look at the deep grooves left by the rusty wire on her wrists and the reddish-purple marks fanning out from each side.

"It's the second time, you know."

"I beg your pardon?" Louise barely waited for an answer. "The second time you've been attacked? Oh, my dear. I'm just so very sad that this would happen to you." She looked up with tears in her eyes and put out a tentative finger but pulled back when Irene flinched. Clearing her throat, she said, "I've never worked for the police before so I hope you and Dr. Altamont will be patient with me and tell me if you think I'm doing anything wrong." She stood and aimed the lens at Irene's wrists, snapping pictures from several different angles.

"Now, I'm going to put another log on the fire so the room will be warm while I photograph your back." Irene nodded and continued patting Queenie. When Louise was ready, she asked Irene to stand facing the fireplace and Matthew to leave the room. "I suppose a male doctor sees female bodies all the time," she said, "but that's while he's treating them. This is different, don't you think? More personal. Now, please stay as still as you can." Louise shifted from side to side, taking photographs from a variety of angles. "This is a lovely, cozy room."

"Ma's been busy getting it ready for my wedding."

"Married? You're getting married. How wonderful. When?" She fiddled with the camera. "Do you have anything to cover your breasts?"

"I can hold up my robe." Irene hugged it against her chest and turned around. "In two weeks. We postponed it to give me a chance to recover."

Focusing her camera on the girl's torso Louise snapped three pictures, the first one close up which eliminated Irene's head and legs. The next focused on the girl's back. Even to Louise's untrained eye, the large areas of parallel lines on her back, ribs and abdomen looked as if the assailants used a thick, straight piece of wood. "Who's the lucky man?" She squatted down and concentrated on the injuries her legs had taken.

"His name is Besaw. He plays baseball for the Carsten's Packing Company team."

"I'd love to take a wedding picture if you'd let me. Okay, I'll do your neck, chest and arms now."

For the following fifteen minutes the only sound to be heard came from traffic on the road, children kicking a can around, and the sounds the camera made. When Louise said she was done, Irene put her robe back on and pulled the collar high around her neck. "The pictures are black and white; how will anyone be able to see the bruising?"

"The bruises will show up as dark gray or black—clearly visible because your skin is so pale. It would be much more difficult if you were swarthy."

"Ma's always after me to stay out of the sun. If I'd listened, I might not have been attacked."

A door at the back of the room opened and Mrs. Carmel poked her head in. "Are you nearly done?"

"Almost. I just have the head gash left." Louise asked Irene to sit down so she could photograph her neck and the place where blood had congealed in her hair. She was finishing when Matthew knocked and entered the room. "Irene was just telling me she's getting married, Louise said while she packed away her equipment."

"Congratulations." He nodded and smiled. "Thank you for letting us take these pictures. They'll be a big help to the police. If another person is attacked, detectives can compare the bruising and see if it's the same person. People who repeat crimes get longer jail sentences."

"If they're caught," Irene said, and Louise and Matthew exchanged looks.

A clock chimed the hour, and they heard a car motor out front. "That will be my ride." Louise tied the piece of rope around Queenie's neck. "You didn't say if you'd like a wedding photo, but you can send word to the Aldrich Photography Studio if you're interested." She led the dog to the front door with Matthew following while Irene retreated to her corner. Mrs. Carmel opened the front door and thanked them.

When it closed behind them, Matthew said, "I'm hoping you'll let me take you to dinner."

"Oh, I would have loved that." The closed door and covered porch created an intimate darkness and Louise felt his warmth. She breathed in his scent and caught her breath. "I really would have, but we have a client, a Mrs. Merritt, who will be in first thing tomorrow to look at the contact sheet, and I promised to have it ready so she can choose her pictures."

Matthew laughed. "Oh, yes, the Merritts are the boy boxers, aren't they? I've seen articles in the paper about them. And contact sheets. That's that piece of paper with little thumbnail pictures on it, right?"

"Yes, and the boys' photographs could be a big thing for me. She's going to use them on posters made to advertise their fights. Goodness, Mr. Aldrich will be so surprised about my working with the police. When word gets around, it will help make our reputation. Thank you for recommending us, er, me."

Queenie yawned and plopped down, and Louise laughed. "I guess all this laying around has exhausted her." She looked at Matthew whose face was disconcertingly close. "Mr. Aldrich is a good employer, but he is old, well, elderly, at least, and I'm trying to learn everything he knows about photography while I can."

"And go into business for yourself?"

"Yes. Have my own studio."

The silence between was broken when a horn sounded. "I'll wait," Matthew said. "I'll wait until you're done and then we can go to dinner." He took her elbow, and in the dark, she appreciated his assistance while walking down the short hill to the waiting car.

With Queenie hustled in and onto the back seat, she said, Two hours, okay?"

"See you then."

When she'd finished, two hours later, Louise stashed her camera bag in the closet and locked the studio door behind her. Matthew, hands in pockets, was leaning against his car looking at lights coming on all over the city. "We're in the war," he said when Louise joined him. "President Wilson just made the announcement."

"Oh, no. Oh, golly." Louise looked unseeing at the lights. The traffic, both street and pedestrian, was increasing, and she felt an enormous weight descend. Shivering, she took Matthew's arm saying, "Let's go to Feeny's. It's just down the road."

Other than three railroad workers sitting at the back of the room, enveloped in a fugue of their own cigarette smoke, Feeny's was empty. Louise and Matthew chose a table in a corner near the front where they could look out the window and avoid most of the fumes. Feeny came over with a pot of coffee and menus. "You can bet your boots a lot of food will be going to the war," he said, putting the menus on the table, "so enjoy your vittles while you can." He raised an eyebrow at the sight of Queenie who had chosen that minute to stand up, turn around, and lay down again but otherwise ignored her as he gestured with his coffee pot.

"Yes, please," both Louise and Matthew said almost in unison and turned their attention to seeing what hadn't been crossed off the bill of fare. "Except for the smoke back there," Louise gestured with her head, "it smells good in here. What do you suggest?"

"Not the stew." Feeny waited and eventually, Matthew chose mutton and Louise ordered a plate of meat scraps for Queenie and chicken with potatoes and cream of celery soup for herself.

"What will happen now, do you think?" She asked after Feeny left.

"There will be a massive draft and a lot of the men will be sent to Camp Lewis for training. No doubt the Red Cross will get busy." He scrubbed his face with his hands. "The deaths will be the worst. Everything's going to change."

"I feel like I should be home."

"Why?"

Louise huffed a half-laugh. "I don't know?"

"Your family knows you're with me, right?"

"Yes. I called to let them know and tell them I'd be late."

"Well then."

They stopped talking and watched milling clusters of people converging on both the sidewalk and on Pacific Avenue. Then they turned their attention to the plates of food Feeny delivered. After a few minutes Matthew said, "Tell me about your family."

"What would you like to know?"

"Oh, how big is it? Where does everyone live, what do they do for a living, that kind of stuff. You're adopted and my uncle is my only family. We're sort of loners."

Outside, people yelled, a dog barked, and Queenie stood up and gave a single woof in response. Shop horns blared and a streetcar hauling freight rattled down the road. Someone from the Tacoma Pipers began playing a bagpipe and was quickly joined by men on coronets and clarinets.

"Why are they so happy when the music sounds so sad?" Louise began crumpling her napkin.

"A lot of people were angry about the sinking of the *Lusitania*," Feeny said as he came to remove Queenie's empty plate and give her a beef bone. "Guess they figure we'll be able to get some revenge." He left and Louise made a conscious effort to control her hands.

"You asked about my family. You will need a baseball scorecard to keep it all straight." She took a bite of chicken and chewed for a minute. "Golly, where to begin. Let's see, I live with Nell and Annie Penny. When she was little, Annie's father beat her so bad he broke one of her arms. She had outgrown the only dress she had and needed a new one only her father wanted her wages for liquor. She and Nell met when they were both helping Mrs. McCarver, down in Old Tacoma at a tea she was having. Even though they'd just met, Annie considered Nell to be her only friend, so that's who she went to for help, and she ended up staying." Louise laughed. "Someday I'll tell you about how Nell made him pay for her upkeep. Anyway, Nell owns a couture establishment and makes the most wonderful clothes, and Annie runs our house. My grandparents, Nell's parents, Obed and Amity and her older sister, Josie, live next door. Obed doesn't work much anymore, only some odd jobs when his aches and pains let him. Josie is hired all over town to play the piano. Their brother, Ike, and his wife Frieda Faye and my cousins live near Stadium High School because D Street is more than Frieda Faye can handle. Uncle Ike likes to change his job as often as he can to give him more time to go fishing. Frieda Faye likes to entertain so finding time to fish isn't a problem. Louise paused, grinned and ate some of the potatoes. "Shall I go on?"

"That's a good size family."

"Oh, heavens, there's more. Now, across the street is a double house. Nell's oldest and best friend, Hildy and her husband Samuel and their twin boys live on one side. Hildy has a bakery downtown and Samuel works for the forestry department. The boys, well, they're not really boys anymore, and they both work on some of the Mosquito Fleet boats. Hildy's mother, her sister, Dovie and her cousin live on the other side of the house. Their father died, and there's a little house in the back yard for Chong. He's been with them for years and sort of oversees the house and takes care of the women."

"Chinese?"

"Yes. "

"Weren't the Chinese driven out of town?"

"Yes, and a lot of other cities, too, but Chong didn't go. He cut off his queue, that's what their pigtail is called, put on western clothes, and stayed. Anyway, next to them, but in another house are Hildy's brother, Reuben, who married Nell's sister, my aunt Albina and they have three children. Nell has another sister, my aunt Indiana, but she and her family live down near Olympia where they have a farm. They have two boys and don't get this way much. And last but not lease is John Calhoun, Nell's beau. He's just the most wonderful, generous man; I don't know why Nell won't marry him. I wish she would."

"The draft will affect your family."

Louise sighed. "I haven't had time to think about that." She looked at Matthew's bleak expression and put a hand on his. "Please don't join until you have to."

But he kept his eyes on the table.

The street noise grew louder, the railroad workers paid and headed out to join the commotion outside, and Feeny started lifting chairs onto the tables and sweeping. "I guess that's a not-so subtle hint." Louise lifted her feet as he maneuvered his broom around their table, poking Queenie as he did so. He grunted something unintelligible, and they grinned and left.

Chapter 5

When Louise got home and opened the front door, she heard Nell and Annie talking in the kitchen. They were sitting at the table, opposite each other each, with a cup of coffee and a plate of cookies between them. Both women with a pad and pencil. Princess, sitting near the food, supervised. "You've had a long day," Nell said, standing to give Louise a hug.

What would I do if I didn't have this place and these two women to return to, Louise thought. She broke away and poured a cup of coffee saying, "Yes, I'm wacked. The poor girl I was asked to photograph, I don't know if scars from the wire cuts on her wrists will ever go away."

"How did you end up doing that?" Annie asked.

"Doctor Altamont was called to attend and he sent his nephew, so I imagine it was his idea, the nephew's, I mean. They wanted a female photographer. Gosh, I just came from dinner and I'm hungry all over again." She gave a piece of cookie to Queenie and ate the rest in one bite. "What are you two doing?"

Annie turned her pad so Louise could read what was written: flour, coffee, sugar, macaroni, soap, rice, the list went on. "The things we'll need to have on hand in case there's rationing. I'm going to the stores first thing tomorrow and buy in bulk."

Nell's list began with McCormack's: underwear, Rhodes Bros.: trimmings, linens, crepe, silk, muslins, cotton, and wool. The list continued almost to the bottom of the page. "When I first went into business, I used to buy used clothing and took it apart to reuse," she said. "I can do that again."

"Shoes should be on the list." Louise took another cookie. "I can buy some tomorrow. The People's Store is right down the street from the studio."

"That's a good idea. As I always say, hope for the best but prepare for the worst."

After a yawn so big it made her jaw pop, Louise took three more cookies and headed of bed. Princess lingered in the kitchen, but Queenie followed the cookies.

During her streetcar ride to work the next morning, Louise listened to various snippets of conversations: women were being asked to enlist though, when one tried, she was turned away; a small colony of Germans living near Ashford at the foothills of Mount Rainier was discovered and arrested because of voicing anti-American sentiments.

"Which, since they live here and not in Germany, seems a pretty stupid thing to do," someone said.

The police were already wanting people to give them the names of qualified men who didn't enlist, and stores were holding knitting classes. Approaching downtown Louise saw that Matthew had been correct in saying men would be flooding into town on their way to Camp Lewis.

"We'll be busy," Mr. Aldrich warned Louise when she arrived at work. "The phone was ringing when I came in; war brides wanting photographs and mothers wanting pictures of their sons." As he spoke, the phone rang again and while he talked to the person on the other end, Louise hurried to the darkroom to develop the Irene Carmel film. She came out to find her boss standing outside looking at the windows and was glad the phone rang yet again. While the caller explained what she wanted, Louise looked in amazement at the appointment book and was hard-pressed to squeeze her in. She made the appointment and looked apprehensively at Mr. Aldrich when he came back in.

"You were busy," he said. He thumbed through the pictures Mrs. Merritt ordered. "You have some interesting ideas." While he was speaking, the lady in question arrived.

"I'm very pleased," she said. "Unlike the last photographer I used, you went the extra distance. These are excellent, just what I wanted."

While she placed an order and left, Mr. Aldrich opened an envelope from the *Tacoma Times* and removed a check. "What's this for?"

Louise went to a file cabinet and found the folder with the Biscuit Eating pictures. "I was the only photographer there, and the paper wanted something to illustrate their coverage, I sent them a couple of pictures I took. Here," she handed him a page from the newspaper. "Here it is."

He was, Louise had come to realize, a very deliberate person, always taking his time before offering a comment. However, after looking at the picture she handed him, his only response was to smile. "Three men want to buy my Mount Rainier photograph," he said.

"Yes, there were calls almost as soon as I put it in the window." Louise did her best to remain calm and collected.

"Well, I must say, you did a fine job. I don't know what I expected while I was gone but it wasn't a window full of pictures, people coming in to pick up photographs, and checks in the mail. At this rate you'll be running the studio."

He smiled and Louise relaxed. She had just enough time to tell him about the photographs for the police when their first appointment arrived. The woman introduced herself as Mrs. Winona Wilcox, a writer for the *Times*. Mr. Aldrich indicated that Louise was to take the picture so, with a cup of coffee in hand, Mrs. Wilcox sat and explained what she wanted while her daughter, Dorothy, tried to interest Queenie in her doll.

"Can you have me overlooking Dorothy while she plays with the dog? I loved that picture of the Biscuit boy."

"Of course, and what kind of background would you like?"

After a spirited discussion, Louise hung a large piece of tapestry to the side of the stove, put a small rug in front of it, added a small pile of fire logs, and pulled a chair over. The trouble started with Dorothy's lackluster personality. She simply refused to look either interested in the going on, or interesting.

"Dorothy, dear, can't you smile for the lady."

"No."

"Why not?"

"I don't want to."

"Why not?"

"I don't feel like smiling."

"I think your doll would like a smile, don't you?"

"She doesn't care."

Louise choked back a laugh and exchanged looks with Mrs. Wilcox. "Is she often this, er, solemn?"

"It comes in fits and starts."

They waited patiently for ten minutes before Louise said, "Well, perhaps you'd like to try another day, when Dorothy is," she struggled to find a word that wouldn't offend, and settled on, "more cheerful."

"I can't. This is my only free day for quite a while."

While they strategized, Mr. Aldrich came out from behind his desk. He walked around, snapping his fingers and humming. Seeing that Louise was looking hopefully into her camera, he gave a sharp whistle. Queenie looked up and barked; Dorothy laughed, and the result was just what Mrs. Wilcox wanted. Taking a photograph to ghost her in was easy, and Mr. Aldrich told her he'd have the picture delivered to the *Times* the following day. For the rest of the morning there were more phone calls for appointments than there were customers. When things quieted down Louise told Mr. Aldrich that she'd promised to go buy some shoes. "Nell is making sure we'll be okay in case there are shortages," she said.

"A very good idea and I suggest you go to Rhodes Brothers rather than People's. I saw they are giving away a free pair for every pair bought. I'll watch the dog"

"Oh, wonderful, thank you." Louise left the studio in time to catch a streetcar for the two-block ride up the hill. The Bargain Department, where the shoe sale was going on, was in half of a large room on the fifth floor, sharing the space with sewing notions on the other side. When Louise arrived, a dozen or so women were discussing yarn with a saleswoman, and two salesmen were talking about a ball game between Rhodes and the Stone-Fisher Store, both were businesses members of the twilight league. She wandered around, feeling the leather and looking at the stitching until one of the men broke away and approached her.

"I don't recommend that style," he said, looking at the white kid leather shoe Louise had picked up. "We won't be wearing them much longer. Now, these," he picked up what Louise could only think of as 'serviceable,' "have been in storage and they're good quality. The war is going to use up all the leather and," he gestured around the room, "before the fighting is over, shoes may be made of shoddy material for all we know." He gave what Louise assumed was meant to be a winsome smile.

He started going through his merchandise, looking for the sizes Louise requested while talking non-stop, and making suggestions. Eventually she chose brown Russian calf, patent leather shoes for each of them, the white ones she'd admired, and three pair of lace ups. With the buy-one-get-one-free offer, the total came to 14 pairs. *This will cause a little chaos at home*, she thought with a grin, whereupon the salesman looked as if he thought she was flirting with him.

After paying for the order, and arranging for delivery, Louise checked the wall clock and saw she still had enough time to take a quick look in the notions department. Two large posters, prominently displayed, immediately caught her eye. "Wanted," read the first one, "Sammies need socks, mittens, bed jackets, bed socks, and wristlets." Each item on the list was illustrated with a picture of a soldier making use of it. The other poster, in bold letters, asked the question, "Is a National Uniform for Everybody on the Way?" Underneath the question were pictures of seven women, each wearing a different style dress. Elsewhere on the walls around the room were pages torn from magazines showing wool helmets, vests, chest covers and fingerless mitts. There was also a magazine cover from *The Delineator* with the words, "Can You Knit Two Socks at Once?"

"The regulations call for Gray 570 or Government Drab," the sales woman was saying to a group of women.

"Cotton or wool?"

"Wool. It's a little more expensive but it's warmer and holds up better. We don't want our boys getting trench feet and gangrenous toes." She went on, saying, "Both the army and navy have established regulation patterns to be followed. They're available through the Red Cross. If you need needles, the organization will give you a pair. It also has labels to be sewn in each sock which reads, 'Gift of the American People thru the American Red Cross."

Louise half listened as she glanced at the suggested yarns. However, she stopped short and went white when she unexpectedly came face-to-face with one of the magazine pictures.

Just as Louise grabbed a table to keep from fainting, one of the shoppers saw her and hurried over. "My dear, are you alright?" The woman's gaze followed Louise's to where a picture of a stump sock hung, and she nodded in understanding. "Oh, yes. I see. It's horrid to think our men might eventually need one or even two of these, isn't it? I've knit a few and it always makes me feel rather nauseous." She looked around, spotted a chair, and led Louise over. "Lean forward, for a minute, dear, and squeeze your thighs together. There, that's better. You'd gone all white."

"It's rather warm up here, isn't it?" Louise said, her voice muffled. "Thank you for your help. I probably just need some fresh air."

The lady nodded. "Yes, probably." She paused. "Do you have men ready to fight? Some of them seem to think it's going to be a lark."

"The draft age is 21 to 31, isn't it?" Without waiting for an answer, Louise said, "Yes, I have family and friends."

"Of course, you do, dear. It was a silly question." The woman took Louise's arm and helped her to stand. "Are you sure you feel well enough to leave by yourself?"

"I'm much better." Louise took the woman's hand in both of hers. "Thank you so much for helping me." She checked her hat and purse strap. "I best be getting back to work. I hope I see you again."

"That would be lovely, dear."

Outside of the store, Louise bought a bag of peanuts from a street vendor and failing to see the streetcar she needed, started down the hill to Pacific Avenue. "She opened the studio door just as the clock was chiming. "Made it." Queenie came up for some pets and Louise gave her a couple peanuts. She scarfed them down then returned to a puddle of sun coming through the window and immediately began to snore.

"A police officer was here," Mr. Aldrich said. "He left this for you."

Louise took the envelope and letter opener he handed her, and slit the flap. The note inside was brief and she read it twice before saying, "There's going to be a court hearing, and they want me to testify about the pictures I took of Irene Carmel's injuries. It says the city will pay for my time." When her employer remained quiet, Louise sat near the stove and put the letter back in the envelope. Sighing, she said, "I'm sorry about this. I certainly don't expect you to pay me while I'm in court. I seem to be causing you no end of trouble."

The phone rang and Mr. Aldrich answered. Louise could tell from his questions the caller wanted an appointment. After hanging up, he looked at her and smiled. "On the contrary, Louise, not only has business has improved, it's certainly become more interesting."

Louise was beaming when the studio door opened and Matthew walked in. At the sight of the young doctor coming through the door, her normally pale skin flushed, and her eyes lit up. The ever-observant Mr. Aldrich immediately noticed and smiled to himself. He watched while Matthew leaned down to rub Queenie's ears before speaking.

"I have a favor to ask," he said and hurriedly continued. "A medical aid station is being set up at Camp Lewis but, right now, there aren't enough doctors to man it. I've been asked to help out with the shots; smallpox, typhoid, and cholera. I need a nurse to assist me." He looked first at Mr. Aldrich and then at Louise.

"Oh, I wish I was a nurse, I would love to help you and maybe take some pictures of the camp at the same time."

"What day?" Mr. Aldrich asked.

"Tomorrow. It's certainly short notice."

Louise sighed. "Oh, well, I just got a summons to testify tomorrow, at court on the pictures I took of Irene Carmel."

Matthew made a noise halfway between a snort and a laugh. "So, did I. And I don't need a real nurse, just someone who can swab arms and hand me things when I ask for them."

"I could do that." Louise looked at her boss. "Mr. Aldrich, is that all right with you; it would mean a whole day off?"

"Of course, my dear." He smiled. "I did once run the business by myself, you know." He looked at her and, to Louise's amazement, winked.

Louise blushed and looked abashed, and Matthew laughed. "Court starts at 9:30. Why don't I pick you up at a quarter to nine. We can go to the courthouse and from there to Camp Lewis?"

"That would be jake. I'm not sure about streetcar routes up to G Street, and a ride would save me from having to walk up the hill. And thank you, Mr. Aldrich. I won't make a habit of taking time off."

"Louise, my dear, not to worry. You're working more hours, now, than I'm paying you for. In fact," Mr. Aldrich closed the appointment book and folded his hands on the cover. "Since all the appointments tomorrow are in the morning, I just might take the afternoon off and deliver the copies of my Mount Rainier photograph."

Matthew opened the door to a man and woman as he left. Louise checked the light meter and saw that she'd have to use a flashgun. Louise was afraid of the magnesium explosion from the gun and made it a practice to place the mechanism on a tripod as far away from the camera as possible. However, as the couple explained what they wanted, she thought how unprofessional that must appear and how important the photograph was to the young couple and tried to ignore her fear. When she was done and the pair had gone, Mr. Aldrich smiled and nodded. She left for the day feeling rewarded. However, her self-satisfaction was short-lived.

The next morning Louise overslept. "Holy cow!" She leaped out of bed, shouted downstairs for someone to let Queenie out, and raced to the bathroom only to discover that there was no hot water. "Son of a gun that's cold." She grabbed a piece of toweling and washed, brushed her teeth and ran back to her room to dress, wishing her new *DeBevoice* brassiere and American Lady corset didn't take so long to put on. A chemise came next and then her dress: a serviceable dark brown with a pleated skirt attached to a wide waistband and a lace collar around a V-neck. "Thank goodness it's ironed," she muttered as she settled the skirt around her hips and sat to pull on some stockings before stepping into her shoes.

Downstairs, Queenie was barking, and Princess began winding herself around Louise's ankles, a sure sign she was hungry. Louise fed them both, then looked at her clock and tried to do something with her thick dark hair. It was very fine and perfectly straight, uncooperative at the best of times and this wasn't a best of times. With a sigh she grabbed a ribbon and worked it into the braids which she pinned up, and scowled at Nell who was at the table, reading the paper and drinking coffee.

"You should have woken me up," Louise grabbed a piece of bread which had been toasted an hour previously and which seemed to protest being spread with butter. "Stupid toast," she muttered.

Nell smiled and turned a page. Louise's seeming inability to get up when she was supposed to was a constant bone of contention. "Don't forget to feed your pets," she said.

"I already did," Louise snapped.

"Don't be rude, Louise, we've talked many times before about you're not getting up when you should." Nell went to the stove to refill her coffee cup.

The back door opened, and Annie came in carrying the egg basket. "The girls have begun laying again," she said.

"Ask around, will you?" Nell stacked her dirty dishes and carried them to the dishpan. "See if anyone needs some. Hildy practically always needs eggs for the bakery."

Hump. Louise shoved the rest of her toast in her mouth creating a lump so big she could hardly chew. *Then why doesn't she raise chickens herself?*

"I hear a car," Annie said as she began cleaning the eggs. "I think your beau is here."

"He's not my beau." Louise shoved half a loaf of bread, some cheese, two apples and several cookies into a bag.

Nell smiled. "Just wait a minute." She unpinned Louise's long braids and twisted them into a coil, anchored it with the pins and within seconds had created a stylish chignon. "There. That will fit nicely under your hat." She patted Louise on the behind. "Now, scoot and answer the door."

After a bit of a hassle involving Queenie, Louise and Matthew left for court later than they'd planned. Annie said she was happy to take the dog with her while she spent the day with Nell's parents, but Queenie wasn't having it. Seeing Annie with the leash, she hid until Matthew opened his car door and then she made a beeline for the back seat and couldn't be budged. "Should we leave her in the car or take her in?" Louise asked while Matthew pulled into traffic.

"She should be all right in the car." He laughed. "After that little display, I doubt if she'd go with anyone."

"That's because I usually give her ham or bacon for breakfast."

"Hah. Then she definitely knows which side her bread is buttered on." He pulled away from the curb and drove to 11st Street. Twice a day the street was crowded with vehicles; going down to the various mills in the early morning and then back up at the end of the workday. However, when Matthew reached it, the hill's street traffic was still heavy and pedestrian traffic was heavier yet, as people jay-walked with abandoned. A woman cut across in front of the car, and he smiled and doffed his hat.

"Who's that?"

"Her name's Ringlish."

Before he could continue Louise laughed and said, "That's the lady who arrested that boy, Paul Levine. She said he was leading her sons astray."

Matthew grunted something and made a U-turn, backing his Model T onto the hill. There he slowed his speed to a crawl so slow that gulls feasting on some food scraps merely shifted instead of flying. He passed a cable car, and Louise briefly heard an underground clockwork pulling steel hemp wires. Almost immediately, they drove under a tangle of overhead electrical, telegraph, and telephone wires which occasionally sent out sparks. Most of the automobiles were gone, having given way to covered horse-drawn wagons, and drays loaded with barrels of beer, women carrying shopping baskets and dragging children behind them, and men going in and out of lunchrooms.

"Can you help me watch?" Matthew asked as he braked to miss a Chinese laundry cart.

Louise soon discovered that she was getting dizzy looking back and forth, left and right, and wiggled around until she was kneeling on the seat facing backwards. Matthew gave her one amused look before shifting into high gear.

"Do you think the automobile will ever replace the horse?" Louise nodded and smiled at a startled-looking woman walking down the sidewalk.

"Not until Ford comes up with something better than a gravity-fed engine." They reached Yakima Avenue, and he gave a sigh of relief.

The Pierce County Courthouse was a four-story wooden frame building covered by brick and light grey Wilkeson stone. Louise looked up when its massive clock began to chime and squinted as the sun bounced off the building's blue Tenino stone tower, and the roof's metallic shingles with a copper ridge. "Pretty, isn't it?"

"Never mind that. We have fifteen minutes to find a place to park and then find the right courtroom."

Matthew scanned the road and made a right turn and then a U-turn, pulling into a spot in front of Central School. Louise decided to take Queenie with her and the three began running down dirt road, dodging two men who were digging a hole on the sidewalk. After reaching the building, a short flight of stairs took them to the first floor where they came to a panting stop and looked around. The county's auditor, surveyor, treasurer, superintendent of schools, and any number of other officials all had their offices along the lengthy corridor. Doors opened and closed and were sometimes slammed. Voices rose and fell as people went in and out of the various departments. A typed list behind a large pane of glass listed four courtrooms on the second floor. Then, suddenly a scream pierced the air and a middle-aged woman burst out of one of the rooms and fell to the floor, all the while shrieking and crying.

"Golly Moses," Louise said, stopping so abruptly Matthew bumped into her.

Doors flew open and people rushed out to see what the commotion was. "Not my son; don't take my son," the woman sobbed as three men tried to help her to her feet.

"Now, madame, don't you fret," said one. "The war'll likely be over a 'fore he gets there." As he staggered under her weight, a severe-looking woman in a black dress, her hair scraped into a bun, came out of an office and stepped forward.

"Here, now. Enough of that," she snapped. The shrieks subsided into wails and moans, and she looked at the men. "I'm the police matron, bring her into my office." She turned on her heel and held the door open. Appearing glad to soon be relived of their burden, they half-carried, half-dragged the upset woman into the matron's office. They all made hasty exits from the room, and the matron shut the door. Immediately the corridor fell silent.

"How terribly sad; how awful for all the mothers," Louise said while they hurried toward a flight of stairs.

"Not to mention families, wives, and sweethearts." When they reached the next floor, Matthew stopped and looked down another long corridor, this one crowded with people. There were yet more doors, most of which, they soon learned, opened into courtrooms and adjacent offices: the judge's room, a jury room, and a retiring room. There were four rooms for court clerks, two for prosecuting attorneys, one yet to be assigned, and lavatories.

"That dog can't be here," said a young, pimple-face man coming out of the men's room.

"She's here for a reason," Louise said.

"I doubt that." The man sniffed.

"We're here for the Irene Carmel deposition," Matthew said.

"Last one on your left," the man said, "but they won't let the dog in."

"Pettifogger," Louise muttered, and behind her back, Matthew grinned. They wove their way through the crush, into the courtroom, and sat on a pew-like bench at the back of the room just before a clerk shut the door. Louise pushed Queenie underneath their seat, took off her coat, and draped it so that part of it hung down and hid the dog. To hold it in place, Matthew added his hat. After their race into the building, Louise was pretty sure the dog would sleep.

Louise, never having been in a courtroom, looked around with interest. At the front was the judge's desk which rested on a platform so that it was off the floor and slightly higher than both the court reporter's desk on one side of him, and the witness stand on the other. Along one wall was the jury box and facing the judge but separated by what looked like a short fence were the attorneys' tables, lecterns, chairs, and then behind that, spectator seating. Everything was polished wood which gleamed in the light. They hadn't long to wait before a door at the side of the room opened and the bailiff came in. "All rise. This Court with the Honorable Judge E.E. Cushman presiding is now in session."

He was followed by a man who entered in such a hurry, his robe seemed to float behind him. "Be seated," he said and gaveled them down.

A courtroom, Louise quickly discovered, was not a quiet place. Warming weather outside made the building settle, causing the casement windows to gape, and that let in street noise. Inside, people's footfalls in the corridor came and went; something fell or was dropped in an adjacent room. The worst, however, was the loud whooshing and clanging noise the lavatory pipes made when a toilet was flushed. Matthew poked Louise and she giggled, which made the judge glare and pound his gavel.

He explained that it was merely a hearing to ascertain the validity of the evidence presented in the case of Irene Carmel. After which, one by one, men were called to testify: the shop foreman, her brother who found her after the attack, several policemen, and finally Matthew. He described Irene's mental and physical state and the treatment both used and prescribed, but when asked about the photographer, he hesitated.

"You called a photographer, did you not?"

"Yes, your honor."

"And who did you call?"

"Miss Louise Tanquist, photographer at the Aldrich studio."

"And why didn't you call the police photographer?"

"Er," Matthew hesitated before saying, "I'm new to Tacoma and didn't know there was one. Also, I was aware of Miss Tanquist's work and felt Miss Carmel would be more comfortable with a young female taking the photographs."

"Humph" The magistrate shuffled his papers. "Miss Louise Tanquist?" Louise stood up and Matthew half-stood, looking at the judge. "Er," he said. "Yes, yes, you're excused. Miss Tanquist, come down here and let's get this over." He went back to fiddling with his papers. Louise heard him muttering something about "the proceedings being a waste of his time" and didn't bother to hid her smile as she walked to the front. The questions she answered were brief: "Yes, I was asked to photograph Irene Carmel's injuries" and "no I didn't use any kind of paint enhancement to make them show up better in the black and white photographs," she said.

A few more questions and the judge dismissed them all, and the proceedings ended.

"I'm not sure what that was all about," Louise said as she rescued Queenie.

"Remember, Irene said she was attacked a year ago, too. For some reason, the police seem to think it might be by someone who moves around a lot, like a sailor. My uncle said that just in case it happens again and we're not around, the authorities will have sworn statements to fall back on and pictures to make comparisons."

"Why wouldn't...?" Louise stopped. "Oh. Like the war, you mean."

It was more of a statement than a question and required no answer. They hurried down the stairs with Matthew holding her elbow and Louise holding Queenie's leash. They were stopped on the first floor by six men carrying what looked like a coffin.

"What the heck?"

"It's a mummy, ma'am." The men had halted and stood looking at the elevator cage. "Not big enough," one said. Groans and not a few mumbled swear words followed as the men shifted their grips and started up the stairs.

"The Ferry Museum on the top floor. I've been meaning to visit, now I'll have to," Louise said. "A real live mummy, golly."

"Live mummy? That would be a first," Matthew said.

They were stopped twice more, first by four policemen who were clearing a passage at the door making a place for a group of convicts to enter. One of the men whistled and winked at Louise and one tried to pat Queenie. Officers quickly put a stop to both and warned them about any further shenanigans, and the men disappeared down a flight of stairs to the basement jail leaving a fading clink of ankle chains in their wake. Next the hallway was blocked by three men helping a woman to stand who'd apparently fainted while the previously-seen police matron held smelling salts to her nose.

"Her husband was in a truckload of men headed for Camp Lewis," someone said.

"I know the family. She's only been married a week."

"The police matron's certainly being kept busy," Louise said. She missed the further comments when Matthew hurried her down the stairs.

"Finally," he said and took a deep breath of fresh air.

The courthouse was surrounded by a small patch of grass of which Queenie made use of and after that they hurried to the car. "I have instructions on how to get to the camp," Matthew said after they were seated. "Here." He handed Louise a piece of paper. "You can be the navigator."

From Yakima Avenue, Matthew drove to Center Street, crossed some railroad tracks and followed a water flume to South 50th, then turned onto Puget Sound Avenue, and from there to the Edison Road, a paved street approximately twenty feet wide. It was all new to Matthew but familiar to Louise. They passed an Orpheum Theatre, the Red Front Saloon, and a little boy standing on tiptoes to drink from a fountain and who waved at them. The road, which changed back and forth from smooth to rutted, was crowded with wagons, cars and military vehicles which Matthew fell in behind.

"I can't believe how much this has changed," said Louise looking right and left. "The last time we visited Indiana and her family, Nell's sister who lives near Olympia, remember? A lot of this was still prairie."

"It stands to reason, doesn't it, what with the county giving 70,000 acres to the government so a military base could be built here?"

Louise appeared not to hear him. "In spring the camas would bloom . . . blue everywhere as far as the

89

eye could see, and the orange paintbrush . . . and butterflies. It was so pretty, so peaceful."

"Did you see the article in the *Times*?" Matthew steered around a pothole and a man hauling a truck load of hay laid on his horn. "Right now," he continued, ignoring the honking, "ten thousand men are building 1,757 buildings and an assortment of other things. Streets, roads, railroad spurs, lighting, heating, it's pretty amazing, don't you think?"

Louise sighed, "I guess."

They continued on, following the military trucks before eventually turning east, passing piles of stones which workmen were using to build an arch. As she continued to look around, Louise thought she'd never seen such organized chaos. Men were taking pickaxes to the hard soil creating a channel. They were followed by others putting down wooden pipes. Voices came from three warehouses under construction next to those already built. Mules brayed, horses whinnied, and Queenie woke up, sat up, and tried to see where the noise came from. When a Chinese man passed in front of them Louise gasped. "That's Dong Chang; he's a dishwasher at his father's restaurant downtown." She didn't know why she was surprised. "Was a dishwasher, I guess. Golly. I can't believe I sort of know someone who's already in the army."

They continued on. Every building, road, and path had a sign, and Matthew eventually found one pointing toward a combination dental and medical aid station. The sign looked official but as they approached others had sprung up around it. "Do dentists give lawyers retainers?" read one. It was followed by "We drill, dentists drill. I'd rather be a dentist." Doctors also came in for their own kidding. "A bladder infection means urine trouble." "Acute appendicitis is better than an ugly one." Louise laughed, poked Matthew, and pointed at one reading, "Call a toe truck if you hurt your foot." He grinned and shook his head. "This ought to be interesting." Pulling onto a patch of dead grass, he got out, and headed for the aide station while Louise gave Queenie a short walk. The pair immediately attracted attention. Queenie sat, wagged her tail, and let men pat her, but as Louise well knew, her main interests were sleeping and food.

"Nice little bitch," said one young man.

"And the dog's cute, too," said another.

"Here now." Matthew came out of the aide station in time to catch the remark. "None of that, you hear me," he said, and the men headed off.

"Are we ready," Louise asked. She didn't know quite what to think about Matthew's remark, *but if I had to guess*, she thought, *it seemed like he sounded possessive*. "What about Queenie?"

"I snagged a spot where we will get a little breeze and has a place for the dog."

Louise handed Matthew the dog's leash and hurried to the car where she put on a white pinafore apron and replaced her hat with a reasonable facsimile of a nurse's wimple.

"That's impressive." Grinning, Matthew took her elbow and hustled her to a building where a shiny new insignia of two snakes entwined around a staff with wings hung above the door. When Louise paused to look at it, he said, "It's called a caduceus."

"It has snakes on it."

"It's actually the wrong thing. It should be the Rod of Asclepius. The army got it wrong."

"Are there snakes on that one?"

"One."

"Why?"

"It has to do with mythology." Matthew had to raise his voice to be heard. "Here's our spot."

"It's kind 'a bare bones, isn't it?" Louise tucked Queenie into an out-of-the-way corner and turned to look around. Each doctor had a table holding cotton, needles, serum, a basin to sterilize the needles, and a small tube of smelling salts. Next to it was a chair and underneath was a garbage can.

"It's all we need; here's what I want you to do. Have a man sit down and roll up his sleeve. Clean an area on his upper arm with cotton dipped in alcohol. Tell me when he's ready and try not to flinch when the needles go in."

And so, it began. Some of the men were stoic; some turned white; a couple fainted. Louise held more than one hand and eventually brought Queenie over to provide comfort, especially when someone on the other side of the room hollered.

"Goodness." One particularly loud shout caught her off guard, and she had to apologize when she stepped on a man's foot. "What are they doing over there."

"Checking teeth." The young man began rolling up the sleeve on his right arm. "We'll all be eating sops with our left hand when this day is over." He left and while another recruit came forward, Louise whipped her forehead with her apron. Queenie whimpered, and Matthew stopped filling a needle.

"Are you alright?"

"Yes. It's just so very warm in here, though. Isn't it?" She looked around. "Is there anywhere I can get a drink of water?"

Hearing her the young recruit handed over a small aluminum canteen. "Here you go, Miss. It'll taste a little funny, but the reservoir is filling up so it's fresh."

"Thank you." Louise took several gulps and put some in her hand to rubbed her face and neck. Then she poured a little on the floor for Queenie and offered the canteen to Matthew.

"Perhaps you should go out to the car." Matthew took a healthy swallow and handed the canteen back with a smile.

"No, I'm fine. The water was just what the doctor ordered, or in this case," she smiled, "the soldier ordered. Thank you so much, ah. . ."

"It's Tommy, Tommy Green." At the sight of the needle, he tensed up and gritted his teeth.

"Best to relax your arm, soldier," Matthew said. "It won't hurt so much that way."

Louise smiled. "And you can tell your mother that she raised a very polite young man." She finished cleaning a spot on his arm and stepped back. When it appeared as if Tommy wanted to extend the conversation, Matthew politely but firmly hustled him out of the way.

The room grew warmer and took on a fetid smell. The lines for inoculations grew shorter but not the ones for dental work, where men weren't shy about yelling and swearing when something hurt.

"They're yanking out bad teeth," said one of the men in line as he waited for his shots. "Ya gotta have good ones. They say we need six incisors above and below each other, and six molars above and below, too. Most none of us never even heard of incisors or knew much about taking care of our teeth and now the army will see that we have to." His words were slow and muffled and when he tried to smile, Louise saw a wad of bloody cloth in his mouth. "I gotta get false teeth," he slurred, and bloody saliva rolled down his chin.

"They gave me a short piece of stick with bristles on the end," said another man. "And a box of something called Colgate Ribbon Dental Cream. We're supposed to brush our teeth every day." He shook his head, "Everyday, you'd think they'd wear out with all that brushing." He'd been so busy talking he failed to see when the needle went in and looked surprised when Louise told him he could go.

"You know," said Matthew as he filled more needles. "You haven't taken a single photograph." He looked at the dwindling line and said, "I can handle it. You go on."

"Oh, gosh." Louise looked flustered. "I completely forgot. Are you sure? I mean, I promised Mr. Aldrich but he'll understand if we're too busy."

For the first time since they'd parked, Matthew relaxed and smiled, becoming more of the young man she was attracted to and less of a serious physician. "Go while there's still some light."

With Queenie in tow, and to the apparent regret of the men still waiting for their shots, Louise hurried to the car where she tossed off her apron and scarf, put on her hat, and grabbed the camera. In September the *Tacoma Times* had printed a short article saying sixty-six surgeons, dentists, and assistants had been assigned to Camp Lewis; but no photograph accompanied the story. When Louise saw a man, his face swollen on one side and his mouth full of bloody rags, leaving the make-shift clinic carrying a box with a picture of a pair of dentures on the side, she asked if she could take his photograph. He stopped and waited until she found the best light. "After General Haig got a toothache and had to wait for a French dentist to come and take care of him, the army got dentists." The words were slurred as he dabbed carefully at his bloody drool. Then, hearing the camera click, he continued on. Louise's 'thank you' hung in the air.

As she looked around, one thing of particular interest Louise saw was a pile of clothes with a nearby sign reading, "Send it home or send it to Belgium." She later learned that as uniforms were issued, some recruits were giving their clothes to the Belgium Relief. Though she was losing the light, Louise took a picture of the clothes including the sign. Then, remembering the food she'd brought, she sat in the car to eat. *Wow. I didn't realize how tired I was*, she thought while munching on bread and cheese. *And just from standing and cleaning arms.* She took a deep breath, and the scent of sawdust filled her nostrils. Looking around she noticed that every structure was made from wood and that in between the two-story barracks were shower facilities and latrines.

The ever-present scavenging gulls and crows hovered near stacks of produce piled haphazardly outside the long, single-story mess-halls. From where she sat peering in the open doors, Louise saw men milling around stoves and sinks. "The kitchens, I presume," she said to Queenie. Large coal bins were conveniently located and, now that she looked, she noticed smoke coming out of roof-top chimneys. She also saw Dong Chang dart out the door, fetch a box of potatoes and hurry back in.

Off to one side, a caduceus was mounted over the hospital structure which appeared to be made of better-quality materials, and had smoke coiling lazily in the air from its chimney.

All around her men hauled lumber, climbed ladders, pounded nails, and yelled back and forth. They dug in the rocky soil, strung telephone and electrical lines between tall posts. She saw boxes labeled 'rifles'; a line of ambulances, and so many men, walking, marching, laughing together as they pushed and shoved each other, or, when necessary, giving directions to the new recruits toting suitcases who piled out of vehicles. She took a few pictures, but her heart wasn't in it. *It's too much for me,* Louise thought. *Too many people and too much noise. How will they stand it, how do they stand it?* She slunk down in the car seat and wished Matthew had parked somewhere less conspicuous. But while she managed to doze, Queenie was bothered by the commotion. She sat half on the car seat, half on Louise's lap, looked out the window, and alternated between napping and growling.

After what seemed like hours, a group of men, which included Matthew, all carrying medical bags, left the aide station. Matthew had pushed his hat to the back of his head and rolled his sleeves up to his elbows. In addition to the bag, he carried his jacket over one shoulder.

"At last," she said to Queenie Seeing him, so unexpectedly and looking so unusually casual made Louise's heart flutter. "Golly, he's handsome," she whispered into her pet's warm, soft fur as she cuddled the dog. "His aunt and uncle will be introducing him to every eligible girl in town." She heaved a sigh and reached quickly to fix her chignon which was drooping and coming undone.

Matthew shook hands with his companions, turning to say one last thing to someone before putting his medical bag and coat in the back seat and getting in the car. Seeing Louise struggling with her hair, he chuckled and said, "Leave your hair like it is. I like it like that." Louise blushed but before she could respond, he added, "It tells people that you've been working."

"Well, really." Louise's mouth dropped open. Ignoring the fact that she'd just been napping she said, "I'm practically never not working. Photography isn't easy, you know." She managed to get the braid under her hat and turned with a huff to face front.

Still grinning, Matthew started the engine. "Well, of course it is. I didn't mean that it wasn't, but it doesn't seem to be that physically demanding."

"It certainly can be, and it takes a lot of—of brain power to decide on the proper lighting and figure out what's best in the dark room. I shift props and climb up and down things to get the best angle. All we—you did today was poke men in the arm."

Waiting at the main gate for the traffic to let him turn, he looked at her ruefully. "I'm sorry, I didn't mean to imply it was an easy job—and, anyway, I think you'd make a heck of a nurse."

However, as Louise had a tendency to hold on to her anger, she merely said, "The road's clear. You can turn now." With Queenie settled on her lap, she shifted to look out the side window. Several times she nodded off, her head dropping down, whereupon Queenie licked her face, waking her up. It seemed like a long time before Matthew pulled up in front of her house. As she started to get out of the car, he took her arm.

"I'm sorry for upsetting you. I heard something about how you got your job, and I know you put in long hours. But I thought we made a great team, and you would make a good nurse."

For some reason Louise's eyes filled with tears and she blinked quickly before saying, "You didn't say anything wrong, I sometimes simply go off the deep end. I guess I'm just tired. It was certainly an interesting day, first the courthouse and then at a military base. I think I have a sensory overload but I'm glad you asked me to help you. Goodness," she gave a small laugh, "those two boys, Gene and Howard, then that poor girl, Irene Carmel, and then today at the courthouse and an afternoon at Camp Lewis. Is your life always this exciting?"

"Only since I moved out here," said Matthew, looking relieved. He slid his hand down her arm and enclosed her hand. "I like being with you." His eyes boring into hers were questioning, and Louise entwined her fingers through his. Her heart pounded and she caught her breath. Could he feel her pulse racing? Maybe. His grip tightened and his eyes traveled slowly down her face, taking in every feature until they stopped on her lips. Keeping his gaze steady, he leaned slightly forward only to jerk back when a voice came from the sidewalk.

"My goodness, Louise. You must have had quite a day." Annie shifted the bag of groceries she carried. "Hello, doctor. Did you shoot up a bunch of soldiers?"

"Yes, ma'am. I think I lost count of how many. Louise, how about you?" Suddenly his hand was back on the steering wheel.

Louise shifted Queenie from her lap to the car floor, and they got out. "I didn't even think to count." Before closing the door, she looked at Matthew and half-smiled. "I'd ask you in but I'm too tired to be polite. Thank you for a most unusual day."

"My pleasure; thank you for your help." He started the engine and followed a wagon down the road, Queenie stopped to make use of a bush, and Annie walked around the house to the back door.

Louise left Queenie to sniff around the yard and hurried inside. "I'm headed for a bath," she shouted, running up the stairs unbuttoning and untying as she did. While hot water ran in the tub, she dropped her clothes on the floor and saw tell-tell spotting on her combination. *Well, that explains the tears*, she thought as she climbed into the water and sunk down to chin level. She hated having to wear a clunky belted contraption stuffed with lard-coated sheep's wool to absorb menstrual blood. Recently, under an ad for menstrual aprons, she'd seen an advertisement reading, "Your late-19th century armory against the Red Baron(ess) crocheted sanitary products." *But it probably wouldn't be any more comfortable*. Laying back and closing her eyes, she remembered when her monthlies first began, and Nell had taken her to see Dr. Clarke. "She's an old friend," Nell had said, "and I think it's important for you to know what is happening to your body."

Dr. Clarke was semi-retired and only saw a few long-time patients and friends. She had an office downtown and, on her way to work, Nell took Louise and made the introduction.

"My goodness," the doctor said while ushering Louise in. "It seems like only yesterday I was telling the same things to Nell." She sighed. "I don't feel old until second generations come to see me. Here," she gestured to a chair. "Make yourself comfortable. Coffee? I made a fresh pot and was just about to have some." She bustled around, talking about how Tacoma had changed since she'd first stepped off of the train from Portland

Louise relaxed, sipping her coffee.

"Now then." The doctor riffled through a pile of corrugated papers on a table next to her and pulled out one. "This is what is known as your genitals area, what your insides look like. Yours and every woman ever born." She pointed at a small round area. "This is your ovary. It releases three things: hormones, estrogen and progesterone. This, "she pointed to a triangle in the middle, "is your uterus. The hormones cause its lining to build up. The built-up lining is then ready for a fertilized egg to attach and start developing. If there is no fertilized egg, the lining breaks down and sloughs off and bleeds." She sat back and waited.

Louise put her hand on her abdomen. "Why does it hurt, sometimes?"

"That can happen when the uterine muscle contracts." Doctor Clarke refilled their coffee cups and held out a plate of molasses cookies. "Did you know molasses cookies date back to before the Civil War?" She bit into one and chewed. "Yum. My favorite." While Louise waited, the doctor looked out a large window: thinking about the Civil War? About the cookies? Just remembering things? Louise had no way of knowing. "Now," Dr. Clarke began, "I expect you'll marry one day and it's important that you know what to expect." She held up another chart. This was always the difficult part—introducing male anatomy. She watched to see Louise's reaction.

After careful examination, Louise merely shook her head. "I don't know what I'm looking at."

Dr. Clarke took her time, "These are the male genitals; this is called the penis and these are referred to as the testicles. They're protected in a sack of skin called the scrotum."

"We have a lot more, uh, stuff in us, don't we?"

Dr. Clarke laughed. "We do indeed. We need more body parts in order to have babies."

And that was the first meeting she'd had with Dr. Clarke. Adding more hot water to her bath, Louise was pleased to know what was happening to her body, and glad that she wasn't alone. However, when it came to thinking of Nell and Annie, and all the other women she knew who were, or had gone through the same thing, mulling over the information had stretched her imagination.

The second time Nell decided Louise should meet with the doctor was on her sixteenth birthday.

It had been a cold, snowy day and Louise sat as close to the stove as she could get, cradling a cup of hot chocolate between her hands. "Someday," Dr. Clarke had said, "you're going to meet a man to whom your body will respond. When that happens, a lot more blood will temporarily flow to your genital area and cause it to throb."

Louise remembered those words as she added a few more bath beads to the water. Scented steam drifted around the room and thinking about Matthew made her throb. He'd wanted to kiss her and she wanted him to. Her thoughts seemed to jump back and forth between Dr. Clarke's explanations and her physical responses to Matthew.

"On your wedding night," the doctor had said, "and thereafter, when your husband wants marital congress, his penis, remember that's this part here," she held up the chart of male anatomy, "will become hard and elongated. At that time, he will insert it in your vagina and release sperm. If the sperm finds one of your eggs, you will become pregnant."

"My goodness." After thinking about it for a moment, Louise said, "that doesn't sound very nice, not something I would enjoy."

"It's natural to feel that way now, but someday you will meet a man who makes your vaginal area feel wet and cause your face to flush. Likely, both your breathing and your pulse will speed up. It's all natural." Dr. Clarke stopped and looked out the window where a man went by shouting, "Rags and trash. Turn your trash into cash. Best price here." A month earlier, she'd found him slumped against a wall in the alley between Pacific Avenue and A Street. His ill-fitting boots had rubbed a raw spot on the heel one foot. She'd treated him and, unable to pay, thereafter, if he had something he thought she could use, she'd find it on her door step, a motley collection of peculiar items, *Tacoma's discards, just like the man.* Recently the *Tacoma Times* carried an article on how the local Jewish community was sending money to the American Jewish Relief Committee to be forward to Jewish War Relief. It did seem, she thought, as if they should take care of those at home first. She'd never learned the man's name, only that he'd fled the Czar's pogroms in Russia and worked his way west. *Faith, hope and charity*, she thought, *the greatest of these is charity. And charity begins at home.*

While Dr. Clarke was mulling over the issue of charity, Louise thoughts were running amok. Every woman she knew who had children, she realized, had gone through what she'd just learned, and the more children they had, the more they'd had what Dr. Clarke called "marital congress." The thought was mind-boggling.

And while soaking in the bath and remembering all this, Louise's scattered thoughts jumped to Matthew and the day they'd had. *I did want to kiss him, but he spoiled the day. Does he really think I don't work hard? He insulted my job. Humph, I forgot to share my food with him. But I'm not sorry.*

* * *

Several days later, sitting in the Perkins Building's Red Cross room, Louise huffed a sigh as she looked at the directions she'd written down: slip eleven, pearl two together, purl one, turn. Slip eleven, knit four… "Why does this have to be so blasted complicated?" she muttered trying to ignore the chatter around her and concentrate on turning the heel of the sock she was knitting.

The young woman sitting next to her giggled. "You can always give it to someone else to finish. There's a whole group of old ladies who do just that."

"It's become a thing of pride. I hate to be defeated by a heel."

"Do you mean a sock heel or a heel as in a cad?" When Louise looked up and laughed, she saw that the speaker was a young woman about her own age who added, "In Seattle, folks are knitting what they call, tube socks."

"Really? What's that?"

"Just what it sounds like. A knit tube twenty-seven inches long with the end purled together."

"Golly, I could whip those out in lickety-split fashion. So much easier. But it does sound like giving a bunch of yarn the upper hand and surrendering to some weird instructions. Thanks for telling me, but I'm not going to let a sock heel get the best of me." She looked at a pile of moss her companion was picking through. "I don't mean to be nosy but what in the world are you doing? And I'm Louise, by the way."

"Dottie," said her companion, "and I'm cleaning this moss so it can be dried."

"Um, why?"

Dottie laughed. "Are you a first timer?"

"Yep. First time since we started meeting in the Perkins Building and first time trying to knit socks. Mostly what I've been doing is making camouflage tarps, but Mr. Perkins happened to come in the photography shop where I work, and I remembered that he'd made a room in his building available to the Red Cross, so I thought I'd come here and learn to turn a heel."

"Did he chase you around the room?"

"What? Good grief, no. Why? Does he do that?"

"Hah!" Dottie pulled a face. "I had to deliver a letter from Mother to him last week and he shut the door to his office and chased me around his desk."

Louise tried to look sympathetic, but she burst out laughing. "Excuse me. I'm sorry but, gosh, he's too old a man to be chasing strange women around his office."

"I know, the old lech."

She had barely finished speaking when a woman Louise later learned was Mrs. McCormack clapped her hands. "Ladies, if I might have your attention for a moment, please." The room quieted down, and she held up a piece of paper. "As you might know, France has commissioned the Foundation Shipbuilding Company here in Tacoma to build cargo ships. The hull of the first one, the *Gerbeviller*, is finished. Before it's hauled to the fitting out yard it has to be camouflage painted. To explain what I'm talking about," she gestured to a young woman standing off to the side, "I'd like to introduce Miss Enid Jackson who has just been accepted in the Aviation Camouflage Department. We are lucky to have her here because she and her family are leaving shortly for the east coast. Miss Jackson."

With the exception of several older women who continued whispering, the room fell silent. "Ladies," Miss Jackson began, "if I was staying here in Tacoma, this is something I would love to do because it takes no artistic skill and promises to be a lot of fun. Just imagine being down near the waterfront on a sunny, summer day with the sky full of singing birds and the air smelling of freshly-cut wood and in front of you are the massive hulls of ships needed for the war effort in France. The Foundation Company has orders for several ships. What the *Gerbeviller*, and all the others involved in the war, need is to have a pattern called Razzle Dazzle painted on their hulls."

"But I can't paint to save my soul," one woman said, and others nodded.

"Well, that's the beauty of it." Miss Jackson smiled. "You don't have to." She held up a large placard covered with bright, bold stripes. "This is an example. All it is, is a bunch of geometric shapes in various colors that crisscross each other. It's not supposed to obscure anything, just make it hard for the Germans to estimate the ship's range, speed, and where it's heading." When her audience continued to look skeptical, Miss Jackson continued. "The Foundation company has a man who will mark out where the lines are to go, and which colors go where and all you have to do is fill in the stripes."

"Well, I can do that," said Dottie. She elbowed Louise. "Beats trying to turn a heel, doesn't it?"

Louise had been recovering from a cold, and the smells of moss and humanity seemed to stuff her head more, but she grinned at the comment and thought about her job. "It would be nice to be outside for a change. And maybe I could take some photographs." When Dottie raised her eyebrows in askance, she added, "I'm a photographer. I work just down the street at Mr. Aldrich's studio."

Conversation started again and, before she could say anymore, Mrs. McCormack clapped her hands. "On behalf of us all, I want to thank Miss Jackson for finding the time to drop by. She'll be here for a bit if you have any questions." Applause, some enthusiastic, some merely polite followed the words. "She has to leave but those of you who are interested should report to the company at 11:00 tomorrow morning. The address is 603 Alexander Avenue."

While several ladies approached the young woman, Dottie said, "We just moved to Tacoma, so I don't know where that is."

"Um, I'm not quite sure, either, but Alexander runs parallel to the Blair waterway." Louise stuffed her knitting in her tote, stood and stretched.

"Gosh, how're we supposed to get there?"

"Streetcar, I guess."

"Sheesh, I don't think Mother would let me. Drat, I was looking forward to it." Dottie made a wry face. "But moss picking isn't looking so bad." She stood, shook sticks and dirt from her lap, and laughed. "Well, not too bad, anyway."

"Why are you cleaning moss, anyway?"

"It's used in medical bandages. When it's clean, it's folded between paper and sterilized, and doctors use it on wounds."

"For goodness sakes."

"Mother learned about it when she visited Scotland once. The moss soaks up blood and oozie stuff real well and there's a cotton shortage because of the war so it's needs must."

"I know about the cotton shortage. My mother has a dressmaking business and is looking for ways to figure out what to do."

"Well, that outfit you're wearing is ducky."

She and Louise joined the others as they exited the room. "Are you going back to work?"

Louise tipped her head back, blew her nose, and took a deep breath. "No, I have the afternoon off." Dottie, who had assumed the same expression Queenie got when she wanted to go for a walk, gave no indication that she wanted to move on, and Louise made what she thought of as a major sacrifice: giving up her free time in order to spend it with a young woman who seemed lonely. "Feeny's is on Pacific Avenue, near here," she said. "Do you want to get a cup of coffee?" Her sacrifice was rewarded when Dottie broke into a big smile.

"You bet."

They waited for traffic to clear and walked up Eleventh Street, turning left on Pacific Avene. As they passed The People's Store, Dottie glanced in a window and then at Louise. "That's a dandy outfit you're wearing. Do you like to shop here? Mother prefers Rhodes Brothers, but I think it's a bit stuffy. I feel like some of the clerks are looking down their nose at me. Wait a minute; should that be 'noses at me?' Mother insists on proper grammar. Sometimes I actually don't say anything just so she can't correct me. When we got to town, here, Mother insisted we stay at the Tacoma Club because she heard a princess once stayed there but I don't suppose that's true."

Louise had to speak quickly in order to put a halt to Dottie's chatter. "Actually, it's true, though she wasn't a princess when she stayed there. In fact, she wasn't a princess, at all. She married an earl and that makes her a countess, and she lives in Scotland now."

"Oh, my goodness, how romantic." Louise pushed open Feeny's door and Dottie followed her inside. "I've never been in a place like this. It's very no frills, isn't it? Is it safe?"

Her words carried and, as one, all the diners looked up. "Of course it is. Tacoma doesn't have a lot of white slave problems," Louise said, her tone turning cold. They found an empty table and when Feeny came over ordered coffee and cinnamon toast which had recently become popular in Tacoma.

Dottie took the reprimand in good stead. "I'm sorry. It's just that Mother will want to know all about where I've been and she can always tell if I'm trying to dodge an issue. Oh, good, you like to sit by a window, too. Mother thinks it's in bad taste, 'common,' she calls it to be seated where people can see what you're eating but I say, the windows are there to be looked out of. Now, coffee is my treat and I will, I can, you know, be quiet so you can tell me the story of the countess. Do you know the full story? How they met and all that?" Dottie rested her head on her hands and looked like a child waiting for someone to read to her at bedtime.

Louise laughed in spite of herself. She'd received a brief note from Matthew saying he was leaving for Buckley and then on to Carbonado, Fairfax and Wilkeson to see to the miners and their families.

The railroad regularly sends my uncle up to the foothills to take care of any medical issues and give the children their shots, he wrote, *and it lends him a company house in which to set up shop. He, my uncle that is, says he's too old to do that anymore, and prefers his own bed so he wants me to go. I'm looking forward to being up in the mountain, it should be quite an adventure. I'll see you when I get back, Matt.*

It's brevity not to mention lack of any sort of sentiment might have put a damper on her day but signing as Matt rather than Matthew felt intimate. She put her feelings aside, added cream to her coffee, and looked across the street at men going in and out of the Monty Gunn Grocery Store while marshalling her thoughts.

"There are a couple of newspaper articles about the marriage," Louise said at last, "but not many about her family." She paused to blow her nose. "Her father was a dentist to the royal court in Rome so the family lived all over—in Rome, of course, and Tuscany but she was born in Florence and educated in Germany and France. She was just Leonora VanMarter back then. His name was George. He was twenty years older than she and had quite a past. I suppose, being a second son and not the heir, that didn't matter. When he was 13, he became a midshipman in the British navy, then, after four years, he left the navy and went back to school. I don't know what came first but he was a lieutenant in a rifle brigade and an A.D.C., that's an Aide-de-camp, to Ireland's lord lieutenant, then after his military career he came out west here and worked as a cowboy. He also made friends with two men, Ira Sankey and Dwight Moody who were revivalists, and the three of them traveled around Britain and then America. According to the newspaper, he had a good voice and sang during the revival meetings and at concerts."

Dottie laughed. "Well, golly gee whiz, flighty, wasn't he? But he was a second son, wasn't he; so, you're probably right; I don't suppose it matter too much."

"Well, there's more and this is the fun part," Louise paused to inhale the steam from her coffee and looking up realized she had an audience.

"He and Leonore met at some social function in New York when he turned a somersault over the back of a sofa and almost landed in her lap. He was really good at somersaults because at some point in time, he'd worked as a circus clown."

"Goodness gracious," Dottie appeared completely flabbergasted. "How romantic. At least I think it is. What do you think?"

Two women having lunch nearby laughed and one of them said, "I'd call it a bit unorthodox."

"But what about Leonora?" Dottie asked. "How did she end up in Tacoma?"

"The story goes that her brother was traveling in eastern Washington and persuaded his father to join him and invest inland there. In addition to being a dentist to the royal court in Rome, their father had been part of a group of men who excavated some tombs in Tarquinia and had also invented some sort of device for teeth."

"Where's Tarquinia?" asked Feeny. By then, even he was taking an interest in the story. He replenished everyone's coffee, leaned against the counter, and folded his arms. When Louise looked up, she saw the cook peeking out of the kitchen. Feeling more than a little uncomfortable, she decided to end the story as quickly as she could.

"Some place in Italy. Anyway, Lorena was teaching music here and working with the Reverand Stubbs down at the seamen's bethel in Old Tacoma." Before Dottie could ask what a bethel was, she said, "That's like a chapel, and the earl, only he wasn't an earl yet, walked in. He had a sister who died, and he had become a street preacher, so I guess he decided to see what was there, at the bethel, I mean. Apparently, he was also staying at the Union Club."

"Oh, my dear," said one of the ladies sitting nearby, "this is just so romantic. I can't wait to write my sister and tell her about it. Go on, please."

"Yes, please." Dottie reached across the table and squeezed Louise's hand.

"There's really not much more to say. They were married in October, 1895. I only know this because Nell made a dress for the bride's sister.

"Are you talking about Nell Tanquist?" One of the table listeners interrupted Louise and asked. "Is she your mother?"

"My adopted mother, yes."

"My, she was young to be making bridesmaid's dresses, wasn't she?"

Louise beamed. "That's how good she was, and still is."

From outside came the sound of a clock. "Oh, no." Dottie pushed her chair back and took money from her purse to pay for food. "Is that the time? Mother will be very displeased with my being so late. But I just have to hear how the story ends."

"Well, that's pretty much all there is, and I'll be brief. It was an afternoon wedding They were married at Leonora's brother's house, I think, or maybe where her parents were staying. That part of her story is a bit vague. The only decorations were flags and palms. Then, everyone sat down to eat, and the newlyweds went on a honeymoon. But George's older brother, who was living in India at the time, caught cholera and died. So, George became the 7th Earl of Tankerville."

"And they left Tacoma to go live in a castle?"

"Yes, but only after Leonora was presented at court to Queen Victoria."

Louise also pushed her chair back and, as she stood, those who had been listening to the story clapped and smiled. Some even thanked her. Nell would have loved the attention, however, it made Louise uncomfortable. *I'm more of a stay-in-the background kind of person,* she thought. But she acknowledged the appreciation with a smile, followed Dottie out the door.

"I've really got to dash," Dottie said, "But I'll see you at the next meeting and get your phone number. There's so many things we can do. Oh, dear, there's my trolly. Goodbye for now."

Louise tried to look pleased when Dottie hugged her. *If we're going to be friends,* she thought, *I'll have to let her know I'm not a hugger.*

Dottie was off in a flash and managed to board her streetcar just before the door closed. Standing under Feeny's awning, Louise soaked up the pleasure of being alone for a minute, then let out a deeply-held breath and wondered if she should go home. Nell, she knew, was going from work to a suffrage meeting at the Commercial Club.

"We're so close to getting the vote, "she'd said that morning at breakfast. "We almost had it in 1854. And the territorial legislature gave women the vote in 1883, but we lost it in 1887." She had sighed and added a generous amount of cream to her coffee.

"What happed?" Annie put a plate of toast down and sat to enjoy the fruits of her labors—mainly poached eggs and bacon.

"The Territorial Supreme Court ruled that Congress did not intend to give territories the power to enfranchise women and we've been waiting ever since. Bloody government." Nell speared a piece of toast and loaded it with jam. "Did you know that fifty or so years ago, if a chieftain in one of our local tribes was recalled, a woman could replace him?"

"What or who are you going to see tonight?" asked Annie. Her scanty education with an abusive father left much to be desired and Nell's interests were a constant source of fascination.

"Walter Davis, he's our own local senator, and he put it to the Congress in Olympia to submit to Washington D.C. a ratification for women's suffrage." Seeing Annie's puzzled look, Nell said, "He got Olympia to ask President Wilson's government to give us the vote. I tell you; it makes me proud to be from Pierce County. The Research Club and the Washington State Historical Society are putting on a program about the whys-and-wherefores. You should come with me; you, too, Louise. After all, it's your future, here, we're talking about."

Annie agreed but Louise declined. Now, standing on the sidewalk outside Feeny's, feeling unusually indecisive, she considered her options for the rest of the day. It was still early and with Queenie at home pouting, Nell at work, and Annie helping Frieda Faye piece a quilt, there was no particular place she had to or wanted to be. Briny-scented fog was rolling in from the bay, and she watched it wrap around buildings creating an ethereal glow where lights shone through windows. *How good it smells*, she thought, in spite of her cold.

Looking up, she saw sea gulls racing in from the waterfront and knew another storm was coming. *Tacoma weather is so unreliable*, she thought. *We'll be begging for some of this rain come August.* She was thinking about that when sounds of hammering caught her attention and she remembered that the Red Cross was building a salvage station one block over from where she was standing. According to the *Times*, men planned to build the whole thing in just one day. *Well, that might be worth a look-see.* A light rain had started but she buttoned her jacket over her camera and hurried down A Street. Approaching the construction site, she saw women carrying food inside where the frame had gone up. The workers immediately started cheering and their shouts of approval carried over music played by members of the Tacoma Musicians Union. *Goodness gracious,* Louise thought, apropos of nothing in particular. Dodging piles of lumber, she managed to get a few pictures, her favorite being of a man sitting on a beam five or so feet off the ground, near a sign reading, *A Gift of Tacoma Union and Business Men.* Louise snapped her camera just as he was in the act of accepting a cup of coffee from a woman who stood on tiptoes to hand it up. Louise took a few more, miscellaneous photographs and then, hearing the streetcar, made a mad dash and swung on board. She arrived home soaking wet and was greeted by an ecstatic Queenie who fretted when Louise was out of her eyesight. Together, they hurried upstairs where Louise put on her warmest robe, and then back to the kitchen for something to eat. There she stopped short.

"Well, that's new," she said to her pet. Along one wall were boxes, each neatly labeled: paper, bottles, rags, and rubber. *Someone, most likely Annie,* she thought, *is already making use of them.* "And that's new, too." 'That' was a chair piled with neatly folded clothing that Nell'd no doubt picked up from various places around town. *Dead people's clothes,* Louise thought, but she knew Nell would respond by saying, it made no never mind to her. And to remember that she'd started in business by picking apart previously-owned clothes and reusing the fabric. Also, with the Red Cross now asking for everyone's unwanted clothing, she wanted to get ahead of things.

Louise filled a bowl from the stockpot Annie kept on the back of the stove and added some leftover chicken, giving a few pieces to Queenie. Princess appeared from the parlor and hopped on the table. With a sigh and pausing to blow her nose, Louise poured some cream in a bowl for the cat. Outside, birds were taking shelter and one thumped against a window. *It's getting too dark for the poor thing to see the glass,* she thought. Feeling snug in the warm kitchen with her hot soup, and only her pets for company, she picked a copy of the *Tacoma Daily Ledger* Nell had left on the table. It was folded open to an article headlined, *Gathering Moss for Red Cross.* Grinning at what she assumed was an unintended rhyme, and remembering all the moss Dottie had been picking through, Louise began reading the article. Suddenly, her Uncle Ike burst through the door. "Get your camera and come 'on."

"Huh?"

"There's big doings at the Oriental Dock; night watchman caught a German he thinks is a spy."

Louise jumped up. "Just give me a minute to get dressed."

"No time. Put something over your robe and come on."

Louise grabbed Nell's old Goodrich raincoat. It was made of tarpaulin, naphtha and fabric, and smelled something awful but it was a useful garment. The phone started ringing and Ike picked it up, shouted, "Call back," in the receiver and hung up. Then he checked the stove, grabbed Louise by the hand, and dragged her out the door. Through a series of swaps involving a cash register and barber chair, he had acquired a beat-up car of unfamiliar ancestry known in the family as the Old Banger. Before she was able to get in, Louise had to clear the seat of pamphlets with the city's traffic codes and speed limits printed on them. Once in, her slippers began leaving puddles on the floor.

"Those pamphlets are gifts from the city's finest." Ike pulled onto the road.

"You have several. Are they helpful?"

"Nah. Just a bunch of laws that don't take the average Joe like me into consideration: how many you can have in the car with you, how fast you can go, how to spin your arm around out the window when you wanna turn." Ike turned down the hill without spinning his arm out the window. "Twelve miles an hour, twelve miles an hour! You're gunna get nowhere fast at that rate."

Barricades blocked the muddy Wharf Road from Pacific Avenue to the waterfront but Ike ignored them, knocked two over, and skidded down to the waterfront. He took more corners without spinning his arm, dodged in and out of traffic, and pushed the speed up to fifteen miles an hour. Louise, holding on with dear life, wondered if he crashed, whether she'd be killed or merely maimed. Then, to her surprise, he drove a block up McCarver Street and stopped on a hill above the Oriental Dock. The massive facility was in front of one of Old Tacoma's longest warehouses. Ike and Louise got out of the car and joined a number of men standing on the hummock. Looking down, they saw a number of police near the Old Tacoma Mill.

"What're they doing?" Louise whispered.

"Looks like they're guarding the tunnel," Ike said.

"That's right," said a man. "He's hold up inside."

"Who?"

Before anyone could answer, gun shots rang out, and everyone ducked.

"Don't know yet. Supposed to be a spy. Night watchman, fella by the name of Erastus Fellows, caught a man creeping along in the shadows and nabbed him. Guy had a gun and before Fellows could take it away, started shooting."

Heavy clouds obscured the moon, but the warehouse had its lights on for the night shift's use. Peering down through the heavy rain, Louise saw piles of lumber, the long docks with ships tied to them: large ships full of cargo to be unloaded or waiting to be loaded, small ships that were part of the Mosquito Fleet, and others out in the bay, each with a lantern to guard against collision. While she inched closer to the edge of the embankment, a man with binoculars trained on the scene below nodded at her.

"They're emptying his pockets," he paused then added, "I can see a flashlight and a bunch of cord."

"Anything else?"

"Wait a minute...yeah, there's the gun...cop just took it away. There's other stuff but I can't see what."

"Le'me look," someone said, and the binoculars changed hands. "Looks like the *Burnside* is trying to make port."

"Must not have heard..." His voice trailed off.

"Blasted rain," Louise muttered. Seeing that she was trying to photograph the arrest, someone held an umbrella over her.

After a few minutes, during which the rain fell harder, Ike asked if she had what she needed.

"Best I can, I'm ready to leave. How about you?"

In answer, her uncle turned and started for the car, When Louise moved to follow, a familiar voice called her name. Turning, she saw Matthew standing next to a well-dressed man, both protected by large umbrellas. With horror she saw the elderly man looking her up and down, taking in her appearance: muddy wet slippers, the bottom four inches of a robe hanging below a smelly raincoat, and hair dripping water in her face, Matthew looked aghast.

"I wondered if you'd be here," he said.

"I thought you were headed out of town."

"Change of plans."

Before she could answer, Ike turned and grabbed her arm. "It's raining harder, and you've been sick. So, shake a leg and get a move on it."

The last thing Louise saw was Matthew's uncle looking at her and shuddering.

Chapter 6

The next morning, Louise took particular care with her hair, creating a French twist, spearing it and, occasionally her head, with enough pins to keep it all in place. Then putting on her favorite blue and white shepherd-checked skirt, she took care to smooth the waist yoke over her hips and make sure the pleats were straight. With it, she generally wore a white blouse and a scarf to match the skirt tied under the collar. "Pretty and business-like," she said to Queenie as they hurried down to the kitchen. The door was open letting in the sounds of chirping birds and the sight of honeysuckle dripping and watering the creeping thyme underneath.

"Umm, smells good in here." Louise picked up a small vase of sweet peas and held it to her nose. "Gosh, I can smell. My cold must be gone."

"You're much improved when it comes to time," Annie said. "Here, I'll pour your coffee and start your eggs."

"I've been working on it."

Nell looked up from her paper and smiled. "You were in bed when we came home."

Louise made breakfast for her pets before adding cream to her coffee and joining Nell at the table. "Do you think any other family drinks as much coffee as we do?"

"I know for a fact that most of the ladies who visit my couture want tea."

"Ugh."

"There's a brief article in the paper," Nell said, "something about a spy being arrested."

"Already? I saw it. In the afternoon, I walked down to see the Red Cross Salvage Building and when I got home, Uncle Ike took me to see the doings at the dock."

Louise forked up some scrambled eggs and swallowed. "Can I see the article? If it's just a brief mention there'll be a longer one today. I took some pictures, but it was raining so hard, I don't know how they'll turn out."

"Are you taking Queenie with you today?"

"No, I feel bad about leaving her home again, but I want to stop by the Red Cross room after work."

"She'll pout."

"I know. Maybe, over the weekend I can take her to Point Defiance and have a picnic."

"Well, she can help me in the garden." Annie put their dirty dishes in a big pan and filled it with hot water. "Them dratted rabbits has been at my lettuce again."

When Louise left the house later, Queenie's reproachful gaze followed her.

Across the street she saw a group of boys piling into her Uncle Reuban's truck bed. If it was handy, he'd often drop them off at Wapato Lake to fish. Ordinarily, they pushed and shoved each other, knocking off each other's hats and untying shoestrings. As Louise watched, Reuban said something, and their demeanor changed. They began chanting, "Kaiser Bill went up a hill to take a look at France. When he came down, he had a frown and bullets in his pants."

Reuban waved at her, she waved and called a good morning, but her thoughts were troubled. *It's as if the war has infiltrated my neighborhood.* She rode the streetcar in silence and disembarked in the middle of a group of men holding cages. Always interested in something new, she asked the first man who looked approachable about what was going on.

"We're answering the call for homing pigeons." He held up his cage so Louise could see the iridescent green and purple feathers on an otherwise light gray bird.

"I never really looked closely at a pigeon before." She started to reach toward the cage.

"Best not," the man said and she pulled back. "Anyway, they're not just your average pigeon on the street. These are Racing Homers."

Someone behind her asked who had put out the call for pigeons. "Major Charles Wyman," the man said. Before Louise could inquire further, another man explained that the major was head of the signal war group at Camp Lewis.

By this time, other interested people had crowded round. And in his element, the first man said, "They're being used to carry messages from the trenches in the front line to headquarters in the rear."

"Isn't there a chance they'll be shot down?"

"There sure is. The Germans know all about them. The British and French have been flying pigeons since the war started."

Always a softie when it came to animals and hating the thought of the birds being shot down, Louise asked if she could take some pictures. *There's something to be said about getting up a little early,* she thought. *I can get these developed and send them off hopefully along with the spy photographs.*

At the studio, Louise found comfort in the familiar chemical smells particular to places where film was developed. Mr. Aldrich was talking to a woman holding a baby and Louise explained that she had film to process but asked if he needed her help first.

"No, you go right along, there's things needing done in the darkroom." Her boss looked both harried and relieved, but his manner was unusually curt. "Take your time." He huddled around the woman talking softly.

His brusque tone was so unexpected Louise, wondering, if she'd done something wrong, found it hard to keep her mind on her work. In the darkroom she spent time straightening everything, even the drying lines. Mr. Altamont had left some film to be developed, and she took care of that along with her own. The photograph of the pigeon man was clear but uninspired, and most of the waterfront scenes were too dark to be of much use. Only one came out clearly. Louise had captured a clear shot of a policeman tying the spy's arms together while other officers and the night watchman looked on. Finally, with no reason to linger, Louise took the pictures she'd made up and returned to the front area. "Mr. Aldrich, have I done something to upset you," she said, putting the pictures on his desk. "If so, I'm terribly sorry. You must know how much I respect you and value my job here."

For a minute her boss looked startled, then he sighed. "No, of course you haven't. You've brought the studio back to life. I just wanted to spare you from the lady who was here."

"Why? Who was she? An, er, a lady of *le demimonde* or something?"

In spite of himself, Mr. Aldrich laughed. "I don't think Tacoma is sophisticated enough to have a lady of that particular position in society. No, it was just that the woman wanted something done that was very popular back in the Victorian era but not anymore."

"Well, maybe I should learn it."

"No, I don't think so. She wanted what was referred to as *memento mori,* a post-mortem photograph." He hesitated. "Of her and her child."

"Golly." Looking dumbfounded, Louise pulled a chair to where she could better hear her boss over an abnormal amount of street noise. "And kind'a creepy."

"Diseases and child mortality ran rampant back then: thyroid, smallpox, diphtheria, cholera. Then, when photography became greatly improved, it gave families ways to remember their children who'd died. It was just a matter of posing them realistically; and that's what Mrs. Grose, this morning, wanted. It's a simple process, just use a long exposure; the living have a tendency to make slight movements which blurs them a little but the deceased, of course, being still, have a clear, sharp image. Fortunately, nobody wants a *memento mori,* anymore." While Louise digested the information, he looked at the developed photos. "This is clear," he said of the man with the pigeon.

"Yes, but banal. I think I was lucky, though, to get a decent shot of the spy action. It was raining so hard."

"You were, yes, and I suggest we send this to some papers back east with a short writeup. Next time, use an umbrella, a tripod, if you can, and open up the aperture wide." Voices from the street were drowning out his words and they looked out the window. "When I was growing up," Mr. Aldrich said, "we had a parade every Fourth of July, and as long as they were able, members of the GAR, that's the Grand Army of the Republic," he explained when Louise raised her eyebrows, "participated. I remember the old soldiers, many of them missing limbs, many of them still waiting for their pensions, riding in the back of wagons waving to the crowds on the one day of the year anyone still pays attention to them. And here we are with the Commerce Club asking for twenty-five thousand people to march in Tacoma's Celebration of War parade. And when the men who make it through and come home, it will be the same thing all over again." He shook his head and turned away. "I'm closing for the day."

Louise wrote notes for her pictures, addressed envelopes, and put them for the mailman to pick up. She followed Mr. Aldrich out and he locked the door. "I'll see you tomorrow," he said and walked away.

"Well, my goodness," she muttered, and a woman passing her and seeing no one else in the doorway, looked startled.

So many would-be marchers crowded the sidewalk, window shopping was impossible. When she eventually pushed and shoved her way to the Perkins Building, Louise found the Red Cross facility closed. *Just as well,* she thought, *I don't want to go there anyway.* Several crows landed a few feet away and began a hunt-and-peck for food. On the tracks below the Eleventh Street Bridge, a slow-moving train picked up speed. *I know,* she thought, *I'll go down to the waterfront and see what's what and get some fresh air while I'm at it. It's just too noisy and crowded up here.*

She walked around to the side of the building and headed for the set of switchback stairs starting on the bridge and ending where she would have been able to see the bay if it hadn't been for all the buildings. Halfway down, where the stairs made the first switchback, she leaned on a railing. Near Seventeenth Street, just out of sight, was the Puget Sound Dry Dock Company where her Uncle Ike sometimes worked. He didn't much like the job but then, at least according to his wife, Freida Faye, he hadn't liked any of the other jobs he'd had. "If Ike had his way, he'd spend all his time fishing," she said. "But thank goodness he's too old to join the army. He, sure as shootin' wouldn't like the discipline." Louise had noticed her aunt's expression when she said that and wondered if she'd been thinking about their sons, Theodore and Grover.

Across the tide flats and beyond the warehouses was the Puyallup Reservation and the mouth of the Puyallup River where Piney lived. "The tribe lost a significant amount of its historical territory," Dovie once said. "Government fraud and greedy developers." While she worked on the early years for her History of Tacoma book, Dovie had been able to interview many of those involved in local history and Piney was one of them.

Watching from the steps, Louise thought the reservation looked peaceful, something that hadn't always been true. Smoke came up from unseen fires, and two men were doing something to their canoes. She shifted her gaze to where an old sidewheeler steamship was moored and smiled. For over a year, steam shovels had dredged the waterway making it broad enough so the ships could pick up cargoes, turn on the headwind in the deep water and sail away. *No big ships today, though,* she thought, *just the sidewheeler.* With the ever-present seagulls which were making for land, it was still an attractive photograph. *Nostalgic and quiet.*

Thanks to Nell, both Louise and Annie knew more than most about the men who worked on the waterfront. "When wives come to me for new clothes, I like to know who their children are and what their husbands do for a living," she said. "Show an interest and they start talking. It's good for business." And, as a result, she shared with them articles from the *Times* and the *Daily Ledger,* where their husbands were frequently mentioned, often reading articles aloud at breakfast or dinner.

Hearing about the mile-long wharf, supposedly the longest in the world, Louise itched to see it for herself, especially the insides of the freight houses which, according to her Uncle Ike, were one hundred and fifty feet wide. "Timber trusses placed every twenty-five feet support the roof," he explained "and beams of Douglas Fir measuring a full 150-foot in dimension are at the bottom of each truss."

"Imagine that, just like when there were massive trees still around. I've never seen a tree that big," Louise had said, listening in fascination as he talked. "I heard that people used to hollow out the trunks of fallen trees and live in them," She regularly nagged her uncle to take her to see the insides of the freight house but so far, he'd refused.

Standing on the stairs, she remembered suggesting to him that he let her go with him to work one day, but he merely grunted. "The waterfront's been ruined," he told her. "What with the wharf, freight houses, the Northern Pacific coal bunkers, and piles of lumber, the views all gone to h... uh heck, he said, "Now adays ya gotta go clear to the Nereides Baths and Point Defiance to find any shorefront."

At his words, Nell had snorted and John promised to take her down when the weather improved. "I'm with you," he said to Louise. "There's nothing like the smell of the lumber, the snap of the ship sails, and the air full of seagulls."

"I love seagulls," Louise had said and John grinned. "Me, too. We can make a day of it, visit the warehouse by foot, then rent a boat so we can go out on the bay and watch the loaded ships turning to head out. Mid-August is a good time because of the southwesterly winds."

But that had been weeks ago and was still weeks away, and she had to hope John would remember his promise. In the meantime, the Waterfront Employers Association's president, Harvey Wells, had been rundown, the fishermen were agitating for a breakwater at Old Town to protect their ships, and thefts at the various warehouses had gotten so bad, the police were posting guards to protect incoming cargoes of food. There was unrest among the longshoremen, too, with the *Times* saying some employers had a blacklist of men not to be hired. Even in the best of times, and this certainly wasn't the best of times, and unless she had a male companion, Nell frowned on Louise going down to the waterfront. "It's a rough bunch down there," she said. "It's not a safe place."

Louise remembered her saying that but decided to go a little way, on the off chance there was something interesting happening. She continued down the steps and turning left, started walking toward Old Town. Sure enough, near the Sperry Flour mill a man stood on a box addressing a large audience of workers. The presence of the sheriff and a number of police officers told Louise the speaker was someone important; the crowd of laborers shoving and shouting told her something important was going on. Next to her, a steep hill dotted with large rocks and low-growing shrubs separated the waterfront from a neighborhood of homes. Looking it over, Louise saw a place where a large boulder and some stunted trees protruding out from the bank created a ledge. *That looks like a spot where I can get a better view*, she thought. With her camera bag hanging around her neck she began grabbing at the low-growing Oregon grape, salal, and at the various exposed roots which Commencement Bay's salty air had sculpted into bizarre shapes. Slipping in the thin soil, rocky soil she managed to pull herself up to where the small patch of land leveled out. Sweating and panting, she ignored the dirt in her shoes and, pausing only long enough to wipe her hands off, took out her camera and focused it on the speaker and the angry crowd.

Out in the bay, what had been a frisky chop was turning to angry swells. Vashon Island which was generally referred to as being twelve nautical miles away, was almost completely obscured by a gray-black colored clouds roiling in. Gulls beat their wings against the briny air as they made their way to safety inland. *Lordy, another storm. This will put a damper on the parade*, Louise thought, and the unintentional pun made her smile. Meanwhile, the no-nonsense wind blew the men's shouts up to where she stood. Though she couldn't make out the words, she had no doubt about their outrage. A few minutes passed, and deciding she had enough pictures, Louise was putting her camera away when she heard a man's voice.

"Well, well, if it isn't the little camera lady I heared so much about."

Louise immediately felt a chill that had nothing to do with the air. "Did you, now?" She said, turning to leave, but he grabbed her arm.

"You been takin' pictures? Why don't you take mine?"

"There's a storm coming and I don't want to get my camera wet, but I will if you want, free of charge. Just stand over there." Louise tugged at her arm, "but I do need to get my camera out." However, the man intensified his grip.

"Not so fast Camera Lady." He moved so quickly Louise had no time to pull away. "You're prettier than that other one and I think you and me should get better acquainted."

Close up she saw his pock-marked face, near-together eyes, and missing teeth; his torn and sweat stained clothes, smelled his sour breath and rank body odor. As he spoke, sharp raindrops burst out of the roiling sky, bouncing as it attacked the soil. Then it hit her. *Oh my God. He means Irene Carmel.* Louise froze in terror. And before she could move, the man yanked her camera bag from her arm and threw it aside. He pulled off his belt and swung the buckle at her, once, twice, three times before grabbing her hair to pull her head back so he could bite her throat. Putting a foot behind one of her legs, he pushed her down. Louise fell back, hit a rock and a piece of bleached root. Stars swam before her eyes. Almost immediately, he was on top of her, tearing at the bodice of her blouse, squeezing her breasts and biting her neck and face. Then he began pummeling her stomach and lifting her skirt to pinch her thighs. The face above her was pockmarked and dirty. The rain quickly soaked his long, greasy hair. Underneath her back, rocks dug into her skin, and pounding rain quickly turned the ground into a muddy quagmire. But the downpour helped bring her around.

"Get. Off. Me." Louise flailed her legs, doing her best to fight him off but, manic in his assault, the man ripped her bloomers, pinched her tender skin, and forced his fingers inside her, twisting and scraping. She managed to scream before he leaned a forearm on her throat.

"Here, now," came a voice from the foot of the bank. "What's going on up there?"

At the sound of a voice, Louise's assailant shifted enough for her to scream again. The feet of the man below brought debris sliding down the embankment as he climbed to where she lay. "What's going on up here?" His nearing presence acted as a prod. The attacker hauled himself off Louise and disappeared.

The last thing Louise heard before she passed out were the words, "Dear God."

* * *

Hospitals, even the best of them, are not quiet places. Three days later, Louise woke to the soft sounds of nurse's shoes going up and down the passage between the beds, to the whisper of their starched white uniforms, and their murmuring to each other. Cabinet doors opened and closed, and water splashed in metal basins. She was in a room full of the stale smells of infrequently-washed bodies, flowers, and antiseptics. Her head and neck were tightly wrapped and almost immobile. And even the slightest movement triggered pain. From the corner of her eye, she saw a table next to her bed. It held a glass and a pitcher of water, an eyewash cup, scissors, a roll of gauze, and a tin of arnica ointment. She also saw a peculiar metal device that turned out to be a Pulsocon Blood Circulator. She was just able to see an empty bed on her left and a woman sleeping in the bed to her right. The two of them were at the end of a long room where patients either slept quietly or writhed and moaned. All the beds had metal headboards and foot boards which clanged when bumped. The more restless patients also had small metal sides pulled up to make sure they didn't roll out. Sunlight coming through sporadically-placed windows created peculiar patterns thanks to imperfections in the glass. Louise licked her lips and found them covered with grease.

"Nurse." The words were barely audible, and she tried again. "Nurse." This time she roused other patients who began making noises. However, the woman who responded ignored them.

Ah, Miss Tanquist. It's good to see you awake."

"I'm so thirsty. Can I please have a drink of water?"

126

"Of course, my dear. Let me just wipe your face and hands first. It will make you feel more alert." The nurse wet a towel and gently dabbed her with warm water. Louise tried to shift and gave a small moan. "Gosh, everything hurts."

"I imagine it does. You were in pretty bad shape when you were brought in."

"Where am I?"

"Tacoma General."

The nurse took a cover off the pitcher and poured water in the glass. "Be careful of the straw. Patients keep biting them and a mouth full of glass won't be pleasant for either of us. I'm Nurse Carmichael and I'll be taking care of you while you're here." She put an arm under Louise's neck and tipped her head up. Pain shot through her body. The water was tepid, but Louise managed two careful swallows.

"I'm was so dry."

"I imagine you were. As I said, you were in a very bad condition when you were brought in. Fortunately, nothing was broken, and no surgery was required, just plenty of arnica on the bruises and antiseptic on the cuts." She re-wet the cloth and carefully wiped around the bandages. In spite of the water's warmth, Louise shivered.

"Do you mind pulling the blanket up?"

"You'll warm up after you've eaten." Nurse Carmichael tucked the blanket around her. "And I'll bring you a hot water bottle."

"That would be lovely." Around them, the ward was waking up with the most frequent request being for a bed pan. Louise was glad she didn't need one yet. "Have I been asleep long?"

"Three days, three and a half, actually."

"Nell, that's my mother, doesn't approve of people, women especially, who complain about their health, but I am well and truly sore. And it hurts to talk."

"I sure you are sore; you are badly scratched, cut and bruised." Nurse Carmichael had to raise her voice slightly as the ward filled with noise. Other nurses entered the room and conversed with patients. One orderly pushed a breakfast cart with a squeaky wheel, and another arrived to fill water pitchers from the spigot on a large stoneware crock. Nurse Carmichael disappeared for a minute and after what appeared to be a somewhat terse conversation with the woman seated at a desk near the front of the room, she returned with a single ice cube and gave it to Louise. While a grateful Louise slurped on the ice, the nurse looked at her lapel watch, took Louise's pulse, and made notes on a chart hanging off the railing on the foot of the bed. "I'm afraid I will have to pull down the blanket for a bit; I need to change your bandages"

Louise sighed, closed her eyes, and tried not to take deep breaths. "Does my family know I'm here?" She asked, and a bit of icy water ran down her chin.

"Oh, my, yes. Your father has to almost carry your mother out of here when visiting hours are over. A lovely pair, though. And the lady who comes with them, too. They cause me no trouble; I can tell you." Nurse Carmichael glared at the woman in the next bed. "Not like some others." She turned to the nightstand. "Now, I'm going to replace your bandages and that will no doubt hurt quite a lot, but after that's done, I'll bring you something to eat and the hot water bottle and then you can rest." She helped Louise sit up and swing her legs back over the side of the bed. I'll start with your back." Louise tried to be stoic while the nurse began removing bandages. "There was a bit of a contretemps here over who your doctor is," Nurse Carmichael said. She wet some of the gauze that had become embedded in a deep scratch and tried to ease it off.

Louise, who was slowly becoming more alert, flinched saying, "Ouch!" Several women looked to see what was going on, so she lowered her voice. "Golly, that hurts. It stings. I'm going to try not to cry but probably will; I can't help it."

"Don't worry about that dear. I'm just sorry, there's no way I can do this more gently." The nurse prodded and dabbed and blew on the cut. "I'm afraid you'll have at least one scar. The man who did this managed to grind your poor back into rocks and your skin is deeply scratched. We had to use tweezers to get the grit out. And Iodine does sting but it's a good disinfectant." She put clean bandages on. "That was the biggest cut, a gouge really, these others shouldn't hurt as much." They did though, and the pain seemed to increase. Louise did her best to remain impassive, but tears flowed, streaking her cheeks.

"There, I'm done with your back. You can lay down now. Here's something for your nose." The nurse handed her a handkerchief and plumped the pillows. "And here's an aspirin which should help with the pain. Believe it or not, your poor chest and neck took the brunt of the assault, so this won't be any easier."

While Louise tried to get comfortable, she said, "What did you mean by 'who is my doctor'?"

Nurse Carmichael examined a particular deep bite wound and made tsking noises. Using a ball of cotton, she cleaned the area with carbolic acid and painted it with iodine. "Apparently, and I wasn't here at the time, the day after you were brought in, a young man stormed in and made a beeline for your bed. After he read your chart, he raised Cain." She sighed and said, "I'm afraid you will have scars here, too. What kind of man does this?"

"A girl named Irene Carmel was attacked in the same way, just a few weeks ago," Louise said. The ice cube was gone and it hurt to talk, but she added, "do go on about the man."

"He demanded to see the head nurse and was very vocal about your treatment. Your parents had called in a Doctor Clarke from retirement and she ordered laudanum drops for the pain. The man said that not only was she not your doctor but that he wouldn't leave until the laudanum for pain was dropped and replaced with aspirin."

"Why?" Louise squirmed a bit, trying to find some comfort. "I didn't hurt as much before."

"Yes, but laudanum can become addictive." The nurse looked at the breakfast cart which had stopped in front of Louise's bed. "I'm afraid your food will be cold, but this has to be done first." She used a copious amount of iodine to clean a deep bite on Louise's breast and Louise sat bolt upright. "Oh, my God, that hurt." More tears flowed down her cheeks and her nose became a fountain.

While people looked to see what was going on, voices sprang up around the room, and various attendants did their best to hush them, Nurse Carmichel eased Louise back onto the pillow. "I'm so sorry, my dear. Really, I am. But you don't want an infection." She applied a wet cloth to the tears and took a cup of coffee off the breakfast tray. "Let's take a little break, shall we?"

The coffee was lukewarm, but Louise drank half of it. She put the cup on the nightstand and ran her hands across her forehead and through her hair. "Best to get it over with."

The nurse gave her the wet cloth and started again, removing bandages, cleaning wounds, applying either iodine or carbolic acid, and binding them up again. Both women breathed a sigh of relief when she was done.

"Now, here's your breakfast tray." She put more pillows behind Louise's back, removed metal lids from the plates of food, and set the tray on Louise's lap saying, "I think we're both glad that's over."

Louise managed a smile, and picked up a piece of toast. She had just enough coffee left in which to dunk it. While she ate, surprised that she could as badly as her throat hurt, and surprised that she was hungry, Louise thought about the interfering doctor. Could it have been Matthew? She wished she'd asked more questions but, in the meantime, she was too sore and tired to care. She ate a few of the scrambled eggs and when she was done, a young woman with a tag reading Student of the Chautauqua School of Nursing stopped to pick up the tray and deliver the hot water bottle. Always curious, Louise asked her name and about the name tag.

"I'm not supposed to interact with patients." The young woman, whispered. She purposely fumbled with the tray saying, "The Chautauqua School is a correspondence course, so before a Matron will hire us, we have to train in a hospital for a year."

Someone cleared their throat and she made slow work of loading Louise's tray on the food cart. "Tacoma General thinks delivering food trays and emptying bedpans is just the hands-on experience we need." She smiled. "My name is Katy Fox." Then she winked and left.

That night, Louise developed a low-grade fever and headache. Her face turned red and became beaded with sweat. With every movement she moaned in pain and the nurses tried not to show their concern. Nell and Annie took turns sitting by the bed, sponging her with tepid water and trying to get her to drink various juices. On a day when Matthew and Doctor Clarke happened to arrive at the same time, they checked her many injuries, and he took her pulse.

"It's thready," he said.

"Yes, I noticed that too."

"I'm thinking she might benefit from full submersion in a bath of luke-warm water."

"Yes, I agree, the aspirin and cold compresses don't seem to be helping."

Behind them, the ward's silence was broken by a nurse saying, "Here now, it's not visiting hours; you can't go in." She called for an orderly. The visitor ignored her and walked softly to Louise's bed. The two doctors were unaware of anyone else's presence until Piney spoke.

"I brought some willow bark tea," she said, handing Dr. Clark a parcel.

"How good of you." She took a bottle out. "Nothing we've tried has worked. Piney, this is Matthew Altamont, the other doctor treating Louise."

"I'm not familiar with willow bark tea," he said. "What's it supposed to do?"

"We use it to treat fevers and body ache."

"Well, I wish we could heat it, but I dare not ask that tyrant of a head nurse so let's see if we can get her to drink some as it is, luke-warm. He emptied the drinking glass into a vase of flowers on Louise's neighbor's nightstand.

"Are you sure about this?"

"The Puyallup tribe has a long history of treating fevers with willow bark tea."

"Successfully?"

"More often than not." Piney poured a generous amount into the glass. "Help me sit her up a bit."

Before the nurse arrived with an orderly in tow, the three of them were able to force the bitter brew down Louise's throat.

"I really must insist on your leaving," the nurse said to Piney. "The commotion is disturbing the other patients."

Matthew's fists clenched and unclenched as he faced the woman. "Mrs. Piney is a consultant we called in. And I will remind you, nurse, that we are the doctors, not you." While the nurse flushed in anger, he added, "We are prescribing a luke-warm bath as soon as we leave. Not merely tepid, but luke-warm, then let her injuries dry before reapplying her bandages."

For the next few seconds, the two had a standoff, then the nurse huffed back to her station with the sounds of several patients clapping following her.

They were never to know if it was the tea, the bath, or Louise's healthy constitution but the fever broke and by the following morning was gone, leaving her feeling limp as a rag but otherwise mentally alert. When Katy came by, she asked for fresh water and coffee which, though out of the regular mealtimes, she got and enjoyed. Twice a day Nurse Carmichael dragged a screen around her bed, applied so much arnica Louise thought she should have bathed in that instead of water. However, she found its strong pine and sage odor pleasant. And once ensconced in a clean cotton gown, Louise slept. She barely managed to stay awake long enough to finish her meals, and during visiting hours, she fell asleep after five minutes. She was asleep the day Nell came carrying a pair of stout scissors and, with the help of Nurse Katy, cut Louise's badly-matted hair into an Irene Castle bob.

"She's been wanting this done for quite a while," Nell said.

"There just isn't time, here, to fuss with a patient's hair," Nurse Katy said, "but in any event, hers was so matted and full of dried mud and pitch, we couldn't get it untangled. Nurse Carmichael said, just wash it so there's no sticks and things in it and then leave it go, that she could take care of it later. Louise, that is, not Nurse Carmichael." Katy looked at the long strands Nell was putting in a box to keep. "It's a lovely color."

"Yes," Nell gently combed where she'd cut. "Dark brown with strands of red when you least expect it. The only other time it's ever been cut was when Louise had scarlet fever. A cargo ship arrived with the majority of its crew sick. My brother, Ike, was working on the docks then, and picked it up. He managed to expose Louise before taking to his bed." Nell combed carefully around a large scab and continued. "If you knew my brother, you might expect him to be a terrible patient, but he wasn't. He'd never gotten that much special treatment before. And he was as docile as a baby lamb, maybe because he felt so bad about making Louise sick."

Nurse Katy sighed. "You must have a lovely family."

"Well, like most families, we have our times, but overall, yes, I do. I've been very lucky that way." Nell looked at the nurse. "You sound a little homesick."

"Yes, ma'am, I am. My family's all back in Vermont."

"I expect you miss them."

"Yes, ma'am. I don't get paid much, being a probationer and all, but what I do get, I'm saving to bring them out here. Pa's a pastor and they don't make much either, but we're working on it."

Nell put the last strand of Louise's hair in the box and closed it with a sigh. It felt as if her baby was gone. However, thinking of Katy Fox, and thinking that if her father was a pleasant as his daughter, she wondered if she could do anything to help bring him out to Tacoma. *I'll ask John; he'll probably know.*

The next day, when Louise woke for breakfast, several of the patients at her end of the ward watched with interest to see what she'd do when she discovered her haircut. More than one hoped for a show of hysterics which would break the monotony of their day and provide conversation for visiting hours. Katy brought her lunch but kept her eyes averted. It was only when a cold draft hit the back of her neck that Louise put her hand up and felt the shorn hair. For a minute she couldn't believe what she was feeling—or not feeling. All the heavy, unmanageable hair was gone, leaving in its place short straight locks combed from the crown to bangs in the front, cut short in the back and tapering in an inverted fashion along the sides. Louise broke into a big grin and laughed. "Well, one good thing came from the attack," she said, and the floor nurse immediately shushed her.

"When, who and how?" She whispered to Katy after being told that "this is a hospital not a place of fun."

"Your mother did it during visiting hours yesterday." Seeing Nurse Carmichael's disapproving look, she lowered her voice. "I was allowed to help."

Louise caught Katy's hand, saying loud enough for Nurse Carmichael to hear, "Thank you, nurse. Between my bath, my hot coffee and now this, the hospital should be proud of you." She took the lid off her plate. "Oh dear, stewed fruit again."

With nothing more to see, the other patients returned to their main occupation: complaining, and the morning went on as usual. Later that day Louise received two pieces of mail: a card, and a newspaper folded open to an article with a circle around it and a note from Nell. Setting the paper aside, she looked at the note.

Darling, I can't come in today, Dovie's been sick, nothing serious but Hildy asked for my help. This story hit the morning paper. I hope Miss Carmel saw it, too. Rest well my little dandelion. Much love, your mother, Nell.

Louise looked at the article and felt her chest muscles constrict.

Woman Accuses South Tacoma Man of Fearful Brutality

Applying to Deputy Prosecutor Seldon for a warrant for the arrest of Andrew Nelson, South Tacoma hardware man on charges of assault. Mrs. Helen Wharton of 5605 South Birmingham told a story of brutality Wednesday that compares with the rack tortures of the medieval ages. Mrs. Wharton claimed that both her hands were clamped between the rollers of a ringer used for wringing clothes and while she was pinioned in this manner she was beaten about the head and shoulders and kicked. He deliberately forced her hands into the wringer, turned the handle until she was held a fast prisoner and then administered a beating.

Suddenly cold, Louise scooted down under her blankets, pulling them up under her chin. Her body seemed to melt into the mattress. She thought she must have been holding her breath ever since the attack and that she was finally able to breath normally again. She asked the first nurse she saw for another blanket and a hot water bottle and fell deeply asleep.

The rest of the day passed quietly. Not until she felt the envelope scrunch under her did Louise remember the card. It was a lovely card with roses on the front and a written message from Matthew inside.

Know that I haven't forgotten you, Louise. I have come to see you more than once but the last time I was stopped at the door due to a bad cold. Recovery takes time, rest, and patience and I miss you more than you know. Matthew

Louise returned the card to its envelope and smiled. She was being discharged the next day and, cold or no cold, she would see Matthew.

The following afternoon Nell and John came to take her home. Nell brought embroidered silk handkerchiefs with swags of flowers surrounding the words, "Thank You" and gave one to each of Louise's nurses. To go with them, John had purchased boxes of a new candy called Almond Roca which was being made by two Tacoma men. Nurse Katy was also given an invitation to the Tanquist and Bacom Fourth of July picnic and then Louise was put in a chair and wheeled out to John's car.

"Gosh I'm glad to be leaving the hospital," she said, taking a deep breath. "The sun is shining and, mmmm, it smells good. Oh, it's so good to be outside."

John Laughed. "Yesterday was Wheatless Wednesday and the bakeries always gear up on Thursdays; that's what you smell. Though, in my opinion, War Bread isn't really worth waiting for." He helped Louise in his car, and she asked about Wheatless Wednesdays. "The bread's mostly made of barley, oats corn, and rice, now."

"The government issued recipes for Wheatless Yeast Bread, not to be confused with Wheat-free Yeast Bread or Wheatless War Bread or Near Wheatless Bread," Nell said. "There's also Liberty Bread and Wheat-free Nut Bread. Actually, that one's not too bad." She laughed when John snorted. "Annie is now keeping containers of barley flour, rice flour, oatmeal flour, rye flour, corn flour, and jars of breads crumbs, and uneaten mashed potatoes. She's part of what is called the Women's Army Against Waste."

Though it hurt to laugh, Louise laughed anyway. John turned down the hill, then right on D street, and pulled up in front of her home. "Oh, it's so good to be home. What a foolish thing I did." While she spoke and John came around to help her out of the car, Annie rushed out of the house.

"Don't you ever scare us like that again," she cried, reaching to hug Louise.

"Not too tight."

"Oh, dear. Do you still hurt?"

"Not too much," Louise lied, "the bruises are about gone but I'm still really tender." They started up the walk and a number of people shouted 'hellos' and 'welcome homes' from their porches. Inside, Queenie wiggled around in circles making funny noises in her excitement to have her favorite person back home, and even Princess looked happy, though, as Annie always said, "You can never tell with a cat."

Louise changed into loose-fitting clothes, and they sat around a table in the garden. Annie carried out a tray loaded with a stuffed chicken, a bowl of mashed potatoes, baked corn, a salad and a gravy boat filled to the brim.

"If this is recommended by the Women's Army, I'm all for it." Louise helped herself. "Hospital food wasn't very good." After a few minutes, however, she stopped eating. "I guess my stomach has shrunk. I'll rest a minute and then see if I can clean my plate." She made a herculean effort, but Queenie came in for her share.

Summer was finally making an appearance, and tired as she was, Louise asked to sit in the backyard for a while. *I'd purely love to let the sun beat on my bare back,* she thought, *but like as not, either someone would see me, or I'd get well and truly sunburned.*

While she dozed in a chair, the others talked: Annie, who loved anything theatrical, had been to see magician Herbert Brooks escape from a small steel box on the stage of the Pantages Theater.

"After he got in, the box was closed and tied up in a canvas sack," she said, wonderment still in her voice. "I know he was in there because he wiggled his fingers where we could see them."

John was pleased that he'd been included in a group of Pierce County Commissioners who met with a group of Bremerton Commissioners to discuss a ferry system that would connect the two cities and Nell said Frieda Faye had called to complain that Ike bought a fishing shack at Salmon Beach.

"Why doesn't he just fish for a living?" Annie asked, but Nell laughed and said that if fishing turned into work, it would take all the fun out of it.

The honeysuckle was in full bloom filling the yard with its scent. Butterflies floated by and a fat honeybee landed on one of the sugar cookies Annie brought out. Louise drifted in and out of sleep until Nell touched her on the arm.

"I think you should go to bed, love."

"Umm." Louise yawned and stretched and the act of moving brought tears to her eyes. She sat to wait it out and when she stood, John did the same and took her arm.

"Let me help you upstairs and the ladies can clean up. You barely touched Annie's cookies, so you better take one or two with you or you'll hurt her feelings."

"Well," Nell's voice quivered slightly. "I'll help take the dishes in and then do some bookwork. I've been it putting off and people tend to forget rather quickly if you don't remind them that they purchased something that has to be paid for."

Sitting on the edge of her bed a few minutes later, Louise thought about how rare it was for her mother to show emotion. *She's always so stoic about things.* Hearing Nell and John's voices at the door, she tiptoed to the top of the stairs and saw John wrap his arms around Nell. Their conversation was too quiet to make out but their love became apparent when he kissed her neck and then lips before leaving. *My goodness,* Louise thought, *they're in love. Why had that never occurred to me before?* Then she heard Annie's footsteps and returned to her room. So much of her body still hurt, she had to pace herself when changing into a lightweight nightgown. She was resting on the edge of the bed but when Annie arrived with a bowl of sops.

"In case you get to feeling puckish," she said. "I'll just put the bowl here in the sun, so it'll keep warm. Do you need help getting into bed?" She put the bowl down and pulled the covers back.

"No, thank you. I'm okay."

"Did you notice your flowers?"

"I did, yes." Louise lifted the vase and inhaled the fragrance of carnations tucked in among the daisies and forget-me nots.

"What an...er...unusual bouquet."

Louise grinned. "I think it's lovely."

"They came this morning, just as Nell and John were leaving for the hospital. Look, here's the card."

Louise eased her way under the covers and put the card next to her. In spite of the open window, the room was warm. Annie pulled up the sheet and tucked her in as if she was a child. "I'll read it later. Right now, I'm going to rest and then have some of your sops; the perfect thing for aches and pains." Suddenly her eyes filled with tears. "Thank you for being so good to me. I know I shouldn't have gone down to the waterfront by myself; Nell warned me, and I ignored her." She sniffed and Annie sat on the edge of the bed and pulled out a handkerchief tucked in her sleeve.

"She hasn't been angry or said anything," Louise continued, "and I think that's the hardest thing to bear."

"Nell has never been one to say 'I told you so.'" Annie said. "She knows you learned your lesson, dear, so don't fret. Look, you're upsetting Queenie." And indeed, the dog was looking concerned. "Princess is here, too so rest and then try and eat. You're fearfully thin."

Louise gave her a watery smile. "Yes, ma'am."

Chapter 7

Though the June weather had been nice, Louise knew Puget Sound summers generally started on, or sometimes even after, the Fourth of July. *Good holiday weather here is never guaranteed.* However, looking out the window a few days later, on the first Fourth of the first summer of America's entry in World War 1, she rejoiced in the bright blue sky and warm sun. With the firm understanding that she would do nothing but sit and enjoy herself, Louise and Queenie found an out-of-the-way spot in the back yard and John carried over a garden seat. Relaxing in the dappled sun, she felt both thankful and guilty that she wasn't involved in the hustle and bustle of setting up for the annual Tanquist and Bacom families' picnic.

The Tanquist backyard was perfect for the crowd expected: it was large, bordered by a wooden fence and flower gardens, with Annie's vegetable garden at the far end. While Annie and Nell were distracted, a small bunny sat there nibbling on the lettuce. *I should scare it away,* Louise thought, *but it is a holiday...* She decided the bunny was cute and entitled to enjoy a feast, also.

In the yellow rose near where Louise sat, fat bumble bees blended in with the petals. She closed her eyes and immediately became aware of the birds fussing about Annie's feeding table. Annie had such a wretched childhood before she ran away from home and ended up being rescued by Nell, that she took pleasure in all the simple things that made a house a home. And she was in her element on picnic day. As people arrived, the men carried out chairs and set up tables, and the women took loaded picnic baskets into the kitchen. Most everyone stopped to greet Louise before they were called away. A squirrel also stopped by, taking its time to look her over before running up an apple tree. Somewhere nearby a crow called to its mates and several answered. They converged in a fir tree next door neighbor and shared secrets, and she was glad the squirrel had taken refuge. Roses, phlox, and the last of the sweet peas perfumed the yard and, with her eyes shut, Louise felt herself drifting off only to give a start when a shadow fell across her chair.

"It's okay, Louise; it's just me."

Opening her eyes, she saw Matthew, smiling his crinkly-eyed smile at her and knew her face light up. He took off his hat and ran his hand through his bushy black hair. Then he pulled up a chair and sat, putting his medical bag on the ground.

"Thank you for the flowers and the lovely card."

He put his hand on the back of hers. "I did try and see you at the hospital almost every day, even if just for a few minutes but then I caught a cold and though I tried mentioning my uncle's name, your nurse stopped me at the door and wouldn't soften up."

Louise laughed. "Probably Nurse Carmichael. She wouldn't even let the probationary nurse talk to me."

Reaching forward, Matthew picked up a strand of her hair.

"Nell and Annie both tried," Louise said, "but it was too matted to comb. So now I have the Irene Castle bob I've been wanting."

"It suits you." He let it go and gently cupped her cheek. "You frightened us."

"I know; everyone keeps saying that." When he took her hand and began rubbing the base of her thumb and making circles in her palm, Louise sighed with pleasure.

"I have to go back up to Carbonado."

"Right away? I was hoping we could go on a picnic."

"When I get back, I promise."

"My Uncle Ike bought a fishing platform at Salmon Beach, and I know he'd let us use it."

With Matthew massaging her hand, she almost missed his next words.

"Thinking about a whole day together, just the two of us on a picnic will keep me going."

"And Queenie, of course."

"Of course."

"I wish I could be here today," Matthew sighed, "but my uncle invited guests for dinner and I'm expected."

"Ah yes, Tacoma's answer to Mrs. Astor's famous 400. To meet their lovely daughters, I imagine."

"I have met some very nice young women, but I promise, none like you. Now," he opened his medical bag. "I'd better look like I have a reason for being here." He removed something from the bag saying, "this is a Mercury Manometer; it takes your blood pressure. I'm going to wrap the cuff around your arm and pump up the pressure."

"What's blood pressure?"

"It's how strong the blood pushes against the artery walls."

"Goodness, that's impressive." Louise grinned. "Makes you look like a real doctor."

"Quiet." When he'd finished, he put the instrument away and started taking her pulse. "Right now, since I work for my uncle, well, he's the boss and then when I get back from Carbonado, with the war and all, and doctors being needed, well I don't know what will happen. But I do know this, whatever it is, I want you there with me, to build a family with me."

Louise smiled and turned her hand, entwining her fingers with his, but before she could reply, she spotted Nell coming across the yard and pulled her hand away. "Dr. Altamont," Nell said as soon as she was within earshot, "are you here to check up on our patient?

Matthew stood and turned around. "Actually, I came to let Louise know I will be going back to

Carbonado, but I thought I could kill two birds with one stone and give her a quick check."

"We'd love for you to stay; you would be very welcome." Nell smiled but Matthew shook his head.

"We've been planning this party for a while so I'm afraid it has to be 'thanks but no thanks'."

"When Matthew gets back from Carbonado, I'm going to ask Uncle Ike if we can use his fishing shack and have a picnic."

"You're his favorite so there is no doubt he'll say yes." Nell grinned. "And with luck, it won't be a good tide for salmon."

"I almost never have any free time, let alone a whole free day so it's something to look forward to. I like it up in the foothills, though. The work's not too demanding and I've been able to explore a little." He stood and picked up his medical bag. "While I'm here, though, maybe I can take a look at the gash on Louise's back, make sure there's no infection."

"That's alright. Dr. Clarke is coming, and I'll ask her to do it."

"In that case," Matthew smiled the smile that made Louise's knees go weak, "I'll be off. Remember, Louise, no laudanum."

Before he could say more, Louise eased herself out of the chair. "I need to move around a bit, and your car isn't far. Let me walk you out."

She took Matthew's arm and with Queenie following, started walking toward the street. Near a trellis which hung heavy with clematis and provided a little privacy, he stopped and kissed her neck. "I wish I could wrap my arms around you and hold on tightly, just feel your body, but since I can't, this will have to do." He put his medical bag down, took her face in his hands and covered it with kisses. When he paused near her mouth, Louise turned his face and kissed his lips. The weakness she felt wasn't from the assault, and she molded her body to his, relishing the feel of his legs and chest through her dress's thin fabric. His hands roamed gently, and she wanted nothing more than to... "What? What did she want? It was hard to remember the things she'd learned about a man's body. *More,* she thought, *I just want more.*

"Louise," Matthew's voice was husky, but before she could respond, they heard voices coming from the front yard. "He kissed her again, picked up his bag, and headed for his car, leaving Louise breathless.

"Uncle Ike," Louise stepped forward. "May I hold your arm?"

Ike turned around and saw the young doctor getting in his car. "Who was that?"

"My doctor, well one of them."

Ike looked at the bushy plant and Louise's red face and grinned. He offered his arm, and they made their way back to the yard. Once seated, Louise thanked him, and he winked. "You're all flushed, Louise, you must have overexerted yourself."

"Uncle Ike, we want to go on a picnic when Will gets back from Carbonado; can we please use your place at Salmon beach? Maybe go swimming?"

"The Narrows is a dangerous place to swim, and the water's mostly too cold, but go ahead. Say," he paused. "You wanta fish? Maybe I could join you." He burst out laughing at the look on Louise's face. "Let me know when and I'll check the tide. Fishing's usually good in late summer and there's generally a run of Silvers." He winked at her again and joined a bunch of men who didn't appear to be doing anything and were enjoying doing it.

Back in her chair, Louise watched a steady stream of friends and relatives arrive. The picnic baskets they carried gradually covered the tables and the yard filled with people. Ike and Freida Faye arrived together. They were followed a few minutes later by their sons, Theodore and Grover, who were tossing watermelons back and forth. They stopped by Louise's chair and grinned at her.

"In honor of the holiday, we liberated these," Theodore said.

They occasionally released things they felt were, as they said, being unfairly held captive in the bowels of a ship. Frieda Faye pretended not to hear them, but Uncle Ike laughed. Nell's older sister, Josie and their parents, Amity and Obed, were right on the young men's heels. Josie hovered protectively over the older couple though they didn't need any help and the attentiveness irritated Obed.

"Go on, Josie," he said. "Give us some breathing space."

Members of the Bacom family had been back and forth all morning. However, Verdita, Dovie and Chong were the last of the family to arrive. Louise thought Verdita must be the oldest person there. She had recently started using a cane and held Chong's arm while walking on the uneven lawn. Chong led them both to a table with chairs which surprised Louise. Yes, for Verdita, but why Dovie? In spite of the warm weather, she wore a long, sleeveless sweater buttoned to the hip and flaring out from there. Then Louise remembered that she'd been ill, though on close examination, her skin was glowing and she'd put on a little much-needed weight. Her thoughts were distracted when, to everyone's surprise, Nell's oldest sister, Indiana, her husband, Lumley and their boys, Elwood and Frank and their twin daughters, Amy and Edith appeared. Suddenly, the yard was noisy with cousins Louise only saw once a year and therefore sometimes didn't recognize, and with bits of various conversations.

"Jack and Murray stayed behind." Edith was saying with Amy adding, "They're in charge of the fireworks in Tumwater." Edith was also introducing Jack's daughters who, she said, were too young for fireworks. Amy was saying something, but Louise couldn't make out her words. They often talked at the same time, and it took some getting used to.

Adults she knew and cousins she didn't recognize converged on her to hear the story of her assault, and to apologize profusely when she winced from hugs. After one too many, she stood and got Ike to move her chair into the shade, near where Mr. Aldrich sat with a newspaper folded on his lap. Smiling at him, she sat, puffed out a heavy breath of air, and eased herself down, making sure Queenie was out of the sight of the littlest children.

"You look a little overwhelmed," she said.

He half-laughed. "It's certainly a lively bunch."

"I'm good with the aunts and uncles, but when I only see my cousins once a year, I can hardly remember who's who." From all around them came snippets of conversations mainly about the war. "Oh, golly, what a strange summer it's turning out to be." Louise sighed and leaned her head back. Queenie sniffed her leg, and she rubbed the dog's head. "Do you remember the draft age?"

"It's twenty-one to thirty." Mr. Aldrich looked at the crowd of uncles and cousins milling around. "Your family might be okay."

"I hope."

"Yes, well." Mr. Aldrich cleared his throat. "I have some things to discuss with you. But, first," he handed her a copy of a two-week-old *Daily Ledger*. "Because of the storm, you got the only picture of the waterfront strike." The paper was open and folded to show Louise's picture at the top above a lengthy article. "And since other papers used it," he said, "we received a sizeable amount of money." He removed an envelope from his pocket and handed it to her. "Here's a check for you."

Louise took one look at the amount, saying, "Holy cow."

Her boss laughed. "Also, I was able to take your camera apart and clean and repair it. I've tried it out and it's good as new."

"Oh, golly, that's just swell."

"I gave it to Miss Annie when I arrived, so it'll be ready when you are."

"Well, every day in every way, I am getting better," Louise said.

"I hope so." He accepted a glass of punch one of the cousins was passing around, thanking her. Taking a long drink, he smiled in appreciation.

They were approached by Dr. Clarke who waved to Theodore and pointed to a chair. "Mind if I join you?"

Soon the three sat in comfortable silence. Gladiolas waved back and forth in a slight breeze and a pair of yellow and brown butterflies fluttered by. "Swallowtails," the doctor said.

Louise nodded. "Annie says just before they die, sweet pea blossoms turn into butterflies. She planted everything here. She goes around everywhere taking cuttings and pretty soon we have a new plant."

"It's a shame I was never able to set her arm quite straight, but it was too badly broken."

"What happen?" asked Mr. Aldrich."

"Her father beat her." Dr. Clarke shook her head. "What a night that was."

Louise had heard the story several times, but the doctor had a pleasant voice, was an eloquent speaker, and new details came out with every telling. When her boss gave the doctor an inquiring look, she began relating the story.

"Annie and Nell were working down in Old Town for Mrs. McCarver who was having an afternoon soiree. Nell was about sixteen, Annie was maybe nine or ten. She doesn't know her birthdate, but she was young; she had to stand on something to do the dishes. When it was all over and Mrs. McCarver paid them, she told Annie she had to use her money to get a new dress, or she couldn't work for her anymore. Only Annie's dad wasn't having any of that. He beat her until she gave him the money. Annie walked, Lord knows how she managed, to Nell's house. She was in a dreadful condition. Nell sent a messenger to fetch me and made her eat something. Together, we cleaned her up and set the arm but it's difficult to set a swollen arm and Annie's was very inflamed." The doctor gave a half-laugh. "The longer we worked, the angrier Nell became. Annie's father liked to drink at a ghastly tavern that used to be in the woods above Old Town and Nell stormed up there, along with her dog and me. There was some consternation when we went in, I can tell you. It was dark and smelled to high heaven of kerosene, spilled liquor and unwashed bodies, but she marched up to Mr. Penny, Annie's dad and demanded money to take care of his daughter and to pay me. When he laughed and tried to bluff her, Nell threatened him with the churches in the area coming to preaching at his house and singing hymns and said she'd make sure none of the waterfront bosses would hire him again."

"She out bluffed the bluffer," Louise said, a grin on her face.

"She did that for sure. Mr. Penny ponied up enough money to take care of my expenses, buy Annie some new clothes, and generally cover what it would cost for Annie to live with the Tanquists."

"And didn't her dog bite someone on the way out?" Louise said and the doctor laughed. "I'd forgotten about that."

"And now she's family," said Louise. "She's Albina's closest friend, that's Nell's youngest sister," she added for Mr. Aldrich's benefit, "and goes around to her family and Grandma and Grandpa Tanquist's house and Hildy and Samuel's place, Hildy and Nell have been friends since school, and Annie just sees what needs to be done and takes care of all of us.

"Well, that's some story," Mr. Aldrich started to say but, one of the cousins brought out his ukulele and drowned him out when he began playing *Abba Dabba Honeymoon*. Soon many of the people were singing the silly lyrics and the youngest children began making up their own dance with the boys joining in and doing their best baboon imitations. One of them began pulling the girl's pigtails and running away, heading for the horseshoes pitch where a player had to grab him so he wouldn't be hit by the flying piece of metal. A baby cried and was whisked into the house to be changed and fed, and the cat disappeared, to take refuge in the house.

"Oh, look," said Dr. Clarke, "There's one of your nurses from the hospital."

"Katy Fox," Louise said. "She's from Vermont, I think, and her family is all back east. Nell thought she'd be lonely on a holiday, so she invited her."

"She's certainly attracting a lot of attention," the doctor said.

"That's because she's so pretty." Louise sighed. "I'm always so envious of women with curly hair and dimples. Poor Nell, stuck with a plain-Jane daughter."

"Hardly that," Dr. Clarke said.

"She seems awfully young to be so far from home," Mr. Aldrich said.

"The Chautauqua school tries to place their graduates and that's how Katy ended up way out here. Before she could even earn a cent, she had to work to pay off the cost of the train ride. Nell's hoping John can find a way to bring her parents out here."

"At the hospital, all I saw her do was deliver food trays and give bed baths," said Dr. Clarke."

"I know, right, or empty bedpans. And she isn't even supposed to talk to patients." Louise laughed. "But Nell would never pay attention to a silly rule like that, and we found out that because she's a Chautauqua nurse, she has to put in a year on the wards before she can be hired as a regular nurse."

"I have to agree that trying to learn nursing through a correspondence course probably isn't the best," Dr. Clarke said. "When I first started practicing medicine, doctors trained their own nurses. I wanted to train Nell, but she would have nothing to do with it."

"Nell started making dresses when she was sixteen," Louise said. "She used to buy used clothing, take it apart and make new things. She already planning for when the war makes a short supply of cloth. We have piles of fabric from picking apart dresses that she's cleaned and ironed."

As she spoke, the guitarist changed to *Ballin' the Jack* and her cousins crowded around, singing and following the silly instructions.

"A good song for Tacoma," said Mr. Aldrich, keeping time with a finger. "It's a railroad song and we're a railroad town."

"How is it a railroad song?" Dr. Clarke asked.

"A "jack" is a locomotive and "ballin'" means going at full speed."

"Well, my goodness, I did not know that."

Her words were interrupted by Annie ringing a brass school bell to announce the food was ready. Louise fidgeted in her chair, trying to get comfortable, and the doctor offered to bring her a plate. "Thank you, but I think I'll go in and get someone to rub arnica on my back," Louise said, "not you, though, Dr. Clarke. You stay and relax. There'll be food in the kitchen, and I can help myself."

"You should be out with your cousins, "Dr. Clarke said.

"I'm trying not to wonder how many of the men will still be alive next year."

"I suppose everyone is. It's a trying time."

For a minute, Louise watched a dragon fly wind its way through the garden, *totally unafraid*, she thought before saying, "I think too many people hugged me."

"Are you awfully sore?"

"Mostly my back. Nell and Annie rub arnica on it every night."

"Can you wait just a minute?" Mr. Aldrich said as she started to get up. "Because I have something I wanted to talk to you about." When Louise settled reluctantly back, he said, "I wonder how you feel about taking a little trip."

"A trip? Golly, I don't know if I feel like going anywhere. When? Where? Why? Can Queenie come, too?"

Mr. Aldrich laughed. "When? Right away. Where? Neah Bay, and why? I want you to take some photographs of the Makahs for a book my friend Father de Rouge is writing, and, yes, Queenie can accompany you. And you wouldn't be alone. You'd be with Dr. Clarke, here."

Seeing Louise's look of confusion, the doctor said, "After I retired, I started visiting outlying areas where people have little or no access to medical treatment. Neah Bay is a place I've visited often, and I know the Father rather well. He's talked about his years among the natives up there and is full of admiration for their resourcefulness. So, he started writing a book and wants some photographs for it. One day he asked me if I knew his photographer friend Wilson Aldrich who lived in Tacoma and said that he'd written Mr. Aldrich, asking if he could make the trip up and take some pictures he could use."

"The thing is, Louise, I have no idea, what with the war and all, what will happen to the studio. Helping Father de Rogue will help me, and I thought you could try your hand at something that came out of Germany just before the war called photo-journalism. It means photographers use their cameras to tell stories with their pictures. They photograph things that would otherwise probably go unnoticed and then write about them."

"Golly. How long would I be away?" Louise rubbed her forehead and then ran her hands through her hair, forgetting, for a minute, that her hair was barely shoulder-length and leaving it sticking out.

"Ten or eleven days."

"And, you'd be doing me a real favor; I can always use a little help," Dr. Clarke said. "Plus, you need to keep moving around or you'll get run down and maybe have nervous exhaustion."

"Could that happen? I thought I was too young." Louise looked horrified. "When is this trip?"

"I plan to leave at the end of the week."

Remembering that Matthew would be out of town at the same time, Louise tried to think it through. "It sounds, uh, lovely, well, interesting anyway, but right now I can't take it all in." She stood, wobbling slightly before gaining her balance. "Let me talk it over with Nell."

"Of course, dear."

Louise and Queenie crossed the yard, stopping to answer questions about the attack, her health, and her hair. Everyone seemed to be enjoying themselves and the air was full of music and laughter and shouts, a far cry from the atmosphere in the kitchen. There it was hot, slightly smelly, and noisy, and crowded with women: aunts and cousins changing babies, nursing babies, finding places for toddlers to nap, fussing with food, and all the while talking. Louise smiled and nodded, making brief conversation as she found a plate. She piled on some potato salad, grabbed a couple of sandwiches, two drumsticks and some of Duenwald's crispy potato chips, which she loved, before escaping to her bedroom with Queenie close behind. Princess had found refuge on the bed but obligingly moved over when Louise collapsed with a sigh next to her. The dog hopped up on the other side and looked hopefully at the plate of food. Louise broke off a piece of chicken for her and took a large bite herself. Then Princess put a paw on Louise's arm. "For goodness sakes," Louise muttered as the cat ate a small bit of the meat but seemed mostly uninterested. "Leave some for me." However, the ever-hungry dog pawed her for more food and Louise gave her another bite before hurrying to finish the drumsticks, diving into the rest of the food, and wishing she had thought to grab something to drink, also thinking that she should have grabbed some pie. She kicked off her shoes and lay back on the bed. Queenie immediately fell asleep, and Louise closed her eyes and listened to the dog's gentle snoring. A warm breeze came through an open window, ruffling the shears. Princess raised her head at the sound of a large fly buzzing around but decided to let it live. Louise was so tired, she almost forgot to think about Matthew. Had he proposed? But sleep overtook here and the three of them were sleeping so soundly they failed to head footsteps on the stairs.

"Louise? Are you here?" Dottie poked her head in the room. "I've brought you some ice cream but it's melting."

"That was nice of you." Louise sighed and managed to wiggle herself into a sitting position. "Can you reach me the aspirin, please."

Dottie handed her a bowl of ice cream and fetched the bottle of tablets from the dresser. "Do you need something to take it with?"

"Yes, lots of ice cream." She took out two tablets, tossed them back, and swallowed them down with a spoon of ice cream. "Hmm, strawberry, my favorite, so good."

Dottie beamed. "They sell it by the brick at the Meadowmoor store. Bringing it was mother's idea. We packed it in ice and straw and your girl, Annie, put it in the root cellar." She pulled the dressing table chair over, kicked off her shoes and propped her feet on the end of the bed.

"Annie isn't our girl, she's family, but you weren't to know." Louise dove into the ice cream and hoped there's be some left after everyone had gone. She let Princess lick her spoon and put the bowl down for Queenie. Gesturing toward some of her injuries, she said, "This has certainly put the kibosh on any camouflage work for me, anything other than knitting socks that is."

Dottie pulled a face. "The meetings sure aren't fun without you there but Mother makes me go. The latest is that she found a house on G Street which Papa says we can't afford, but she made him buy it anyway and she joined the Kindercraft Club which Mrs. Rhodes runs, and she—Mother, I mean, not Mrs. Rhodes—has decided I will train to be a kindergarten teacher." Dottie leaned her head back and groaned. "I don't even like little children. They're noisy and sticky, their noses are always running, and something always needs to be buttoned or tied."

"Oh dear." Louise pulled Queenie onto her lap and laughed. "That could be a problem."

Footsteps pounded down the hall and three children stopped in her doorway. "What are you doing?" one asked. She took a few steps in the room, her eyes on Princess. "I love cats."

"I sustained several serious injuries and I'm resting," Louise said. She put a restraining hand on the cat. "She bites."

When the little girl looked unconvinced Dottie said. "I'm her nurse and I must ask you to leave." The child rubbed her runny nose and wiped her hand on her skirt.

Dottie gulped. "Scoot now before I call your mother." When their footfalls faded away, she looked at Louise. "Ugh. See what I mean?"

Louise laughed. "You'd better decide what you yourself want to do and get started."

"I have. I found someone to tutor me in typing and stenography. I took them in school but got rusty. I thought I could find some classes in night school, but the courses offered were unbelievable: swimming is one and basket weaving is another. I mean, can you believe it? The military is crying out for office workers and Lincoln High School is offering raffia work, knotting, and basket making. Hey, Kaiser, you can't shoot me; I'm needed because I weave baskets. I mean, honestly."

She was so indignant; Louise hooted. "Oh, that's funny."

Dotti grinned. "Well, to cut to the end, the civil service is crying out for clerical workers, and I mean to join." She stopped abruptly when they heard Nell's voice in the corridor.

"Louise. Are you up here?" Nell stopped in the doorway when she saw Dottie who stood and for some reason looked guilty. "I brought her some ice cream," she said.

"Oh, how kind of you. No one else thought to do that and it was gone in a flash."

Drat, thought Louise.

"Well, Indiana and her family are leaving and I just thought you might like to come down and say goodbye."

Louise knew better than so say what she thought which was, not really, I hardly know them, but she dislodged the dog and swung her legs to the floor. "Of course I will." While putting her shoes back on and making herself presentable, she and Dottie, but mostly Dottie, chatted away.

Out in the yard, the picnic was breaking up, and others were also making ready to leave. Louise knew that, as in the past, Hildy and her family would stay behind to relax and talk over the day. After saying a lot of goodbyes, and seeing that the kitchen was almost clean, she retreated to the bathroom.

"I don't care how hot it is outside," she said to Queenie. "A hot bath always feels good." She added a Rose Glycerin bath tablet and let the scented steam fill the air. The dog cocked her head when Louise added, "I suppose I might as well go with Dr. Clarke. I owe it to Mr. Aldrich and besides, it will make time go faster."

Out in the hall, and hearing her talking to Queenie, Annie laughed. "Does she ever answer you?"

"All the time, with her ears and her tail and how she tips her head."

"Hmm, well, I just popped up to see of you need anything."

"Is there any potato salad left?"

"A little."

"Could you put some on a plate and some ham, if there's any of that, too and some potato chips and whatever dessert there is. I want to soak for a while, but for some reason, I'm really hungry." She lay back in the tub and looked at her stomach and legs. On the surface the bruises were gone but she knew there were still telltale signs of the bitemarks on her neck. Nell applied Arnica nightly on the gash on her back and said it had left a long, jagged scar. *If anyone ever sees it, I'll have to come up with a good story,* Louise thought. When the water cooled, she drained the tub and ignored the mirror while carefully applying the towel. After putting on a soft, flannel nightgown and wiping down the tube, she was in bed and reading *Seventeen*, a book John had given her to help pass the time while she was in the hospital. Louise was deep in the antics of the love-sick hero when Nell came in carrying a tray.

"I'm trying to give Annie a rest," she said.

"You do remember that she's younger than you, right?"

"Don't be cheeky."

Louise put the tray on her lap and looked with approval at the plateful of food. "If I eat all this, even my corset won't help me, but I've been so hungry since I got home. . .." She let the sentence end and concentrated on loading a slice of ham with the potato salad."

Nell sat on the bed, leaning against the footboard. "The ladies I make clothes for are certainly of two minds about how they should look, thin as a rail or the traditional hourglass shape." She watched as Louise gave Queenie a large piece of ham. "That dog is going to get fat if you keep feeding her like that." Louise, her mouth full of food, grunted something and Nell changed the subject. "What do you think about going up to Neah Bay?"

"I really haven't had time to think about it." She crunched on some potato chips and when she'd swallowed, asked Nell what she thought about it.

"I think it's a good idea. You've never been anywhere and won't be going anywhere until the war is over. Not that spending a week on an Indian reservation is any great shakes, but it will give you a chance to see a whole different way of living." She leaned over and took the last potato chip. "Indiana is so afraid for her boys."

Louise scooted over to the edge of the bed and put the tray on her desk. "I was trying to think how old everyone is, but I couldn't remember."

"What about Matthew? He's the right age."

The room was getting dark and Louise turned on a light. Within minutes insects were flying against the windows waking Princess up. An owl which had been coming nightly and taking a position in a nearby tree suddenly swooped past the window and within seconds they heard something screech.

"The family eats tonight," she said. Nell waited, knowing Louise was considering the questions and looking for an answer. "We haven't talked about it," she finally said. "We're pretty much never together long enough to talk about anything." She sighed and pulled Queenie on her lap. "I think he's reluctant to enlist and if we actually get to go on a picnic when he gets back, it will be a miracle. His uncle will no doubt come up with something he thinks is more important for him to do. Odious man."

"His wife is a regular customer, but I've only met him once. She's lovely, at least on the surface, but him—not so much." Nell paused a moment, and Louise could see her gathering her thoughts, considering the best way to go on. "And when you come back, assuming you do, in fact, go, you may see Matthew in a whole new light. Travel can do that. Now don't bristle up, it can do the opposite, too." She got off the bed and kissed Louise and ran her fingers through the shorn hair. "Your haircut was all the talk in the kitchen and," she added, "the envy of many of the women. Now, I'm going to take the tray and retreat. I promised you would call tomorrow and tell Dr. Clarke and Mr. Aldrich if you're going or not so you have overnight to decide. Goodnight, love."

Louise moved the dog and pulled the overs up. *Golly,* she thought, *some decisions are so easy, but this isn't one of them. I love home. But maybe I should go; what do I have to lose except sleeping in my own bed?* She kissed Queenie's head and turned on her side. "You'd like a little adventure, wouldn't you?" She said and then fell asleep and slept deeply, failing to hear the screech of another rodent which had fallen victim to the owl, or to see a falling star cut across the darkened sky. And sometime during the night her subconscious decided going to Neah Bay with Dr. Clarke would be an interesting thing to do. She caught Nell who was on her way out to work and told her and then caught Annie sitting at the kitchen table.

"Are you tired after yesterday?

"A bit." She seemed dispirited. "Are you going with the doctor to Neah Bay?"

"Yes. I guess so."

"Goodness, seems like you just got home and now you're off again," Annie said. "What does Nell think?"

"She thinks it's a good idea. She's always said travel broadens the mind."

Louise fed her pets and then sliced some Wheatless Nut Bread. "I'm sure glad butter isn't rationed," she said.

"Not yet, anyway, or peanut butter. Do you want some? The Roger's Company just made it"

"No thank you." Louise poured a cup of coffee, added cream and sat to dunk her toast. "I suppose we should be thankful that sugar isn't rationed."

"It is in some places and likely to be here, soon."

Louise sighed. "Oh, gosh. What next?."

Annie opened the door to let the animals out and then darted out herself to chase the rabbits out of her vegetable garden. "Knee high by the Fourth of July is what they say about corn," she said a few minutes later as she began wiping the counters. "But what with the rabbits and the crows, I'm beginning to wonder if there will be produce left for us. And you asked 'what next?' Well, the Aids are already working out how to use honey to replace sugar." Annie was a devoted member of the Methodist Ladies' Aid Society and regularly shared what the members were doing with Nell and Louise.

"That will be good for Reuban," Louise said around of mouthful of toast. When he was young, Reuban started working for a farmer who also had bee hives. He'd eventually taken over the farm and regularly made honey butter which his sister Hildy sold at her bakery.

"I'm going to call Dr. Clarke and see what clothes I'll need." Louise cleaned up her toast crumbs and added more coffee to her cup.

"Before you do, do you want me to put some Ozonol on your back?"

"Oh, yes please."

Louise turned sideways and lowered her chemise. Ever since coming to live with them, Annie had favored a salve called Ozonol. She said it helped her hands if she been overdoing and she liked its faint camphor scent. As she applied the cream, Louise all but purred. "You're always so gentle, Annie."

"If you're still hurting, do you think you should be headed off for parts unknown?"

"Not exactly unknown and I will have a doctor with me. And, it's only my back that hurts much anymore, and a few places where I have bone bruises." She twisted around and looked up. "I just purely love to have you rub my back."

"Ah, get on with you." Annie gave a piece of Louise's hair a gentle tug, clearly pleased with the compliment.

With her mind made up, Louise called Dr. Clarke to see when they would be leaving and asked what clothes to bring and then phoned her boss to tell him not to expect her after the following day.

"I'm sending you a letter of introduction," he said, "and don't bother about coming in tomorrow. To tell you the truth, Neah Bay can be a bit cold and damp for my old bones. You're agreeing to do this is a load off my mind. The Father and I grew up together, then sort of drifted apart. But he was a good friend when we were young and did me many favors so I'm happy to do this for him."

"Well, it'll all be new to me and it's actually kind 'a exciting. If I can, I'll send film to be developed, otherwise, I'll just bring it back."

They chatted a few minutes more before Louise hung up and headed for the rarely-visited attic, a catch-all loft under the pitched roof containing any number of forgotten items. Mismatched dishes, furniture needed repairs, old toys and a collection of luggage Nell used when traveling. Dust motes floated down shafts of light and cobwebs clung to wherever they could get a foothold. The air was only slightly musty, thanks to gaps in some of the boards but as she waited for her eyes to adjust to the dim light, Louise heard birds on the roof, chatting among themselves. *No doubt planning mischief in Annie's garden*, she thought. After lifting the various pieces of luggage, she chose the one that was lightest in weight, a Gladstone carpetbag. *In case I have to carry it any distance.* It needed a good cleaning and once out of the attic, Queenie greeted her as if separated for hours. Together they went downstairs and took the valise out into the yard to air out. Dappled sun warmed her back, and the smell of roses took away the lingering musty attic odor. A load of wash hung on the clothesline, and she heard mooing from a cow who lived on the street below. Since it was almost too peaceful to go back inside, Louise sat on one of the wicker chairs and propped her feet up on another. She'd been unable to tell Matthew where she was going. She'd called but his aunt said he was already gone; that if he called, she'd let him know. And in the back of her mind was the scene she'd witnessed between her mother and John. It was hard for her to know what, if anything, to do. Should she ask Nell or Annie or John? Come to think of it, Hildy would know, but then if there was something they wanted her to know wouldn't they have told her? In the end, Louise decided to take a wait-and-see attitude and went to clean the bag. A copious use of vinegar eliminated the odors it had acquired in the attic, and she left it in the sun to continue airing. Grabbing a glass of lemonade, she went up to her room to consider clothes: combinations, corset covers, two petticoats, stockings. A long-sleeved nightgown and robe; several serviceable skirts and blouses, a sweater, and a pair of boots. Of course, while traveling she'd be wearing a hat, but she added a tam-o-shanter to wear outside.

"Wow, that's a lot of clothes," she said to Queenie.

"You have to roll them," said Annie who'd come upstairs with some of the freshly dried laundry.

"Really?"

"Yes, you can get more clothes in a bag if you do. Wait a minute 'til I put this away and I'll show you." Annie disappeared for a few minutes, and when she came back, Louise asked how she knew that. "I went on a trip once with Nell, and an actress staying in the same hotel told us. Apparently, it's an old theatrical trick." She looked at the clothes Louise had laid out. "No slippers?"

"I'll wear heavy socks." Louise watched Annie fold the sleeves in on her blouses then roll from the bottom, tuck stockings in the shoes, make tidy folds of her skirts and roll them from the bottom up.

"Where did you take a trip with Nell," she asked.

"Um, someplace in California. Now watch. Heaviest things in the bottom and then line up the rolls like logs." When she was done, Louise remembered writing paper and envelopes, a few toiletries and a new Sherlock Holmes book. Then she closed the bag and carried it down to the front door. John was taking her and Dr. Clarke to the depot early the following morning. *Let the adventure begin,* she thought.

Chapter 8

Dear Will;

I imagine you are in Carbonado by now and if you looked at the postmark on the envelope, you will see it came from Elma. I called your home to tell you about my trip, but your aunt said you'd already left. Dr. Clarke was going to Neah Bay for ten or so days to inoculate the children there and Mr. Aldrich asked me to go with her and take some photographs of the reservation for a friend. So, the doctor, Queenie and I left Tacoma early this morning on a freight train headed for Elma. Initially it was only two cars long, but the doctor persuaded the railroad to add a caboose, and we had it all to ourselves. She seems to know a great many important people, or maybe just the right people, and can be very persuasive. She had a fair amount of medical equipment, and I had my photography bag so, along with our luggage, we were glad not to have to share space. Before I left home, Nell practically drowned me in Arnica and also put a bottle in my bag. I was glad because the train seemed to vibrate every which way, and it wasn't a pleasant trip. The caboose was a big, old wooden affair with a coal stove in the middle and benches on each side under three, not-very-big windows. A small comfort station was in the back. We swayed along and the scenery was pretty. I thought maybe I would see Camp Lewis, but it was hidden behind trees, except for a corral of horses. Since the freight was intended for Elma, that's where we stopped. Dr. Clarke wanted to stay at the Hotel Wakefield which was only half-a-mile from the depot, so we walked, which made

Queenie happy. It's a pretty town with wide streets, both sides lined with trees. I think Elma must look like Tacoma used to because there were lots of wagons loaded with logs going someplace, and others almost bulging with produce. The only thing is, almost no seagulls. There is going to be a fair in a week, and signs were posted everywhere. Apparently, there is a big new racetrack and we could hear men shouting and lots of noise from their work. I caught a glimpse of the grandstand and several new buildings. Most of the noise came from fences going up and the track being graded. I wanted to take my camera over, but Dr. Clarke was expecting several female patients and was in a hurry to reach the hotel, which is on main street, and is quite big. Being July, the temperature was high, and I was glad to reach it and then my room. I took an aspirin powder and lay down. It was a good time to think of what you said to me at the picnic. Our time together hasn't let us really talk much and get to know each other. A few minutes on a bus when we met, rescuing some boys, going to Camp Lewis; perhaps our letters will help. Then when we're both home, we have our picnic to look forward to. I was thinking about this, and it seemed like no time at all when I had to get up for dinner. I'd just as soon have had a tray in my room, but Dr. Clarke says it's important for me to keep moving so we went to the dining room. The hotel is owned and run by Mr. and Mrs. Wakefield; his first name is Leonidas; isn't that a mouthful? They moved up here from Alturas, Oregon. Anyway, enough for now. And now that you know where I will be for the next ten days, I will expect a packet of letters from you when we reach Neah Bay.

Devotedly yours, Louise

* * *

Dear Will;

We left Elma early for the trip to Aberdeen and it was nothing if not "an experience." The hotel provided us with transportation to the depot. There, the first thing we noticed was steam escaping from some cracks in the train's boilers which scared Queenie so much I had to carry her. A group of senators and legislators had recently taken this train to Seattle, and the passenger car was clean and fairly comfortable, but our speed never got higher than eighteen miles an hour and the car reeked of smoke from cigarettes, pipes and cigars. The smell made Queenie sick and when she threw up her breakfast, more than one man complained. I mean, the very idea and I told them it was due to the foul funk they were making and that I had half a mind to be sick myself. A few of the men quit smoking, but one started to get nasty and Queenie gave him such an ominous growl, he moved to a seat as far away from us as possible. Then someone opened the door connecting the passenger car to the baggage car and a lot of the smell blew out. We had a fifteen-minute stop at a town called Cosmopolis and were able to get out. There wasn't time to see much, mostly logging trucks because it's where the Weyerhaeuser Company has a big pulp mill. There were posters announcing a trap shooting competition next week, but it was such a brief stop there was no time to look around. I was glad because the whole area smelled like rotten eggs from the mill. When we got back on the train and Queenie was being so stubborn about that, I had to carry her on, Dr. Clarke had a newspaper with a story about a wild man named John Tornow who lived in the woods near here and had killed several people, so I was doubly glad to leave town. And now, off to Aberdeen and the night train to Neah Bay.

As always, Louise

***

Dear Will;

As it turned out we had a three hour stop-over in Aberdeen, plenty of time for me to take Queenie on a good walk. Aberdeen is at the mouth of two rivers, the Chehalis and Wishkah and has a lot of Filipinos living there because they're cheaper to hire. Queenie and I had barely started our walk when a little boy decided to come along with us. There were a couple of sailing ships on one side of the harbor, and the hill opposite was covered with houses. I thought the area was pretty but then the little boy pointed out a place known as Billy's Restaurant. He, the little boy not Billy, took a great deal of pleasure in telling me about Billy. It seems Billy kept an office he let sailors use so they had an address where folks could send them mail and where they could safely store their possessions. He also had a bar built on pilings over the Wishkah River. He'd pick out someone to rob, kill them, and dump their bodies through a trap door directly into the river below. As the rivers were regularly frequented with vessels of all sizes, nobody could tell where the bodies came from, and floating dead men were found for years. Eventually, so many corpses were found, and because they were mostly sailors, people got suspicious of Billie. His last name was Gohl, but he got the nickname of Billie Ghoul. Well, I can sure say that after hearing that and even though Billie's in prison, I decided Aberdeen wasn't a place to linger in even though it was pretty and anyway, I needed to get Queenie and me some dinner. Naturally, the boy, whose name I found out was Herbert, knew just the place and I ended up back at the train depot with a bag of something called Lumpia. They're a sort 'a roll with filling that the Filipinos like. Queenie ate three, Herbert had four and I ate the remaining five. They were very good, and I wished I had more but there wasn't time to buy any. Soon we were on our way again and I was glad to leave behind the murdering bar keeper and the wild man who lived in the woods. Hopefully, Neah Bay won't have any of those types of men.

As always, Louise

* * *

Dear Will;

Well, here we are at Neah Bay. The train rattled and swayed all night, and I am dreadfully tired. And as soon as our car door opened, we were greeted with wind and rain and the smells of smoke and low tide and fish, the fish being in various states of decomposition. The first thing I saw was a very old woman with a blanket over her head to try and keep dry, using a cane to walk, and carrying a bundle of sticks on her back. Before we left, Uncle Ike gave me an old copy of "Scientific America" because it had an article on Neah Bay which called it "a most dreary and unattractive place." All I can say to that is that nothing looks nice when it's raining, and raining it definitely was. Fortunately, we didn't have far to go. Every year, just before she comes, Dr. Clarke arranges to rent a house where she can stay and see patients. She hustled us there and the Makah native she rents it from had a nice fire going. The house is a rectangle with four very small bedrooms along the back, each of which has a narrow metal bed with a thin mattress, and next to it, a box holding a lantern, also there's a table with a basin in which to wash, and a chipped and stained chamber pot. I have a corner room with uncovered windows on both sides, but good views of the hills and shacks. The entire front of the little house, from one end to the other, is a combination front room-kitchen-eating area and treatment place. Everything was clean but smelled and felt damp.

A young man wheeled our luggage down and Dr. Clarke gave him a big hug. "This is Peter Hay," she said. "Peter was my first patient, so to speak. The day I arrived, the first thing I did was deliver him. The first year I came, it was by land because the train didn't come up this far, and I was still in the wagon when a man came running up telling me his wife needed help. I grabbed my bag and followed him to a house where I found her in labor. It was her first baby, and she was scared. There were a lot of women crowded around and I shooed them out. I had just enough time to wash my hands and put down some clean cloths when he came out. Peter was a big baby, and he was ready to face the world. He just needed some help." When she said that, Peter laughed saying, "And Ma told everyone you never even took off your hat. A great big one with all kinds of feathers and flowers on it." Dr. Clarke's response was that one must keep up the style.

The next thing I knew, I jumped a foot when the door flew open because it got caught in the wind and banged against the wall, and a little girl carrying a basket came in. She kicked the door shut behind her and put the basket on the table saying, "Ma sent this" She was the prettiest little thing, very petite with pale skin like Peter's but black eyes where his are green. He said her name was ShiShi which, I learned, is a Makah word for a small, silvery fish.

* * *

Louise put her pen and paper on the box-cum-nightstand. Hopping into bed, she wiggled down under an assortment of quilts and animal pelts, the largest of which had once belonged to a brown bear. They were warm but the bed was hard and would take some getting used to. Queenie immediately crawled up and snuggled as close as possible and together they listened to the storm pummel the house. Cold wet air squeezed in wherever it found gaps; the wind picked up bits of debris and threw it against the walls, and puddles of water crept slowly onto her windowsills. ShiShi's basket contained bread and butter, fish and baked potatoes, all still warm from having been recently cooked. It was at the same time familiar and strange. Louise wasn't used to eating a lot of fish. Peter and ShiShi left the women to their meal with Peter saying he'd be by the next day to see how they'd fared. In spite of herself, Louise felt tears beginning to roll down her cheeks. She rubbed her face on Queenie's soft head and tried to get comfortable. *I think I'm just going to wallow in misery for a bit.*

All night the storm gave its best and by the next morning was down to a fading drizzle. Louise hurriedly dressed and wrapped the bear skin around her. Dodging the puddles on the floor, she walked to a window in the front room and looked out. The tide was low, and it seemed to her as if Neah Bay's entire population had converged on the shoreline. Other than women gathering firewood, Louise had no idea what everyone was doing. She turned away when Dr. Clarke entered the room.

"You're up early," the doctor said and laughed. "Did you get any sleep?"

"Off and on." Louise added wood to the fire from the dwindling supply. "Do we get our own firewood?"

Before Dr. Clarke could answer, someone knocked at the door. "Are you ready for a busy day?" Peter and ShiShi came in and put a parcel on the table.

"I am." The doctor unwrapped the packet. "Eggs and bread, wonderful."

"Shouldn't I help pay for this?" Louise asked.

"We have a bartering system," Peter said. He started a fire in the cook stove, filled a coffee pot, and added grounds. "The food comes from someone who wants to see the doctor. "Here," he handed her a toasting tool. "Why don't you toast some bread while the coffee heats up."

"Goods for services works very well here," said Dr. Clarke who had been laying out medical supplies in one of the rooms." Louise gave her a piece of buttered toast, Peter poured her a cup of coffee, and she sighed in satisfaction. "This is lovely."

"I can hear all kinds of commotion outside," Louise said. She was surprised to see Peter cracking eggs into a pan. When they were ready, he put them on a platter and carried it to the table. Louise put a pile of toast and the hot coffee next to the eggs, the four of them sat to eat. "I guess everyone's happy the storm is over," she said. Queenie pawed her leg, and she got up to feed her.

"That, and the fact that the men brought in a whale." Peter smiled at her showing a dimple in his right cheek.

"You should take some photographs of that, Louise." Dr Clarke helped herself to more eggs, "and send them right away. It's so interesting to see how the people use pretty much every part of the whale."

Before Louise could ask what they did with it all, Peter's eyebrows went up. "Are you a photographer?"

"Yes. I work for a man in Tacoma and I'm here to take pictures for a book on the Makahs Father de Rouge is writing."

"Well, I'm free until school starts so I'm happy to show you around."

Dr. Clarke laughed. "I'd take him up on it. Peter knows everything there is to know about Neah Bay." As she spoke, they heard people at the door and Louise jumped up.

"Thank you; I'd love your help. I'll just clean up here, won't be a tick if you're free this morning." Peter waited as she filled a basin with water from the stove's back boiler and washed the few dishes they used. In the meantime, the doctor went to the door. The room was immediately full of adults and children jostling about, warming up in front of the fire, staring curiously at Louise and patting Queenie. ShiShi went to join a friend and both Peter and Dr. Clarke greeted people while Louise changed into her boots. She put on a coat, then with the dog's leash in one hand and the camera in the other, she hurried outside where the air was fresher but no less pungent.

"I wasn't expecting to see so many people," she said.

"Most everyone turns out when there's a whale being butchered." Peter smiled. "The meat, oil, skin, we use just about every part."

The tide was far down the beach and dozens of canoes lay high and dry on shore. "Why are there so many different kinds of canoes?" Louise asked.

"Each one has a different use." Peter pointed to one. "That one there is for salmon and halibut fishing. The long ones are what the men use when they go whaling. A whaler can measure up to 30 feet and war canoes are even longer. Canoes are sacred to the owner and both the canoe and anything in it are safe. We're taught to respect other people's possessions."

Louise turned away from the water and took her first glimpse of the reservation. "Goodness. It's much more crowded than I expected." She could see, now, that the house Dr. Clarke had rented was in the middle of dozens of others, some crowding the shoreline and others dotted around hither-thither on the land behind. Some were small, others quite large, some were made from odds and ends of planks and others were teepees. Poles and rafter beams protruded from sides and roofs and on some of the closest houses, Louise saw thick planks of wood either slotted between the poles or tied on. Several of the smallest places had large stones on the roof, holding it down.

"I didn't expect to see so many houses," she said as Peter steered her around a pile of bleached wood to where seagulls were fighting over the remains of discarded fish. The birds flew a short distance and glared at the interlopers. Louise found a driftwood log and attempted to climb up. Peter watched her struggles for a minute, then scrambled up and extended hand. Not liking that she was left below, Queenie began barking. Immediately, several dogs who'd been nosing around the shoreline came to investigate.

"They know the other dogs and want to see if she's a threat," Peter said, and after a few seconds they took off leaving Queenie whimpering and trying to get on the log with Louise. Eventually giving up, she hunkered unhappily down and bit at the sand fleas. Suddenly, Peter gave a piercing whistle, catching the attention of a little boy sitting in a small canoe. He looked up, broke into a gap-tooth grin, and waved. "That's my nephew, Little Joe," Peter said. "His dad, Big Joe, is trading up north. He told his dad he'd learn to row while he was gone. That's why his canoe is so small, it's a practice canoe." For reasons she couldn't understand, Louise found Peter's closeness comforting but also disconcerting.

"Photography would be so much easier if I didn't have to hold the camera at my waist." She aimed her camera at the boy, capturing the determined look on his face as Peter continued talking,

"It's too bad you couldn't see the sails Big Joe uses. They're real pretty."

Louise wobbled as she tried to get better footing and Peter took her arm.

"You'll be steadier if you lean against me."

"Thank you. I'll just take one or two more."

"Take your time. Anyway, as I was saying, Big Joe will be looking for spruce root hats, adze handles made from madrona, abalone shells—items not readily available here."

While he talked, Louise focused on men wielding knives on the massive whale carcass. "What, exactly, are they doing?" she asked. Queenie was tugging on the lease and Louise handed it to Peter. Looking through the camera, again, she snapped indiscriminately, hoping for the best. The men were pulling off large strips of the animal's skin and cutting away the meat underneath. They made separate piles for the bones and the innards. As they did, a viscous odor of spoiled meat and bile covered the area. Louise tried to breathe through her mouth but the sight of people going through the piles, pulling out bones and pieces of intestines, became more than she could stand. Becoming both nauseous and faint, she leaned over to vomit, at the same time losing her balance. Peter grabbed her before she fell and lifted her down to where she could sit on the sand and put her head down. Queenie pushed her cold nose under Louise's arm and barked.

"Gosh, I'm sorry." Peter jumped down and sat next to her.

Louise didn't know how to respond. *What in the world were the people doing pulling bones out of the dead animal?* She took a deep breath and started counting the days until she'd be going home. "I think," she said after a moment, "I think I'd better go back to the house."

"I really am sorry." Peter repeated as he helped her up. "I sure wasn't thinking straight about how this might look to, uh...?"

"An outsider." Louise managed a small chuckle. "Not to worry. I got a couple—um—interesting pictures, I think. I can send them tomorrow if you tell me where the post office is."

After helping her to stand, Peter kept a firm grip on her left arm, putting his other hand firmly on her back, walked her to the doctor's office-cum-house. Two children and a woman paused in front of the door and the woman surprised Louise by stopping to light a pipe. They moved on and Louise apologized.

"I'm terribly ashamed, Peter. I don't quite know what came over me."

"It was just too much too soon, I guess." Peter ran his fingers through his hair. It stood up, giving him a rakish, boyish look.

Golly, I didn't know an Indian could be so handsome, Louise thought as he went on.

"But there are a lot of other things to see. How canoes are made, carving, basketry. The women are making baskets to send to Washington D.C. for the war effort. They set up a workspace in one of the long houses..." His voice trailed off, and Louise briefly closed her eyes, inhaling the clean pine smell that his body seemed to emit.

"Father de Rouge has asked me to lunch tomorrow, but those things sound really interesting." She reached for the door and smiled ruefully. "But I only speak for me, not for my stomach."

Peter grinned. "Well, it's going to rain again, anyway."

"Again? More storm like last night?"

"No, just a squall. Maybe the day after tomorrow, then, and I'll show you the other things."

Louise was both glad and sad when he left. Glad because she still felt queasy and tired but sad because, in spite of herself, she felt comfortable with Peter, finding him, on such a short acquaintance, pleasant to be around. *I must take his picture,* she thought, *so I can remember him.* For a minute she closed her eyes and tried to remember how it felt when Matt held her face and kissed her neck and lips. *I'm too far away, I can barely remember.* With a sigh, and dreading the crowd that had been there earlier, she opened the door. To her surprise, only two people remained in the room, Dr. Clarke and a young woman. They sat near the fire knitting and drinking coffee.

"I didn't expect you back so soon," the doctor said.

"I disgraced myself and vomited by the whale carcass." Louise hung her coat on a hook and hurried to the stove to see if there was any coffee left.

"Are you sure your stomach can take coffee?"

"Yes. I'm not sick, it was…"

The other woman completed the sentence. "Too much for a first time. It was the sight of the men cleaning the whale, wasn't it?"

Louise found a small bowl of thick cream and added a spoonful to her coffee. Spotting some drippings, she spread a small amount on a piece of bread and put it down to Queenie.

"Yes, it was." Giving a rueful chuckle, she said, "I was okay until people started going through the innards." She took a quick sip of coffee and tried to forget the scene. Then she went to her room for her own knitting bag and sat in an old rocking chair near the fire while Queenie curled up on a piece of old blanket and started licking her paws.

"Louise, this is Martha Stanup," Dr. Clarke said.

"Nice to meet you." Louise looked at the partially-completed, yellow garment Martha was knitting. "Lovely color."

Dr. Clarke smiled. "It's a happy color for a baby."

Martha nodded. "Do you know why the people were going through the guts?"

Louise flinched at hearing the crude word and shook her head. She pulled out a partially-completed sock and picked up where she'd left off.

"Is that a new sock?" The doctor looked surprised. "What happened to the other one?"

"I thought you could teach me how to turn the heel on one and then the second one would be ready for me to do it on my own." She began rocking, enjoying the rhythmic squeaking her chair gave off.

"You can't turn a heel?" Martha asked. Seeing Louise stiffen slightly at the remark she said, "I thought all white women could do that."

"Not this white woman. I can sew and crochet and embroider, though."

"Well, I just learned myself."

176

"And," said the doctor, "never mind socks, you were going to tell Louise about how the Makah use all parts of the whale."

The rain Peter predicted thumped outside, once again seeping in various places where the caulking had fallen away. Martha's quiet, low-pitched voice suited their fire-lit room. She counted her stitches and then began.

"When the men bring in a whale, we perform ceremonies and sing traditional songs to welcome its spirit. You probably didn't notice, being sick and all, but when the men are cleaning the whale, it's done in specific way." She looked at Louise, her eyes twinkling. Louise, who had taken in a lung full of air and clenched her teeth, let out the breath and relaxed. "Different families are entitled to specific parts," Martha explained. "The rest is handed out. We tan the skin and make clothes out of it. We also make the blubber into oil which is worth a lot of money."

She paused and the clicking sounds made by three pairs needles combined with rain bouncing off the windowpanes and the snapping sound of pitch on the firewood seemed almost musical. The room felt snug and cozy. Queenie had begun to snore; Dr Clarke refilled the coffee cups and Louise looked at Martha.

"Please continue."

"The intestines are big enough to use as storage containers and the stuff that holds the muscles to the bones is what we use for rope." Martha pulled a comb out of her hair, and it cascaded down her back in a lovely black wave. Holding the comb up she said, "This was made from a piece of bone."

"It's lovely." Louise leaned closer. "May I photograph it?" Martha nodded and put it on her lap. Louise took several pictures, including one taken in profile of the young woman putting it back in her hair.

"We'll have a big potlatch in the longhouse to celebrate the life and death of the catch. Dr. Clarke came once." She looked up. "Do you know what that is—a potlatch?"

"Yes," Louise was happy to say. "My friend, Piney, belongs to the Puyallup tribe and they have them."

"Did you know potlatches are illegal in Canada?" Dr. Clarke said.

Louise put her knitting down and shifted to a more comfortable position. Rubbing her eyes she said, "For goodness sakes, why?"

"They think that it's a non-essential tribal ritual and totally inappropriate. The government wants to eliminate anything that prevents the natives from pursuing what is considered to be a 'healthier, European mentality.'"

"For us, a potlatch is a way to keep the dead alive," Martha said. "When my grandmother died, we gave a potlatch so that the people would remember her. We make a living by what the land gives us, but we make a life by what we give away."

After considering Martha's words, Louise said, "I don't think I could give my possessions away, but it's certainly a lovely way to live." The room grew quiet again and then, as Martha began to put her knitting away, Louise asked if the baby she was expecting was her first.

"Yes. I'm due in January."

"I promised to come back and help with the birth," Dr. Clarke said.

"And I suppose you want a boy."

"My husband does, yes, but I want a girl." Changing the subject, Martha held up her bag. "This is made from gut. So is my raincoat. My father traded a Yupik man for it. It's my mother's, to keep her dry; she's sick, but she lets me wear it."

"Ouida, Martha's mother, has consumption," Dr. Clarke said. "I've been reading about something called vital amines and brought some Mastin's Yeast Vitamon Tablets with me for her to take."

Martha nodded and smiled. When the door closed behind her, Louise got up to look for something to eat. "Is there a general store here?" she asked after a fruitless search.

"West, at the end of the houses. The post office is in it, too." Dr. Clarke propped her feet up on Martha's chair and closed her eyes. Seeing her that way, Louise thought she looked old and tired. *But what purpose she's given to her life.*

Well, the rain is letting up so, I think I'll walk down." Hearing the word "walk," Queenie looked up. "No, you stay here and keep the doctor company." Louise laughed when her pet seemed relieved and snuggled back down.

"Would you like a blanket? Is there anything I can get you at the store?"

"Just my shawl, please; it's on the hook." Dr. Clarke was already asleep when Louise tucked it around her.

Outside, the briny air cooled her hot face and smelled wonderfully fresh though it was smoke-filled from fires which every kind of makeshift chimney seemed to emit. Louise took a deep breath, knowing that as in Tacoma, the tide would always make changes to how the reservation smelled. *Life on the water*, she thought. Since the rain had stopped, people were back on the beach again. Seagulls swooped above where the men were finishing the whale, fighting each other in the air. Some of the women and children were prying mussels off logs, others were wading for seaweed and draping it on driftwood to dry. Dogs chased each other, ignored by a wading osprey that was looking for fish. Louise took a last look before heading to the store, thinking the people she saw looked as happy as she was to be outside.

The path she followed was half dirt, half wooden walk, so close to neighboring houses, she could see through their windows. *No lights*, she thought, *so they must be empty*. And she was being so careful not to trip that she failed to notice a garter snake until it slithered in front of her. Seeing it, she jumped and gave a yip and a little boy snickered and ran to tell his friends.

The store, though looking as if it was built from salvaged wood, was, nevertheless, a substantial building with large windows and an awning across the front. Several men stood under it talking. Opening the door, Louise saw a number of women looking through bolts of cloth. As she entered, they all stopped what they were doing and gawped.

"Good morning, ladies," she said. They nodded, some smiled, then everyone went back to what they were doing. Louise inhaled the combined smell of furs and spices, tools and cloth, and a myriad of other things. "Tacoma doesn't have general stores like this one, anymore," she said to a man standing, with his arms crossed, behind a counter. "Can I browse a bit?" And he nodded.

A large wood-burning stove in the middle of the room puffed out heat. Shelves lined the walls from floor to the ceiling, and a narrow walkway separated them from waist-high counters. Both counters and shelves held a dizzying assortment of apparel and hardware, canned goods, drugs, animal feed, beverages, and dried meat and vegetables. There was a coffee bean grinder, a large wheel of cheese, a glass jar of candy, odds and ends of kitchen ware. Spices, a big jar of pickles, and boxes of straw holding eggs. In one corner was a pile of pelts; nearby Louise smelled barrels of kerosene.

"I didn't think to bring a basket," she said.

"Not to worry. Pick out what you want, put it in this box and I'll have someone deliver."

"I'm staying with..." Louise began.

"Doctor Clarke, yes. No problem."

Under the women's covert stares Louise picked out a dozen eggs, a loaf of bread, some canned chicken, and asked for two pounds of cheese. She also chose an assortment of candy for the children who were getting smallpox shots the next day, and a meaty bone for Queenie. The door opened and closed; people came and went, some buying and some selling: salmon, halibut, shellfish. One man had a sea otter pelt, and a little boy came in with a rabbit skin. Louise stood in a corner and watched until she couldn't remain still any longer.

"May I take a few photographs?" At the storekeeper's nod, she wandered about and eventually stopped in front of the piles of furs. They had been separated by type: otter, seal, deer, and some she didn't recognize.

Seeing her interest the storekeeper strolled over and picked up one of the skins. "Deer make nice gloves," he said. "You'd likely get three pairs out of one hide.

Louise laughed. "I don't think I have enough money for a whole hide, and I wouldn't know how to make gloves. I'm rather useless at that kind of thing."

"Well, now, the ladies could likely teach you. They tan hides and make gloves."

"They tan the hides. Golly." Louise thought back to deer her uncle had shot when visiting her Aunt Indiana and wondered what happened to that hide. "They certainly have skills I don't. That seems like a lot of work."

"It is." He caught the eye of one of the women. "Grandma Sadie, here, is an expert, aren't you, Grandma Sadie?"

Grandma Sadie's brown and weather face resembled a dried apple. She wore wire-rim glasses, and a beaded headband to hold her white hair off her face. She was well-wrapped in a variety of clothes and blankets, so much so that she walked with a rolling gait. Flipping through the pile, she said, "This is one of mine." Her voice was soft, almost monotone, neither pleasant nor unpleasant. *Just different,* Louise thought.

"See how there's no hair left on it?" the storekeeper said. "That's the first step to making a pelt like this, isn't it, Grandma Sadie?"

"No." The elderly woman looked at Louise out of dark, raisin-like eyes. "The first step is to kill a deer."

Louise wasn't sure if she meant that as a joke, but it was funny, and she laughed. "Yes, I imagine it is."

Satisfied with the response, Grandma Sadie said, "Mostly it's the men who kill the deer so we have food for winter. Then they skin it and bring everything back home. The hair is left on if we want to use the hide as a rug; otherwise, we scrape it off. We use a tool made from stone or bone."

Louise nodded. "Martha Stanup showed me her bone hair piece."

"We scrape and scrape until every bit of flesh is off, and we soak the hide to help loosen the hair. The sinews make good thread for bowstrings, and boiling the bones makes good broth." Louise wasn't sure about the broth, not being a fan of game animals but she tried to look respectful. "When it is all clean, we start the tanning." Grandma Sadie looked at Louise. "You vomited, didn't you?"

"Yes, ma'am. I'm ashamed to say I did." It was an abrupt change of topic and Louise didn't know why until the woman said," We tan it using the deer's brains."

Everyone within hearing distance in the store looked to see Louise's reaction, but, disappointingly, she merely nodded. *Out of sight, out of mind.*

"We mash the brains in some warm water until it gets like soft soap and begin rubbing it in the hide. It takes a long time because we have to put it on a frame and stretch and pull the skin to loosen all the fibers. When it's ready, we smoke the skin.

Louise put a tentative finger on the pelt Grandma Sadie had made, then looked at the speaker and those around her. "I think you all are entitled to every cent you earn. Such hard work; I'm quite sure I couldn't do all that. Grandma Sadie, may I take your picture while you continue your shopping?"

Hearing her, some of the women smiled and some merely nodded, but with the storytelling over, the group broke up. Louise meandered around until she was able to take some random shots of the elderly woman and then turned her attention to a collection of baskets. "My," she said, moving on, "these baskets are beautiful."

"They're being shipped to the Department of the Interior in Washington tomorrow," the shopkeeper said.

"Yes, I think it was Peter who mentioned that."

"For the war effort. Many of the tribes are donating artifacts to be auctioned off."

"Gosh." Louise hesitated before saying, "I think, considering how the government has treated the various tribes, that that is quite generous. I know the Puyallup Reservation near Tacoma where I live used to be much bigger. So many government decisions shrunk it." She sighed and under her breath said, "Money always talks, doesn't it?"

Several people heard the remark and nodded, and after carefully repositioning some of the baskets into a better arrangement, Louise took several pictures, paid for her purchases, and left. A frisky breeze blew off the bay. Looking up, Louise saw three eagles soaring on the thermals. But as day faded to dusk, the temperature dropped, and she was glad to reach the house. Her groceries soon followed, and Queenie happily retreated to a corner with her bone.

Dear Matt,

It's midnight and though Queenie is on my bed, snoring away, I can't sleep. I wish we had a bathtub, trying to wash in a basin of rapidly-cooling water is very inadequate. Tomorrow, I meet with Father de Rouge to find out what photographs I'm supposed to take but today I went to the store and then had my first look around. The reservation is like nothing I've ever seen before—messy, crowded, noisy and happy. On the beach I saw several women tending a fire which was surrounded by fish fillets held upright between thin wooden stakes to cook in the smoke. I'm not a fan of seafood but I hope we get to have some because the smell was wonderful though I'm not sure if that was the firewood or the fish.

There are a lot of long logs bobbing around in the bay. They've been polished to a silvery smoothness by the salt water. Today the water had only a slight chop and two of the larger logs were lined with small boys attempting to push each other off. Only the youngest children seem to have toys. I saw a girl with a doll made of wood, and some of the boys, too small to play on the logs, had miniature bows and arrows. The cutest thing on the beach, today, was a tiny little girl playing with a lamb. And one of prettiest things I saw were two horseback riders racing each other in the surf. I said it was noisy, and it was. People were singing, either alone or in small groups, or shouting at the children and at each other There was so much to see, hear and smell that I was overwhelmed.

Louise put her pen down and rubbed her forehead. She closed her eyes and sighed.

I'm ashamed of myself but I'm homesick. There isn't a single comforting thing here, except Queenie.

Since it had only happened that once, she didn't mention the fainting spell she'd experienced when Peter had to grab her, and instead continued writing.

Neah Bay is a cove, of course, with crags poking out of the water here and there, and on the land behind our house and down as far as the eyes can see, there are dozens of other houses standing cheek-by-jowl. Between them are tree stumps and short boardwalks. Laundry on rope clotheslines and, everywhere, fish hanging on drying racks. There are always quite a number of dogs on the beach, but I often hear more barking coming from the houses behind us. Some people have cows and, from the smell, don't seem to muck out their cow yards very often. There are so many eagles here, too and I saw one swoop down, aiming for a baby chick. Chicken distress calls apparently alerted its owner because while I watched, a woman with a gun suddenly appeared. Its blast shook the air and that's when I went inside. I'd say, 'went home' but nothing feels like home. Oh, dear, I am whining and I shouldn't. I have a job to do, and I'll only be here for a few more days.

Chapter 9

Had it not been for a cross on the roof, Father de Rouge's house would have been indistinguishable from all the others: weather-worn wood, small windows, and smoke puffing out of a pipe on the roof. At Louise's knock, a squat, elderly woman opened the door.

"I'm here to see Father de Rouge," Louise said. "I think he's expecting me."

"Let her in, Awena" said a man, the voice coming from somewhere inside. Awena smiled, stepped back, and gestured Louise into a room very much like the one in the house where she was staying. The voice came from a man of advanced years ensconced in a large, over-stuffed chair by a fireplace. As Louise walked in, the first thing she saw was that his right leg was well-wrapped on a board and propped up on the chair opposite where he sat.

"Sorry about not getting up," the Father said, "but I've had a little accident; slipped on a piece of driftwood; it rolled under my foot, and broke my leg. Brittle bones, my dear, brittle bones, come with age. The good doctor Clarke says I'll be six weeks down for the count. I asked Awena, in my nicest voice, to put a chair here so we can talk, and she did. She mostly does what I ask, don't you, Awena, but sometimes she gets a bee in her bonnet and makes me suffer. She can be a little tyrant sometimes, isn't that right, Awena, just like Napoleon."

Awena grunted, Louise smiled, and Queenie headed for the hearth. "Well now, you've brought your dog and a nice looking one it is. The people here used to knit dog hair into clothes, didn't they, Awena? Might still do. Well, now, you're the person who's going to take my photographs. Didn't expect such a pretty young thing. Sit, sit. Coffee or tea?"

Louise managed to ask for coffee, and milk or cream if there was any, and Father de Rouge continued.

"I prefer coffee, but Awena likes tea, don't you Awena? And she does the shopping. Now then, are you Catholic? No? Then you've probably not heard of Reverand Mother Katherine Drexel. She's a stout supporter of both the Indians and the colored people and in 1891 founded the Congregation of the Sisters of the Blessed Sacrament for Indians and Colored People. That's a mouthful, isn't it? But, of course, things of that nature cost money to maintain and it is her idea to put together a book about the various Indian tribes and sell it. I actually maintain the Coleville mission, but the Reverand Mother asked for my help since I'm the closest priest to the Makahs. She wants a brief history and pictures. I put my own book aside to help her. That's where you come in: I will give you a brief outline of the history and we can decide what photographs you can provide."

Louise waited to make sure Father de Rouge was done. "Alright. I don't know much about the reservation, but between you and Awena," she smiled at the woman, "I'm sure we can work something out."

"Not Awena, though. She's a Nez Pierce; she came with me from Coleville where she's my housekeeper."

Louise put her tablet on her lap and got out a pen. "Well, we'll just have to do the best we can."

The priest leaned forward. "That's certainly an interesting pen."

"Isn't it?" Louise handed it to him. "It was a gift from my mother. It's called a Trench Pen." Taking it back she said, "See, this part in the barrel holds ink pellets. You put one in and add water."

"My goodness." Father de Rouge was so astonished; he almost forgot to talk. But the silence was short-lived. "I must see about getting one. Now, let me give you some background."

... believe it or not, Matt, he talked for four hours. I got a short break when I had to take Queenie out, but the Father actually talked through lunch—between bites. Lunch was delicious, though, pheasant and small potatoes with plenty of butter, a green vegetable, too but I managed to avoid that and then berry cobbler for dessert. I was trying to eat, listen, and write down ideas for photographs. I sure learned a lot, and I always love learning something new. The Makah's land used to include islands I never heard of: Waadah where they grew potatoes, Tatoosh which has a lighthouse, Ozette which had a major mudslide, three islands on Lake Ozette, and Cannon Ball Island which also had a mudslide and which the Makah use for what they call vision quests. That's where a young person goes alone out in the woods, somewhere, looking for spiritual guidance and their life's purpose. I'm pretty sure Father de Rouge would like some pictures of them, the islands, that is, but I don't plan to go island hopping. The Makah also used to have summer camps on the beach at the northwestern-most point of land by the ocean. I don't know if they still do. Dr. Clarke says I'd have to hike out to a place called Hobuck Beach if I want to get an unobstructed view of the ocean. Where we are outcroppings with trees actually growing on some of them obstruct the view. I'd love to see ocean breakers but don't suppose I'll get to on this trip but, anyway, there's lots I can photograph here, like the cedar longhouses. Right now, there's a potlatch going on in the biggest longhouse that I've seen so far. In the olden days, every village had several and it's said that hundreds of people lived in them. I can't imagine that. How does anyone ever get a moment to themselves? The longhouse here where the potlatch is going on in is

only about seventy feet long and maybe thirty feet wide.

In her bedroom, Louise's make-shift desk had just enough room for her to put her head on her arms. She moved the lantern, closed her eyes, and immediately noise from the potlatch seemed intensified. *Lord, love us,* she thought, *but they're noisy. Not the city noise I'm used to, no men shouting and street cars and Princess licking her paws. I don't understand how the people here seem to like always being around other people. I certainly don't.* The sudden realization of that fact gave her pause. "Maybe that's why I like working in the studio darkroom," she said to Queenie, "because it's quiet and a one-person job."

With a sigh, Louise picked up her pen.

* * *

I used my Trench pen when talking to Father de Rouge. It was certainly handy not to have to carry a fountain pen and bottle of ink. I've already taken photographs of some of the things he wants, so I'm ahead of the game there, but since Mr. Aldrich thinks I can make my own book, a photo essay book, I have my work cut out for me to find some additional, really interesting things to take pictures of.

And now, fair warning, I will tell you more about the Makahs. Their longhouses have cedar-plank walls which can be tipped or even removed to provide ventilation or light. Cedar trees are important to the tribe; they use the roots to make baskets, carve whole trees into canoes and, at least according to Dr. Clarke, actually make hats and clothes out of the bark. Cedar smells so good. Have you been to Wright Park yet? It's not far from the Gypsy Smith Tabernacle and has a really large, hollowed-out cedar stump in it. It's been used for all kinds of things. Right now, it's a bandstand, but that's where President Roosevelt stood when he visited Tacoma, right on top.

Tomorrow I am going to help the doctor give vaccinations to the children and talk to their mothers as best I can. I'm hoping one of them will show me the plants and roots they eat. The next day I will finish taking the photographs on the Father's list and not long after that I start back home and then our picnic. A whole day together. It seems too good to be true. I've not heard from anyone since I got here which is very worrisome to me; I just have to assume that no news is good news.

As ever,

Louise

P.S. I have learned how to turn a heel on my knitting.

* * *

Louise was shivering when she crawled in bed. She pulled the bearskin on top of the blankets and snuggled next to Queenie. The owl she'd heard the previous two nights had apparently moved on to somewhere where the noise from the potlatch wasn't scaring away the rodents. Occasional smoke smells seeped into her room which was half-lit by the moon. Her last thought before falling asleep was to wonder if her cat was missing her.

Though the smell of coffee was a good way to wake, the water in her pitcher was ice cold. Louise washed and dressed as quickly as possible and hurried to the kitchen. First things first; Queenie had to go outside, and Louise grabbed a cup of coffee on her way to the door. The tide was halfway up the beach, and a number of women were toting baskets of shellfish, leaving behind holes from which they'd dug clams. However, it was the house next door that caught her eye. A thick tree limb about five feet long had been nailed outside on to the wall and extended parallel to the ground for about four feet before being attached to a post at the other end. The limb had five ropes tied on. They were attached to a small bed in which a baby slept. Periodically, a young woman sitting near it put down a small chisel and the bone she was carving to tuck in the baby's blankets and pushed the bed into a gentle rocking motion. *When did that go up?* Louise wondered, as she asked for permission to take a picture. *How very clever. Innovative? Well, something, anyway.*

"Best hurry if you want some breakfast before the children come," said Dr. Clarke when Louise rushed in for her camera and then back out. Fortunately, Louise had time to take several photographs, make and eat some hot buttered toast with cheese on top, and feed Queenie. She was cleaning up the kitchen area when the first of the women and children arrived. Without exception, they all looked apprehensive.

As they filed in, Dr. Clarke smiled and clapped her hands. "Please sit down everyone. You children, if you would, sit on the floor so your mothers can have the chairs. No, not that one, that one's mine. Yes, I know, there's not enough for everybody, but you won't be here long. Don't cry Abby; the shots will be over in lickity-split time and then my helper here, Miss Louise, will give you a piece of candy. I know you don't want to be here, but the shots only take a minute and a half, and having cholera, smallpox or typhoid is much, much worse and will keep you in bed for weeks."

Or be fatal, thought Louise but felt it better not to say. People milled around for a bit and sat where they could while Queenie retreated to the bedroom. When everyone was mostly settled, Louise was surprised to see the doctor sit in her favorite chair.

"Now," Dr. Clarke began, "what is the smallest animal you can think of"

Immediately, the children began waving their arms and shouting. "Puppies," "kittens," frogs," and poking and shoving each other if they thought an answer given was wrong.

Dr. Clarke laughed and clapped her hands. "All very good answers, but the tiniest animal there is, is called bacterium. Just think, Queenie, Miss Louise's dog, is made from millions of things called cells, but bacterium has only one, one cell. That's how small it is. Now, more than a hundred years ago, a bunch of bacterium got together and decided to be bullies. What better way to be a bully, they thought, than to make people really, really sick, maybe even die? So, they started traveling around and began living in the water that people drank, and a lot of people did get sick, and a lot of them did die. That made some very smart men very sad, and they wanted to see what could be done to fight the bacterium. Yes Jacob, fighting a bear is hard, too, but just imagine fighting something you can only see in a microscope. How would you know where it was hiding?" Dr. Clarke paused to let that sink in.

"Then, about thirty years ago a Spanish man named Jaime Ferran found something that would go after the bacterium and attack and kill them, and he made a liquid out of what he'd found so people could put it in needles. That's what the shot is and that's what it will do," the doctor raised a fist and in a loud, sinister voice said, "attack the enemy so they can never ever make you sick." Speaking normally again, she added, "Even your mothers are going to have the shot but they probably won't get a piece of the candy Miss Louise bought just for today."

While Dr. Clarke talked the room had gone quiet. Once she stopped, the woman began rolling up their sleeves and those of their children. "Now, Miss Louise, are you ready? Who's to be first?"

While Louise took a mental count of her pieces of candy, reluctant woman dragging equally reluctant children walked one by one to the table holding needles, serum, alcohol, and cotton balls. The actual procedure itself didn't take long but the needle was large. More than one woman flinched while the babies howled, and the smaller children cried. Once the torturous event was over, though, both boys and girls scrubbed off their tears as quickly as they could, grabbed a piece of candy and raced outside.

Dr. Clarke's process was much like what Matthew and Louise had done at Camp Lewis, swabbing a spot on the arm with alcohol, administering the serum, and cleaning off any blood. Even with Louise doing the swabbing and then applying a small piece of cotton gauze with adhesive tape to the wound, the vaccinations took up most of the morning and the time dragged on. When the last patient left, the doctor heaved a heavy sigh and helped herself to a leftover piece of candy before collapsing into her chair. "Land sakes but I'm glad that's over, and Louise, many thanks for your help. Usually, inoculations take me all day. Lordy but I'm tired; maybe I'm getting too old for this."

Louise added tea leaves to some hot water and after a few minutes strained them out. "Here's a cup of tea; I'm going to build up the fire and fix you something to eat; that should help."

She rooted through their food supplies and found a small and very old jar of honey. *Just needs softening,* she thought and put it on the stove. Once soft, she spread some on a piece of buttered toast, added some cheese, and then another piece of toast. Then she cut the sandwich in half and carried it to where Doctor Clarke sat, half-asleep and gently rocking.

"My goodness but this is good," the doctor said talking around the big bite she'd taken. "I didn't realize how hungry I was."

Returning to the stove, Louise started toasting bread for her own sandwich. While she scraped honey out and spread it on her own toast, she said, "Dr. Clarke, have you ever noticed that some of the people here look almost Chinese?" On her way to her own chair, she picked up some of the loose candy wrappers and threw them in the fire.

"Not Chinese, dear, Japanese."

"Really?"

"The *Hojunmaru* was a Japanese ship that was caught in a storm on the Pacific Ocean and drifted until it was shipwrecked near Cape Flattery."

"When was this?"

"Um, in the eighteen-thirties, I think. Three men survived and the Makah held them captive for a couple months, then turned them over to authorities at Fort Vancouver."

Louise laughed. "Seems to me like there was some hanky-panky before they did."

"Good grief." The doctor also laughed. "That's not an expression I hear very often. It used to have something to do with magic tricks."

"Well, it sure wasn't magic that caused Japanese features to show up."

"Truer words were never spoken."

Louise finished her sandwich and the tidying up. When Queenie got restless, they went out and walked a short way among the houses, waiting for Peter. Everywhere she went, people were working, mostly doing tasks she couldn't identify. Why, for example, were they pounding bark? Why were they weaving cat tail leaves and bulrushes into mats? Was that really dried seaweed they were rolling and packing in baskets with leaves? As the two of them walked, dogs came to visit, and Queenie made some potential friends and a few enemies. Louise had hoped to encounter one of the Woolly Dogs whose hair tribal members spun into yarn, but none were to be seen. There were, however, chickens, a few cows and goats. Only later on did she learn that the appearance of domestic animals on the Reservation was relatively recent.

"Europeans introduced them," Dr. Clarke told her when she returned to the house and sat near the fire. *Fires always feel good,* Louise thought. Ignoring her knitting, she picked up Queenie and began rubbing her back. They rocked in companionable silence until someone knocked on the door before opening it and walking in.

"Hello, Peter," Louise said. "Did everyone survive their shots?"

Peter laughed and bent to scratch Queenie's ears. "So far. I think the candy went a long way towards healing."

"It often does," Louise said.

"Well, what brings you here?" the doctor asked. "You've had your inoculations."

"Louise and I have a walk planned for this afternoon, and I was wondering if, tomorrow, she'd like to take a hike tomorrow out to Cape Flattery," he said. "It's not much more than a mile and we could take a picnic."

"Gosh, that sounds wonderful. I'd see the ocean, wouldn't I? I never have. Oh," she stopped. "I have to take the photographs Father de Rouge wants."

"What does he want?"

'Umm, making a canoe, the women making baskets, a picture of the reservation." Louise stopped. "Not many others because the Makahs are only one of the tribes to be included in the book, but I have to check my list."

Peter leaned against the edge of a table. "If we go out in a canoe, you can get a good shot of our village, and I saw some of the women headed for the longhouse to work on their baskets. The carving of a canoe will be hard because—oh, wait. Charlie Tahola is putting new gunwales on his whaling canoe. Maybe that will work. Look, Louise, it's only two o'clock. Let's see how much of your list we can take care of now so we can go to Cape Flattery tomorrow. What do you say?"

Peter looked so happy with his plan; Louise felt obligated, though, truth be told, she was easily persuaded. "That sounds wonderful."

"Get your camera, then, and let's see what we can do."

In the end, finding what the priest wanted proved easy. It started with a short walk to one of the longhouses. Once there, Louise tied Queenie's leash to a stump, Peter opened the door, and the two entered a room overheated from a fire in the central hearth. Several women sat on floor mats near where some shelves were piled high with a variety of plant materials, and others with completed baskets. When the door opened, they stopped talking and glanced up. Louise looked at the accumulation of reeds, strips of bark, dried Bear Grass and other items and then turned her attention to what they were making.

"My goodness. I can't imagine how you can turn all this," she gestured toward the plant materials, "into such beautiful baskets."

As the weavers went back to their work, one said, "Here, I show you."

"Louise, this is Ramona. She teaches the young girls when they're old enough to start learning." Ramona set her partially-completed basket aside and picked up some pine needles. Louise hunkered down to watch.

"You start by holding bunches of pine needles together like this," Ramona said, "and lay some thin lengths of gut along them. Then you wind the gut around the needles until they're covered and fold the wrapped needles to make a circle." Her circle was ready at the same time as she quit speaking, and she held it up. "Next, you wrap the gut around the circle a couple of times and stitch through it. After that, you lay some needles alongside and start wrapping and stitching."

Louise touched the circle gingerly. "Doesn't it hurt your fingers, using all this plant material?"

Ramona picked up her half-completed backet and began incorporating beads. Finding her rhythm again, she said, "What hurts is the ache my hands get."

"Oh, my. I never even thought about that." Louise stood, staggering slightly from the warmth. Peter grabbed her and she leaned against his chest for a moment before expressing her thanks. The heat, the smells, and the unsettled feeling Peter's body gave her were disconcerting, and she welcomed hearing a couple of barks from Queenie. "If it's alright with you, I would like to take a few photographs." She snapped several, but before she could put her camera away, Peter asked if he could take one.

"If you would kneel down again, just as you were before." Louise knelt down again and watched as the new basket took shape, and Peter took three pictures, one when he made a joke and Louise and the women looked up and laughed. "I'd like a copy of that one," he said.

"And I'd better rescue Queenie." Louise thanked the ladies and hurried out to find a showdown between her pet and a large cat. Seeing humans, the cat darted under a nearby building scattering a flock of birds pecking in the soil. Some flew to rooftops where smoke crept out of the chimneys and hugged the roofs. Realizing how heavy with moisture the air had become, she said, "Is it going to rain again?"

"Probably. Being so close to the ocean we get a lot of rain." Peter surprised Louise by taking her hand. "Come on,"

"Where to?"

"To take one of the pictures on your list." He started off, keeping a firm grip and Louise had no choice but to follow dragging poor Queenie behind her. Peter led them in a crooked route around weather-worn, whitewashed buildings, some with windows but many without, some with flat roofs, some with peaked, around large rocks, bleached logs, and a few gardens. They passed a substantial-looking building where stairs led to a covered porch. A boom-town front faced the water, put up, no doubt, in the hope that it added class to the structure.

"The Presbyterian mission and reading room," Peter said without slowing down and before Louise could ask.

"Goodness," said Louise, as she tried to extricate her hand. "Are we in a race against time or something?"

"In a matter of speaking."

On the bay, a seal snoozed on a piece of driftwood. Some of the ever-present gulls lit on floating logs, and others flew into the trees. Ahead of them, people of all ages, birds of all types, and an assortment of dogs went about their business on the shore. Hurrying past a flock of Black Oystercatchers, sending them into aerial indignation and heading to where an older man was doing something to a large canoe, Peter stopped so abruptly, Louise staggered, struggling to keep her balance.

"Uncle," he said, "thank you for waiting."

"Had to finish fixing the gunwale." The older man, wearing baggy pants wet to the knees, a faded sweater, and slouchy hat, was fitting a piece of cedar on the rim and fastening it in place.

"Louise, this is Uncle."

"It's nice to meet you, uh, Uncle. Do you mind if I take some pictures?"

"That's what Peter said you wanted to do."

Louise got her camera ready and walked around, looking for the best angles.

After a moment she asked Uncle to look up. He had a thick head of black hair and a beetle brow over a white mustache and beard. His sweater was more holes than yarn, and fish scales on his pants sparkled when the sun hit them. The sun, however, was intermittent. Clouds were rolling in from the ocean bringing more birds with them. Uncle gave Louise approximately thirty seconds before continuing his work. She thanked him and turned to look at the houses. "Why are there so few vegetable gardens?" she asked.

"By tradition, the women forage for food," Peter said. "Wild greens, mushrooms, all kinds of berries which they dry."

"I'm partial to boiled seal flippers and eelgrass stalks," Uncle said.

I beg your pardon?" Louise was aghast. A few scattered raindrops hit her arms, and she snapped a picture of the houses and picked up Queenie's leash. "I think we best get back."

"Rain on the way; storm will be here before dark," Uncle said. He began putting his tools in an old sack and stood to stretch his back. Louise wondered if his bare feet were sore and cold, or if he was used to the salt water and piles of sharp-edged shells.

"Come on, let's head for the mission." Peter took Louise's hand again and they ran to the building which, unfortunately, was locked. However, the porch awning provided protection, and they hunkered down against the wall. Queenie was shaking and Louise picked her up and cuddled her under her sweater. At the same time, Peter put his arm around the two of them pulling Louise close. "I don't think we'll get our picnic tomorrow," he said.

"Well," Louise sighed. "I guess the ocean's not going any place, is it."

For a few minutes they watched the rain, then Peter said, "You don't like it much here, think much of us, do you?"

"What?' Louise tried to pull away but he held her firmly against his side."

"I said..."

"No, I heard what you said; I'm just surprised that you would think that. Have I said anything, done anything to give that impression?" When Peter remained silent, she sighed. "If I have, I'm truly sorry. Everyone had been nothing buy polite, but it's so damp and wet, and has been ever since I arrived. I just got out of the hospital and came here for my job but also to recuperate. The cold air makes me ache. And," she gave a rueful laugh, "I'm a little homesick. I miss my family and my cat, and then there's the war." When he remained quiet, she moved Queenie off her lap, pulled away from him and got to her feet. "I think it's letting up."

Peter stood and pulled her close. He kissed her and Louise melted into his body. How strong he felt and how good it was to be held firmly against a man's body. He pulled her closer and kissed her neck and she turned her face to meet his lips again. Giving into the feeling, she enjoyed his passion. But the memory of Matthew was never far away. *This can't be,* she thought and drew back. *I'll be headed home soon and, besides, there's no life here for me.*

After a moment, Peter let her go. "He's a lucky guy."

"Huh? Who?"

"The fellow you're thinking about." Louise blushed and Peter took her hand." Let's make a dash for it."

They parted at her door, with him racing for home and Queenie beating Louise inside. Both hurried to the fire which Dr. Clarke had blazing. "Heavens, Louise, you're soaking wet. Best change. I won't let you on that train if you're sick."

Louise hurried to her room and returned in less than ten minutes with a towel in one hand and her wet shoes in the other. Putting the latter on the hearth, she began rubbing Queenie who was trying to lick her fur dry. Looking up, Dr. Clarke laughed. "Good heavens, girl. I knew it was just a matter of time. What, exactly, do you call what you're wearing?"

Louise grinned. "Nell adapted them from Carhartt work pants but made the legs extra wide so they're almost like a skirt. And the fabric is called flannel. Civil War soldiers wore a lot of flannel. It's soft and warm." She spread the towel out to dry. There was some sliced bread left over from breakfast, and she spread a piece with butter and joined the dog by the fire.

"Nell made her own pattern." Louise went on as she gave Queenie, who was partial to butter, some of the bread. Then she picked up her knitting and began casting on stitches for yet another sock. "It's called a bifurcated skirt. Mostly, they're for riding horses but she says that with all the men going to war, a lot of women will be doing their jobs, and they will need something sensible to wear. And she wanted the fabric to be soft so she's making these from flannel."

"Well, don't let the natives here see them. The Makahs are a conservative bunch." Dr. Clarke finished sterilizing some instruments and joined Louise in front of the fire. Every once in a while, a lighter-knot popped and hissed, sending up sparks. Other than that, all they heard was the storm raging outside.

"Gosh, it's not like summer at all, is it?"

"It's being so close to the ocean and that brings in a lot of storms," the doctor said, echoing Peter's words, "but it has been an unusually wet summer."

"I hope it's not like this at home." Louise put her needle work down. "I'm still hungry."

"There's some cheese and a tomato in the icebox. Best eat it; the ice is about gone."

"I'll make a sandwich. Would you like one?"

"No. I ate earlier."

Louise made a sandwich and put it on a plate, added a cup of coffee and returned to her chair. The sandwich was fat, giving her permission to dunk it. She chewed a bite and swallowed before saying, "Have I been an okay guest? I haven't said or done anything that would insult the people, have I?"

The doctor looked startled. "Not to my knowledge. I've not heard anything. I think some of them are pleased at the interest you're showing. Why do you ask?"

"Um," Louise tore off some bread and cheese and gave it to Queenie.

"You're spoiling that dog."

"I know but I don't think she had a happy puppy life, and she deserves to be spoiled." Louise bit her lip before answering the question. "It was just something Peter said."

"Peter?" Dr. Clarke shook her head. "You've seen a lot of him. How are the two of you getting on?"

"Fine, as far as I know. Why?"

"Since Sally's been away, he's been breaking a few hearts."

"Who's Sally?"

"She's what, in my youth we called his *inamorata*."

"What?"

"She's his intended. From what I've heard, after he starts teaching and has an income, they're getting married."

Louise choked on her sandwich. "Well, what a bounder" Then she looked at the doctor and forced a laughed. And Dr. Clarke was wise enough not to ask for an explanation.

The storm continued for the rest of the day and onto into the night. When it finally wore itself out, the quiet woke Louise. Snug under a pile of blankets topped by the bear skin, she stared at the bedroom window watching clouds race past a full moon, leaving behind a starry sky. Queenie wiggled in her sleep and just as she drifted off again, Louise heard an owl. *I hope he gets a rat or mouse*, she thought.

Chapter 10

Dawn was breaking when shouting voices filled her room and Dr. Clarke pounded on her door. "Get up, Louise. Get dressed. I'm going to need your help, and this is something you'll want to photograph."

Glad to be awake after a restless night, Louise crawled over Queenie and pulled on a sweater and the bifurcated skirt. She grabbed a pair of socks and hurried to the fireplace hearth where she'd left her boots to dry. "What's going on?" She had to raise her voice to be heard over the noise outside.

"I just got word that the storm played havoc with the *Retriever*," Dr. Clarke said, "and she had to have a tug bring her into the bay. I'm going to see if anyone is hurt. Leave Queenie here but stay close; It may well be all hands on deck."

Outside, though dawn was turning the sky a lovely blue and the pair of young gulls that had sought refuge in some Sitka spruce were deserting the tree and taking up their usual positions. The frisky wind kept a chop on the bay. The storm had brought in massive logs through which the damaged barkentine limped, and through which many of the Makah men steered their canoes. It looked as if the entire village had turned out.

One of the *Retriever's* three masts was listing, and tattered sails hung off the other two. As she snapped pictures, Louise saw injured men in canvas hammocks being lowered over the side to waiting dugouts. Men brought them to shore and ignoring the water, Dr. Clarke waded out to meet them and make quick assessments of their injuries. Without being asked, Louise put her camera inside and joined her at the canoes, helping those who could walk up to the house. There followed a day like no other she had ever experienced.

Directing men with cuts and gashes to one side of the room, Dr. Clarke told Louise to clean the injuries with carbolic soap in clean, hot water and then dry and bind them.

"You may have to do a little stitching," she added. "Let me know and I'll bring you some sutures and a needle. Right now, I'm going to check for broken bones."

"Stitches?" Louise filled a basin with hot water and carried it to the table. "Do you mean sew up the cuts?

"Just pull the skin together and suture it. Try to be neat." She turned to a man who cradled his left arm. "Now then, sit here and let me take a look."

Affectively dismissed, Louise gestured toward a grizzled man whose canvas pants were torn from his ankle to his knee. She folded the fabric up, revealing a ten-inch gash which bled down his leg, the blood disappearing in his boot. Sitting in a chair facing him, she lifted his leg onto her lap and washed the cut until the dried blood disappeared into the water. Then, before she could move, one of the men removed a bottle from his pocket, poured some of the liquid it contained on the cut, and took a large swig. The patient hollered and everyone looked up.

"Whiskey," the miscreant said.

"God damn, that stings. Parden me, ma'am." He began blowing on the wound.

"Not to worry." Louise threaded a needle, took a deep sigh, and pulling the skin in place, began stitching as best she could. "What's your name?" she asked, hoping to distract him.

"Roscoe, ma'am. Roscoe Kamell." He took a deep breath through his teeth.

"We call him The Camel," said a young man with a French accent. He grinned and a number of men, probably those who weren't in too much pain, Louise thought, laughed.

"Well, I'm about done here, Mr. Kamell." Louise wound his leg with cotton gauze and tied it off. "You can change chairs with the whiskey-drinker, and I'll bring you a cup of coffee."

I'm Jacque Jacob," the Frenchman said after the two swapped seats. "And what do I call you, *mon cheri?*"

"Nurse," said Louise as she left him to get the coffee, and he laughed.

And so, it went for the balance of the day. With every new patient, Louise added more water to the stove's boiler, refilled her basin, and treated a host of cuts and abrasions. She sutured two more cuts and bandaged several others, found flat pieces of wood for splints, and held limbs so the doctor could set the broken bones. In between, she made coffee and poured numerous cups. Several people dropped off pots of venison stew, and she doled it out. There weren't enough bowls so as each man finished, she washed them and dished out more. By late afternoon all the wounded had been treated; most of them lay on the floor, and both the doctor's and Louise's bed held the worst of the injured. Queenie had lifted everyone's spirits by walking around soliciting pets, but now she was asking to go outside.

"Are you packed, Louise?" Dr. Clarke asked. She was sitting at the table writing in a small pad.

"The carpet bag is ready and tomorrow I'll finish the small portmanteau."

"Well, why don't you and Queenie take the carpet bag down to the depot now. Your train leaves very early and it will make things easier come morning."

"That's a good idea. I'll just get my sweater and camera."

The sweater Louise belted on had a hem reaching almost to her knees and she pulled on the matching tam-o-shanter. The Frenchman whistled making her laugh as she hooked up Queenie, picked up her camera, and pushed her bag out the door with her foot. She was glad of the sweater when salt-laced, fresh air rushed to greet her. A few deep breaths and Queenie's tugging at the leash brought her to the realization that carrying her camera and holding the leash would make getting the carpet bag to the depot difficult. Luckily, she saw a boy playing on the beach and waved him over.

"I'll either pay you or buy you candy if you'll help me get this bag to the train station," she said.

"Candy." He gave her a gaped-tooth grin and hoisted the bag up using both hands. His frequent rest stops gave Louise opportunities to see how long strips of bark clogged the bay; gave her time to enjoy the sun glistening off the rocks, and to watch a pair of otters frolicking in the surf. The *Retriever* still listed heavily to its starboard side, its rigging skewed, but, already, one or two men were doing something on her deck. Then Queenie tried to roll on a rotting fish, and she tugged her away, hurrying to catch up with the boy. They were all glad when they reached the bustling depot, but the boy, in particular. With her bag stowed safely away, he had a sufficient spurt of energy to run to the store and was well inside the store when she reached it.

"Well, now," said the proprietor, "I hear you're leaving us."

"Yes, sir." Louise smiled and turned her attention to the candy.

"And Aluk tells me you're paying him in candy?"

Louise laughed. "His choice, cash or candy."

After careful deliberation, Aluk chose a Hershey bar and a bag of Cherry Mash and she threw in a new candy called Mary Janes. He left with a big grin while Louise bought some candy to share with the patients, to take on the train, and some bread and cheese to share with Queenie.

Outside, at the edge of the boardwalk, a path meandered away from the houses. Queenie tugged, wanting to investigate and Louise let her pet lead the way through low-growing clusters of salmon berry, Oregon grape, and other wind-stunted plants. Western red cedars started on her left up a hill, then the trail leveled off, straggling along the edge of a bluff. Winded, Louise sat on a large rock and stared down at the bay. People looking no bigger than ants were again either digging clams or picking mussels off old pilings.

"It'll be a long time before I want any seafood again," she told Queenie. Above her, a hawk with wings spread wide floated on an updraft of warm air. Smaller birds chased it, protecting their nest. Louise took a deep breath, letting it out slowly. Queenie sat at her feet and inspected interesting odors on the path. *Deer,* Louise thought, *or elk, or even bear.*

A small bird joined them, hopping down and probing the dirt. After her brief rest, Queenie stood, scaring the bird and indicating she was ready to go on. A few hundred yards later, the path ended at a place where the bank had broken loose and a scree of stones slid down onto the beach, giving Louise an unobstructed view of the sad-leaning ship. She dropped the leash and stepped on it, then got her camera out and took several photographs, the last which caught an unexpected ray of sun reflecting off the masts. *That will be interesting,* she thought. Behind her, something rustled in the bushes and when the hair on Queenie's back stood up and she emitted a low growl Louise decided it was time to head back.

Coming within sight of the beach, she saw that most of the people were gone. A gentle breeze pushed the briny smells around and they mingled pleasantly with the smoke. Wavelets teased the shore, advancing and receding as the tide crept up. Queenie's nose never stopped twitching, and her silky ears blew back. When they reached the house and Louise pushed the door open, they both were glad of the living room's warmth.

"It's getting chilly out there," she said looking around.

"I'm afraid you'll be giving up your bed tonight," said Dr. Clarke. She was cutting potatoes into cubes and adding them to a pot on the stove, and Louise sniffed appreciatively.

"I bought some candy for the men," she said, putting a sack on the table. "Can I hand it out?"

"I think they'd like that." The doctor put a lid on the pot and rinsed her hands off. "Awena brought us a pot of stew but if we're going to feed the all patients and have some ourselves, I decided I'd better add more vegetables."

Louise mentally scrambled before remembering Awena was Father De Rouge's housekeeper. "What kind?" she asked.

"Venison." Dr. Clarke laughed knowing Louise's aversion to it. "And I'll take a piece of that candy."

"I'll just eat the potatoes." The floor was covered with men sleeping or just resting on sagging pallets. One or two snored and Louise gave candy to those who were awake. Then, while the stew simmered and the fire snapped and crackled, the two women took their accustomed chairs near the warmth and picked up their knitting.

"Louise," Dr. Clarke broached a subject she'd been pondering. "You did a good job with the injured men, and I checked your suturing; it was spot on. What sort of things did you do when you helped Matthew out at Camp Lewis?"

"Um," Louise, who was prone to picking up extra stitches in her knitting, stopped and counted what she had on her needle. "I cleaned areas on the men's upper arms for the shots, cleaned the used needles, waved smelling salts around where needed, and rubbed Arnica on bruises and lumps." After a minute she looked up. "Why?"

"I think you'd make a good nurse. Funny, I said the same thing to Nell. Did she ever tell you?"

Louise dodged the question. "Nurse? But I want to be a photographer. That's why I'm here."

"There's a desperate need for nurses overseas and it's just a matter of time before Matthew has to enlist."

"Matthew." Louise made a rude noise. "I haven't received a single letter from him. Anyway, I'd have to go back to school, probably for several years, and by the time I graduated, the war will be over."

"There's a new class of nurse now called an auxiliary nurse. They're part of the Red Cross, trained to assist the full-fledge nurses."

Before Louise could answer, a voice came from one of the nearby pallets. "I'd let you nurse me, *mon cheri*." And both women laughed.

They rocked and knit in companionable silence until Dr. Clarke said, "I think it's time to see about dinner." She went to the stove, lifted the lid on the big Dutch oven, and stirred the contents. The room immediately filled with the comforting aroma of meat and vegetables. "Let's take care of the patients first," she said. "I think only two of the men will need to be fed."

Louise sliced and buttered some bread and found enough spoons and bowls for everyone who was awake. Those who were able, sat up to eat but, with a thin draft of cold, foggy air creeping under the door bringing in an early-evening chill, they remained where they had been sleeping so as to snuggle back down again. They talked quietly among themselves while the two women made ready to feed the bedridden.

"You can't eat while flat on your back," Louise said to the sailor in her bed.

"I'm not hungry." He turned his head away.

Louise put the bowl she carried on the table and blew on her hands to cool them off. "You have to eat to build your strength back up. I wish we had more pillows, but we don't so I'm going to slide you up a bit and bunch up the bearskin behind your back." She slid her arms under his. "I'll be as gentle as I can."

"Every movement hurts."

"I know and I'm sorry."

"How would you know?"

"I just went through something similar myself and I have a big scar on my back to prove it. Now, bear with me and it'll be over in a moment." Sweat broke out on his forehead and Louise tried to ignore his groans.

"This is your bed," he said, "isn't it?" he said while she wiped his face with a cool cloth.

"It was."

"I can smell your perfume in the bedding."

It was a strangely intimate thing to say, and Louise began stuffing the few things left in the room into a small bag. "Think you could eat something now?" She sat on the edge of the bed, picked up the bowl and gave him a small spoonful. "What's your name," she asked and then laughed. "Best swallow first."

"Luke Peasley." The young man took his time and chewed carefully before swallowing. "Good."

"And where were you headed?"

Over the next half hour, he told Louise that the Koala Company had contracted with captain of the *Retriever* to deliver copra to a number of ports on the west coast.

"What is copra, exactly?" Louise asked while slipping Queenie a piece of venison. "Never mind; you're getting tired, aren't you?"

"I'm okay. Just give me a minute." Luke relaxed into the bearskin before speaking again. "It's the white stuff inside a cocoanut."

"Really." Louise handed him the slice of bread and lit the lantern. "We use that for cookies. Who would want a shipload of it?"

Luke started to laugh but pain made him stop and take some shallow breaths. "Some companies press it and make soap out of the oil; some make feed cakes for livestock. This is all headed for Portland." He sighed and closed his eyes. "Can you do me a favor?"

"What is it?"

"Would you send a note to my wife and tell here where I am? She didn't want me to come on this trip."

"Why did you?"

"I have a twin brother. We had a fight, and I want to bring him home." Before Louise could respond, he said, "please."

"Of course I will. Let me get some paper."

Luke dictated a short letter and managed to give her the address before falling asleep. He'd finished all the stew which returned color to his face, and Louise blew out the light and joined Dr. Clarke in the main room. A log in the fire burned through sending smoke into the room. Louise opened the door until the air was clean. She filled a bowl of stew for herself and picked out all the venison for Queenie. Shadows were dancing on the walls while she asked, "Will you be able to manage by yourself after I leave?"

"By tomorrow I'll just have the men who currently occupy our beds." She gave a gentle push to start rocking but, for once, her hands were idle. "I have to admit it's been a long day, and I will miss my bed."

"I'll be as quiet as I can when I leave." Louise yawned, stretched, and pulled her sweater over shoulders. "I miss my bearskin."

"It's always dank in here. In fact, a lot of the houses are. It doesn't help ward off all the TB."

"Don't you ever worry that you'll get sick?"

"I suppose I should, especially considering my age, but I don't. As a child, my dream was to live a good and useful life and both of those depend on good relationships. If I got sick, I've no doubt that the people here would take care of me."

"But what about your own family?"

"I have none, well, maybe some cousins back east but I was an only child, and my parents were older when I was born."

"Goodness." Louise considered her words. "I never thought about it but I'm an only child myself." She set her own chair to gently rocking and closed her eyes. "But at least I'm surrounded by family."

"And friends. I thoroughly enjoyed the Fourth of July picnic."

A single lantern and flames from the fire provided the only light; the smells of burning wood and remains of the stew circulated pleasantly. The doctor gently snored and the floorboards protested as the men shifted on their makeshift beds. Queenie's head shot up when something scooted along the porch and Louise shivered. *What a different sort of place this is, so isolated, so wild but happy; the people seem content, food isn't a problem, and there's always someone around if you need a helping hand. But it's not a very healthy place, and why isn't there electricity or running water?*

"Excuse me, Miss." The voice coming from the back of the room belonged to Mr. Kamell. "Could I trouble you for a drink of water?"

"Of course, and there's some stew and coffee left if you like." Louise stood quickly hoping Dr. Clarke wouldn't be disturbed. He drank half-a-glass.

"Well, a bit of stew would be real warming." Louise brought him a bowl and a piece of bread. Between bites he said, "Is this your first time away from home?"

"Yes. I came here to take photographs for a book."

"Well now, isn't that something. You a photographer." Mr. Kamell ate quickly and set the empty bowl where Queenie could lick it. "I remember my first time away from home. I was fourteen, gone over six months, missed my family something awful."

"Why did you go?"

"Ma couldn't afford to feed us all." Louise's whispered response went unheard. "My first trip—a train load of buffalo hides came in, and we took them to China. I never saw such a place, and I didn't get to see much because the captain kept an eye on me. But there were little boats with families living on them and people on the wharf cooking. Men rode in funny little wagons pulled by other men, and they all had a pig tail handing down their back. And everything smelled like smoke and fish and a bit like opium. We weren't there long because we were taking some Chinese people who had the money, from China to Hawaii and they were impatient to leave. They had servants who cooked their food. And then when we got to Hawaii, a prettier harbor you never saw. Some of the men threw pennies in the water and kids there dived down for them. Sometimes the waves were good sized, and men rode down them on boards. The whole place smelled like sugar cane and flowers." Mr. Kammel stopped talking and sighed. "We were only there long enough to buy supplies and load up the copra before we headed to San Francisco. When I got paid off, I sent most of my money to Ma and let her know I was signing on for another voyage. I tell you, Miss, on that trip I caught something called wanderlust and I been sailing ever since." He sighed again and pulled his blankets up. "Beggin' your pardon Miss, I didn't mean to bend your ear like that."

"Not at all. Coming here is the only trip I've ever taken. You've given me a lot to think about. You'd be welcome at my home in Tacoma, and you could tell us some of your adventures."

"That's mighty kind of you." He yawned and immediately apologized. "I think I can sleep now. Thank you for..." He fell asleep, the sentence unfinished.

Louise washed the dishes he'd used and returned to her chair wondering what time it was. She woke to the sounds of Dr. Clarke moving around the room.

"I heard you and Mr. Kamell talking last night."

"Yes." Louise fed Queenie and then washed her hands and face. "He wanted a drink and then ate some stew." She checked to see that the men were still asleep and quickly changed her blouse, then hooked Queenie up to her leash, and shrugged on a sweater coat. It would be a long trip home.

"I've made you a couple sandwiches and put them in your bag."

"Oh, how kind." Louise's eyes filled with tears, and she hugged the tired-looking woman. "I'm at sixes and sevens about leaving you."

"Don't be dear. I will be leaving in a week or so myself. Now, go." She gave Louise a little push. "Have a good trip."

And, with her camera and bag in one hand and the leash in the other, Louise stepped out into the cool, morning air.

Chapter 11

The morning train to Neah Bay arrived late in the afternoon, after which it stoked up, ready for the return trip. Queenie balked at having to board and Louise lifted her in and tied her leash. A man waiting to board helped her with her bag and camera case.

"Thank you."

"I'll take it to where you're sitting."

"I'd appreciate it. Queenie doesn't like trains."

"I can see that."

Louise found a seat close to the coupling where the air would be freshest and hoisted her shivering dog next to her onto the seat. Though the air was fresher where they sat, men were already puffing away on an assortment of smoking paraphernalia. Their voices filled the car, Queenie crawled onto Louise's lap, and she tucked her sweater around both of them. Once, looking out the window, she thought she saw Peter standing near the track, staring at the train. Before she could wave, the train was already moving and picking up speed as it rumbled down the tracks, rolling side to side, clattering when its wheels struck joints in the rails. With a sad heart, she dozed off and on, pausing only to share a sandwich with her dog.

Late in the day they reached Aberdeen. While Queenie made use of the first thing she found, Louise learned that there was a train leaving for Tacoma in an hour and bought a ticket. The depot had a small kitchen counter which sold food specifically to be taken aboard.

"What's biscuits and Sawmill gravy?" she asked when it was her turn to order.

"The gravy has sausage in it," said a man standing next to her. They were at the end of the line, and they both heard the release of steam as the train prepared to start.

"Wonderful. That's what I'd like." Louise started fishing around for money to pay for it.

"Let me." The same man passed some bills across the counter, and the waitress handed them each a wooden spoon and a Morton salt container with enough of the top cut off so that it could be filled with food. Louise and Queenie quickly reboarded, her benefactor behind them, just as a man closed the train doors.

"I'm happy to pay for my food." The train shuddered and Louise fell into her seat. "Where are you sitting?"

"It's my pleasure, Miss." He made his way down the aisle and Louise wondered how bad she must look if a man she didn't know chose to buy her a meal. *Charity begins at home*, she thought, *or in this case, in Aberdeen*. She took a spoonful of the food and couldn't believe how good it tasted. Queenie pawed her knee, and she gave her some sausage. Between the two of them, they finished it in a matter of minutes, and Louise was sure she could have eaten the contents of two more containers. "Still," she said to her pet, "we have two sandwiches left. Shall we?" Queenie cocked her head and watched Louise get out another sandwich. Each ate half and then Louise alternately looked out the window at the passing scenery and tried to read her book. However, scratchy eyes and a throbbing headache from a lack of sleep made reading difficult. *Why is it so hard to relax when I'm so tired*, she wondered? Somewhere behind her a card game had started up, filling the car with shouts and accusations as players slapped the cards on a table. The train rolled through a rain shower; the scenery changed from heavily wooded to grassy prairie and, occasionally, to pastures. Children, bringing cows home for milking, paused to wave; women removed laundry from clothes lines, and once, Louise saw a doe and two half-grown fawns. The passenger car's swaying gave her nausea and Queenie spit up. When, finally, they pulled into Tacoma's Union Depot, Louise wondered how many hours they'd been traveling.

"Home at last," she said to Queenie while gathering her things.

"Been away long?" It was the man who'd bought her the biscuits and Sawmill gravy.

"Two weeks." Louise took the porter's hand and stepped down. She'd only been in the large brick and terra cotta building once before, and after trying to ditch the man, took a minute to stand on floors that were highly-polished marble and look with pleasure at the arched windows and stone columns under the station's copper-clad dome. The noise, however, was overwhelming. People pushed their way to barbershops, newspaper stands, and to a ticket office. They crowded around the telegraph office or went to get their shoes shined, ordered sandwiches at a lunch counter and looked for family and friends. Hoping to evade the inquisitive man, Louise looked for the telephone, only to see that it was out of order.

"Would you like to share a cab?" The over-friendly man was right behind her.

"No, I don't think so."

"After I bought your meal and all, it's the least you could do."

Louise looked at him. "I didn't ask you to pay for my meal, and I offered to reimburse you. Now, go away and leave me alone."

The man grabbed her arm. "Well, aren't you the little uppity thing."

"And you, sir, are no gentlemen. Now, let me go."

He might have continued to grip her arm had not Queenie lost her temper and bit him on the ankle. With a howl, he jerked back and hearing the commotion, the station master hurried over.

"Is this lady causing you trouble?" he said to the man.

"The very idea. I most certainly am not." Louise drew herself up. "But he is certainly causing me trouble. He keeps following me around and won't leave me alone. Perhaps you can help me find a cab. I am returning from a business trip and I'm tired and want to go home."

By this time, a crowd had gathered, and a man worked his way up until he was standing near the station master. "Seems to me," he said, "if she let him buy her dinner, the least she could do is share a cab in return."

Others in a group nodded and spoke among themselves. By this time, Louise's fatigue was replaced by red-hot anger and she spoke loudly so her voice would carry. "I don't know who this man is, nor do I want to. As I said, I offered to pay for my food, but he refused. Your phone is broken, or I would have called my uncle Ike Tanquist to pick me up, but since I am unable to do that, I want a cab which I have no plan of sharing. It seems to me that this station isn't safe for a woman, and I fully intend to make that fact known."

"Excuse me," said someone who had just walked in. "I have a cab, and I am happy to take Miss Tanquist home." He picked up her bags. "If you'd like to follow me."

"With pleasure." Walking away she heard some of the men talking and heard one of them say "Ike Tanquist?" *Well,* she thought, *for whatever reason he has a reputation in town, and it saved my hide. I wonder what he'll say when I tell him.*

Fifteen minutes later, when the cabbie reached her home, the house was dark, and he was reluctant to let her out of the car.

"Are you sure you this is right?" he asked.

In answer, Louise let Queenie out and, after taking care of business with a plant, the dog raced up the walk and sat on the doorstep wagging her tail.

"I guess it is."

"If you'd just leave my bags on the step, I'll take care of them." Louise paid the driver generously and called Queenie. She waited until the cabbie drove away, then walked around to the back door and let herself in. While the dog headed for her water dish, Louise went to the foot of the stairs. "I'm home," she shouted and within minutes was joined by Nell and Annie.

Ten minutes later they sat around the table drinking hot chocolate and catching up on each other's news. "Maybe that explains the broken phone at Union Depot," Louise said after learning that City Council members were surprised and angry to learn that the phone company had been replacing all the phones in downtown business offices with nickel-in-the-slot phones. Princess had jumped on her lap and she cuddled the purring cat. "It's probably why someone broke the one at the Depot—kids, maybe, trying to get the coins out." Meanwhile, a group of Tacoma women were trying to get some much-needed comfort stations installed at various places in the main business district, and a gasoline stove exploded in the People's Store tea room. Louise washed her cup, yawned and stretched. "My bags are still out front, and I desperately need a bath not to mention a good night's sleep. No, no hugs. I'm definitely not fresh as a daisy."

Lousie put Princess down and fed Queenie. She brought her bags in and carried them upstairs, then took a much needed bath. Annie made her a thick, meaty sandwich and brought it upstairs with a glass of cold milk and a handful of cookies all of which Louise thoroughly enjoyed. With a full stomach, she dropped into bed wide awake one minute and sound asleep the next.

The next morning, she found a cup of cold coffee someone had put on her nightstand. Downstairs, Annie was singing in the kitchen, and Nell was chastising Princess for something the cat had done. Louise put on an old, faded, and very comfortable dress and ran downstairs. Queenie rubbed her legs, asking for food and she filled a bowl with table scraps.

"Are you going into work today?" Nell asked.

"No. I'm going to eat, do laundry, and call Matthew. First things first, though. I feel like I'll never be full again." Poking through the icebox, she found the last of a package of sugar-cured bacon and put it in a pan to fry. While it cooked, she peeled and diced a large potato and added it to the pan.

"Didn't they feed you up north?" Annie asked.

"A lot of fish and game."

"Well, enjoy the bacon. The price just keeps climbing."

Louise filled a plate with her food, then added buttered toast, and a glass of milk.

"I can start your laundry."

"No, Annie." Louise said. "I'll do it. I don't have much planned for today." She was busy splitting a slice of bacon between Queenie and Princess and missed the surprised look Annie and Nell exchanged.

Louise had just hung up the last of her laundry and was enjoying how the warm grass felt on her bare feet when Queenie stood and gave one woof. Looking up, Louise saw Matthew walking slowly across the yard.

"You're home," he said while removing his hat. "I thought you'd call."

Truth-be-told, Louise didn't know why she hadn't called and decided to dodge the comment. "Oh, my gosh, you're so thin." She took him in her arms, and he buried his face in her hair. "What has happened to you?"

"Can we sit down first?"

The kitchen was the favorite family gathering place and taking his hand, she led him there. Sunlight filled the room, mingling with the smell of the apple strudel Annie was taking out of the oven. She put it on a large plate to cool. "Wait a bit before cutting that," she said, "and dust it with a bare minimum of powdered sugar. I'm going across the street and see to Dovie. She's been feeling a little fragile lately."

Annie left and Louise poured two cups of coffee. When she sat down, Matthew took her hand. Princess jumped on the table and Queenie wore her best hung-dog look. Both went ignored.

Matthew's pale face and the circles under his eyes frightened her but before she could comment, he said, "I've been ill." His thumb rubbed her palm until eventually he kissed it and held it against his cheek. "I wasn't feeling all that well before you left but I no sooner got to Carbonado than I collapsed. One of the men taking the train down to Tacoma told my aunt and she immediately sent word that I was to return home. Uncle wasn't best pleased I can tell you. He has some sort of arrangement to provide medical care at Carbonado and the outlying towns. Without me there, he lost a fair amount of money."

"He could have gone up himself."

"Uncle prefers taking care of local society."

For lack of a ready response, Louise sputtered and her face flushed in anger. "Will he let you stay home?"

"He says I can take care of a few of his Tacoma patients until I get some meat on my bones."

"And then?"

"If he has his way, back to the same old grind, I guess. Ever since I graduated, I've saved everything I could, but I don't have near enough to start my own practice. And I have put out a few feelers, but no one wants to take me on. Of course, in all likelihood I'll be drafted."

"Does your uncle have anything to do with no one wanting to hire you?"

"Probably." Matthew released her hand and rubbed his face. "God, I'm so tired."

Louise stood and wrapped her arms around him. Neither said a word and then the phone rang. Muttering under her breath, she left the kitchen, and Matthew, hearing her side of the conversation, knew almost immediately who she was talking to.

"Louise Tanquist speaking." After a few seconds of silence, she said, "Yes, we were just having a cup of coffee . . ."

"...no, I won't. . . I'm sorry, but I think it's better if he stays here where it's quiet, and rests awhile. . ."

"Well, again, I am sorry but, perhaps, you could do that yourself. . ."

Louise was doing her best to remain civil but perhaps it was her own lingering fatigue or perhaps it was her desire to protect Matthew, but after a few minutes during which she listened to the caller's words, she lost her temper.

"I was with Matthew when we went to rescue those two boys living in neglect on the tide flats but the *Times* had an article about it and heaped praise on you—your efforts, not his, and calling it a job well-done. I spent the day with him inoculating recruits out at Camp Lewis and, once again, the papers praised your work, not his."

There was another pause and then Louise said, "No, you listen to me. You have worked him to the bone and taken all the credit. You've paraded young women you think are socially acceptable in front of him in hopes he'll make a marriage that will enhance your reputation. You don't think much of me, and I don't really care because I think even less of you. After I hang up, I'm going to feed Matthew and then I'm going to make him lay down and rest. You, sir, may go to church religiously, but obviously the lessons aren't taking."

Louise hung up and, feeling faint and shaky, sat on the nearest chair, wondering, for a minute if she'd pass out. Since childhood, scenes such as this had always affected her in the same way. Queenie nosed her leg, and she patted the dog, grateful to have her nearby.

Annie came in the front door, saying she'd come for her knitting but would be going right back across the street. She hurried up the stairs and Louise returned to the kitchen. To her surprise, Matthew was laughing.

"I think the last time my uncle was talked to that way must have been when he was a child." He pulled Louise onto his lap. "I love you, Louise. Have I told you that?" Suddenly his lips and hands were everywhere and not until they heard Annie coming back down the stairs from her room did they break apart.

"Like I told your uncle, I'm going to feed you and then you're going to rest."

Louise found a bowl of eggs, decided to make creamed eggs on toast. While the eggs became hard boiled, she made the roux and toasted and buttered several slices of bread. Princess jumped on Matthew's lap, and he stroked her and drank his coffee.

"Have you ever had a canary?" he asked.

"No." Being careful not to burn her fingers, Louise peeled and diced the eggs and added them to the roux. "Why?"

"We had one, once, when I was growing up; we kept it in the kitchen. It was always singing while I was eating breakfast and getting ready for school."

Louise put his toast on a plate and covered it with the roux. It smelled good and she was glad she'd made enough or two. "I've been hungry ever since I got back from Neah Bay," she said, putting the two plates on the table."

"Didn't they feed you up there?" Matthew took a bite of his food and smiled. "You'll make a good wife and mother."

"Well, I have too much I want to do so I don't want to be a mother anytime soon. But, in answer to your question, yes, everyone was really generous and there was plenty of food, but it was generally either fish or game. That's what the locals used to pay Dr. Clarke with, and I'm not crazy about either."

Matthew grinned and his eyes almost vanished into laughter lines. "How can you live on Puget Sound and not like seafood? I'm not sure that's even legal."

Louise snorted. "Have you ever read the book, *Heidi*? She pretty much lived on goat's milk, bread and cheese. The perfect diet I always thought."

The two exchanged looks and simultaneously broke into laughter. When they finished the creamed eggs, Louise wiped their plates off and cut the strudel.

"Well, that's different," Matthew said. "No dessert plates?" Using his napkin, he cleaned his fork.

Taken aback, Louise thought about his words. Then, while they ate, Matthew asked her to tell him what all she'd seen while at Neah Bay, and so Louise described the whale harvest and the size of the longhouses, the many different kinds of canoes and the sounds of the potlatch and how it went on all night. What she didn't tell him about was the pair of deerskin gloves she'd found in her bag while unpacking: soft and delicately trimmed with shells, just right for a woman's hand. And tucked inside one was a piece of paper on which was written, *When someone becomes a memory, the memory becomes a treasure*. Peter, of course. *How lovely*, she'd thought. But the gift and the note had made her feel conflicted. She'd send him a thank you and possibly a book but her trip there was only that—a short trip she'd taken for a job. Then she remembered that he'd asked for a copy of the photograph he'd taken and quickly turned to Matthew and asked about Buckley.

"It feels old," he said. "Maybe because the houses are wooden with coal stoves for heat. There's no indoor plumbing; I could tell that on my first trip there." He stopped and laughed. "I think one reason my uncle doesn't like to go up there is because everyone has an outhouse. "I can't say I like them much myself." Hearing that, Louise vowed never to take him to visit her Aunt Indiana.

"As near as I can tell," he went on, "it's laid out in a grid. And since it's a timber and coal mining town, and a company town, the company owns and rents out just about everything from the houses to the stores. Also, because it'd small, there don't appear to be any cars; everyone walks or rides horses."

"But what about the people who live there? What are they like?"

"They're pretty much all immigrants: Welsh, Italians, Eastern Europeans. There's a public school, but the boys generally quit when they're old enough to start working in the mine." He sighed. "I'm always glad if there isn't an explosion; the black lung disease is bad enough." He stopped and tried to prevent a yawn, but Louise saw it and saw that he was very pale.

"That's enough," she said. "I meant it when I told your uncle that I want you to rest. So come on. Let's go upstairs." Louise took him to her room where he took off his shoes and jacket and lay back against the pillows. Almost immediately he was asleep.

Louise returned to the kitchen and saw Queenie pushing her dish around and laughed. "More food?" She gave her a cuddle and let her lick their plates. By the time the dishes were done Louise was also yawning and decided to lay down. Matthew had turned on his side and was sleeping soundly so she laid next to him and was soon asleep herself. Coming home an hour or so later, Annie saw them and was careful not to wake them. She pretended to have seen nothing but made a mental note to tell Nell.

Later on, when Louise walked Matthew to his car, he asked her if she would be growing out her hair.

"I don't think so, why?"

"Long hair is just so womanly, that's all."

She lingered outside for a bit, to think about that, and to enjoy August's warm weather. A hummingbird zipped by and began poking its beak into some morning glory blossoms clinging to the fence. The faces of three children popped up over the flowers, and it flew off.

"We have stilts," one of the boys shouted before tumbling off whereby his companions burst into laughter.

When Louise returned to the kitchen, the smell of beefsteak with onions and mushrooms had replaced that of the strudel. "Sit down, Annie," she said. "You rest and I'll peel the potatoes."

She was putting them on to boil when Nell came home. "Ah." Nell removed her shoes and wiggled her toes under the table. Louise brought her a cup of coffee. "Did you ever notice how much coffee we drink?"

"I have," Annie said. "I'm the one who does the grocery shopping."

They laughed at her wry tone and Nell took a deep swallow. "So, Louise, we hardly heard anything last night about your trip. How was it?"

"Eventful." Louise put a lid on the pot of potatoes and started getting out plates and silverware. "The people were kind and generous. Father De Rouge seemed pleased to have someone take the photographs he wanted though I'm not sure he trusted a female to do the job."

"Did you get to see the ocean?"

"No. There was a bad storm that damaged a ship, and it came into the bay for repairs. Dr. Clarke and I spent a day treating injured sailors. One had to take over my bed, and one woke up in the middle of the night and wanted to talk, that's why I was so tired—am still so tired. I didn't get much sleep."

"You look thin," Annie said.

"I found out that I don't like venison," Louise said. "Every time we had venison, I gave mine to Queenie, and you get tired of fish real fast." She finished setting the table and poked a fork in the potatoes. "Done and I'm starving."

Over dinner Louise learned more of what had happened while she'd been gone: Antoinette Rosin, well-known in Pierce County for illegally selling liquor, became the first female prosecuted under the prohibition laws. In Germany, people thought to have secret maps on their skin, were having lemon juice rubbed on them; closer to home, men were using City Hall's steam room to sweat out their colds.

"What a good idea," Louise said. "There ought to be days for women and children, too."

"Someone broke into the Sullvan sisters house and stole most of their clothes. And the police actually had the nerve to question me," Nell said. "The very idea; as if I would stoop so low."

We all focus on our own areas of interest, Louise thought while listening to Annie talk about flour prices, "...and so now the *Times* has printed a recipe for bread using grated potato," she was saying. "I swear, it fair boggles the mind."

Long after they'd finished eating the three lingered in the kitchen laughing and talking and knitting socks.

"I think it was Benjamin Franklin who claimed to have never left home without a good pair of socks," Nell said.

"Wearing or carrying?"

"He didn't say."

Louise laughed. "Well, if you tell me where to take them, I'll drop the socks off after work, tomorrow."

Nell put her needles down and rubbed her eyes. "They go to the Red Cross building on Eleventh Street not far from the bridge. You were there, I think, when it was being built."

Louise began clearing the table, loading the dishpan, and adding hot water. "I wonder if anyone is actually wearing the heel-less socks Dottie told me about." She gave an enormous yawn and Annie said she'd do the washing up.

Louise hugged both women, remembered to take care of her pets, and yawned again. "Gosh, it's good to be home."

After a hot bath, she snuggled down in bed with a new Sherlock Holmes book. Queenie made herself comfortable on one side and Princess sat on the windowsill, well-lit by a full moon. Frogs conversed with each other and an owl hooted, reminding Louise of her Neah Bay owl. She had laughed with Dr. Clarke over Peter's philandering, but truth-be-told, it didn't seem like him. *I guess sometimes good things just fall apart,* she thought.

Chapter 12

"Louise?" Nell poked her head around the open door. "Can I come in?"

"A 'course." Louise nudged the dog. "Queenie, move."

The dog climbed onto Louise's lap, and Nell plumped a pillow, and joined Louise on the bed. "Annie said Matthew was here today."

Louise sighed. "Oh, Nell, it was awful. I'd wondered why I didn't hear from him and then I found out that he's been sick, and he's so thin and pale. He said he hadn't been feeling well but his uncle made him go up to Buckley anyway and by the time he got there, he was so sick, when one of the men came down to town, he told Matthew's aunt who sent for him to return him."

"I remember, once, when Hildy was really sick," Nell said, reflectively. "Samuel was just a boy, then, about twelve or so, but he built a tent over her head and kept hot steam in it until he sweated the sickness out."

"Matthew's uncle never would have allowed that" Louise wiped her eyes and rooted around for a handkerchief.

Nell pulled one out of her pocket and handed it over saying, "You're very fond of him, aren't you?"

She was surprised at how long Louise took to answer, and then, at her answer. "I'm fond of Mr. Aldrich, too, but I always figured I'd stay single and live here with you an Annie."

Nell laughed. "I felt the same way when I was your age. I was just going to create beautiful clothes and swan around town making the women jealous."

Louise looked at her. "But you never married. Why didn't you marry John?"

"Well," Nell smiled at her daughter. "I guess I just wanted to always sail my own ship. Which brings me to some things I want to tell you." She handed Louise a small bag. "I'm not such a fool as to think you have no need for this."

Louise opened the pouch and removed some small sponges and a little beaker of what turned out to be vinegar. What's this?"

"It's so you won't get pregnant."

Louise made a startled noise and felt her face turning red. Before she could think of what to say, Nell exhaled as if releasing a long-held breath. "I hear all kinds of things at work, you know. That's why I'm not surprised Matthew's uncle made him work when he was ill. He, Dr. Altamont Sr., that is, worked hard when he first set up practice, I'll grant him that, but he's a nice-looking man who turned, first, into a dandy, and then into a first-rate lothario."

"So, he encouraged Matthew to join him in his practice but actually to do all the work?"

"It seems that way. Now, I want you to listen to what I'm going to tell you and not interrupt until I'm done." She paused for a minute. "I was very young when I went to San Francisco to buy fabrics, and Annie went with me. It was the year of the big football accident. Did you ever hear of that? No? Well, it was the eighth annual football game between Stanford University and the University of California at Berkeley, which was always played at the end of November or in early December. Across the street from the stadium where they were to play was the San Francisco and Pacific Glass Company building. A lot of people, the paper said from 500 to 1,000, who either couldn't pay the dollar to get into the stadium or just didn't want to, climbed on the glass company's roof to watch. The roof couldn't hold all of them and gave way. The lucky ones fell four stories onto the factory floor and were pinned down by binding rods. About a hundred were badly burned when they fell on the top of the furnace. And then the fuel pipes were severed, and many people were sprayed with scalding oil. Bodies were actually set on fire." She paused and looked at Louise. "And you're wondering why I'm telling you all this, aren't you? Well, it's because that's when I went into labor."

"What?" Louise quit stroking Queenie. "You went into labor? You had a baby?"

"We, that is, Annie and I, barely had time to make it back to our hotel and then we couldn't get a doctor to come because they were all busy with the accident victims. It ended up that Annie handled the delivery."

Louise's brain churned with questions but before she could speak, Nell said, "it was you. Did you never guess?"

"But I don't look at all like you."

"No, you look like John."

"John? John's my father?" Louise started to sit up, then fell back on her pillow. "Heavens to Betsy. I'm blowed." She pulled Queenie up and buried her face in the dog's head. Dog intuition made Louise's need known, and Queenie licked her owner's face. "First Peter being so unexpectedly attractive, then Matthew being so sick, and now..."

"Peter?"

"Someone I met at Neah Bay." She fingered the strings attached to the small sponges. "What's this all about?"

"Birth control." Nell put them back in the little pouch along with the vial of vinegar.

"And I suppose if you had known about birth control you wouldn't have had me." Louise flat out didn't know what to think.

"Oh, darling, please don't think that." Nell put her arm around Louise's rigid shoulders and tried to pull her close. "I always wanted you, that's why Annie and I went to San Francisco. If I'd stayed here, I'd have been shamed into trying to get rid of you or having you in secret and giving you up." She gave a rueful laugh. "Or Mother might have sent me to stay with Indiana on some pretext or another. Can you imagine what a horror that would have been?" She continued holding Louise until Louise sighed and relaxed.

"Do you know what the Comstock Laws are?" Nell asked.

"No."

"They came after the Civil War. They make anything having to do with birth control, that's what Margaret Sanger calls it, illegal. But now though, with the war and all, everything will be changing, society will change, and the Comstock Laws might change or even go away. After all, it was after the Civil War that gave all men, not just white men, the right to vote."

"That didn't do women much good, though. Did it?"

"No, but there will be changes. That's what war does. Anyway, I have some copies of *The Woman Rebel*. It's a magazine that Margaret Sanger publishes, that you might find interesting." She sighed. "Dovie might not be in the fix she's in right now if she'd had access to the magazine."

"Dovie? What's ailing Dovie?"

"Oh, Louise. You innocent. Dovie and Chong are expecting a baby."

"But—but. . ." Louise, who had half sat up, fell back on her pillow. "They're not married and Chong's Chinese, and Dovie's old."

"Well, obviously not too old." Nell gave a small laugh.

"But what will they do with a child?"

"They'll have to hope it looks enough like Dovie that it can pretend to be white, I guess."

"Is that possible? I never heard of such a thing. My goodness; poor Dovie."

"I actually think she's quite happy to be having a baby, but that's beside the point. I don't want you to be tied down with children unless that's what you want.

And being with a man is wonderful. You shouldn't be deprived of that for fear of an unwanted child. Matthew will no doubt go to war and before he does, he may have, er, expectations…" She let the sentence drop.

For a moment the room was quiet. Outside, a moth, attracted by the bedroom light, fluttered against the window catching Princess's attention. Then, squawking chickens followed by a shot gun blast broke the silence. "Poor Mr. Boylston," Louise said. "It's a nightly battle to keep critters out of his hen house." She sniffed the small vial of vinegar. "How did you learn about this?"

"From a couple of prostitutes, friends of Hildy."

Louise felt her chest tighten and uttered a high-pitched sound. "Prostitutes. Friends of Aunt Hildy. My sweet, kind, gentle Aunt Hildy once consorted with prostitutes. Oh, this just keeps better."

"Stop it, Louise. You're being overly dramatic, and I expect better of you. In the first place, you don't know the story and in the second, it was a different time and times were different. Tacoma was a rough frontier town. The ladies were kind and did Hildy a great favor. Ask her about it sometime, she'll tell you."

"Jiminy Crickets." Louise shook her head. "But won't Matthew know all this, about the sponges and vinegar, I mean?"

"From what Dr. Clarke has told me, I don't think this is a subject taught in medical school."

"Why not?"

"The Comstock Laws. However, he's young enough to probably know about French Letters. And before you ask, it's something a man wears to prevent pregnancy. The British army gives them to the men so they don't get diseases." When Louise looked as if she wanted to ask about the diseases, Nell said, "I'll bring you some magazines. Margaret Sanger can do a better job of telling you about them than I can." She squeezed Louise's shoulders. "I think that's enough for now. Good night, baby."

'Enough for now?' How could there possibly be any more? Alone again, Louise's thoughts swirled, and with all she'd just learned, she didn't think she could sleep. But sleep she did until dawn's chattering birds woke her. She'd hadn't had time to iron the clothes she'd washed the previous day but found a yellow tunic dress with short, cuffed sleeves pushed in the back of her closet. "Why haven't I worn this lately?" she asked Queenie. The dress's wide collar extended on down to the waist band and she examined it for tears. "It's one of my favorites."

No one else was up yet so she let Queenie out and started a pot of coffee. When they became available in Tacoma, Nell bought an Excello Power Washing Machine "Because," she said at the time, "house work is hard and time consuming so we might as well take advantage of everything that makes it easier." While the coffee heated, Louise loaded the washtub with dirty clothes, soap, and water, and cranked the lever until the agitator started. That done, she made sure everything she needed was in her camera case.

"You're up early," said Annie who'd joined her in the kitchen. "Thank you for starting the laundry. She looked in the icebox. "It'll be slim pickin's for breakfast, I'm afraid."

"I think I'll just have toast. I want to get to the studio early." Louise fed the animals and looked around. "Do you think we should get a canary?"

"I hadn't thought about it. Why?"

"Just something Matthew mentioned. It might be nice to have a bird singing."

"And throwing feathers and seeds around."

"Hmm. Matthew didn't mention that."

"It's not something men usually think about."

Louise cut two slices off a loaf of bread and put them on the toasting fork while Annie poured the coffee. "Henry Mohr's down on Commerce is selling electric toasters but they only toast on one side."

"I like toasting with a fork; I can feel the heat on my face." Louise turned her bread around. When it was golden brown, she added butter and jam and wolfed her food down. Nell was coming down the stairs and, on her way out the door, Louise shouted "goodbye."

The streetcar was crowded and Louise waited until everyone else boarded, before she lifted Queenie in, paid the conductor, and managed to squeeze onto one of the wooden benches. From there she enjoyed a favorite pass time: listening to snippets of conversations. A group of men sitting close to each other were discussing the baseball teams which local businesses sponsored. The planned parade for members of the G.A.R. and Spanish-American War Veterans came in for some pithy comments, as did the parking problem in town. Of more interest to Louise, though was a whispered conversation between two women about a chain gang working at the White Shield Home for Unfortunate Women. "It's just not seemly," one murmured.

"I don't suppose the girls'll be tempted by the likes of men from the jail, though."

"Nevertheless..."

While they got off, Louise thought about the White Shield Home and about her conversation with Nell, about Margaret Sanger and about The Comstock Laws, and about Dovie and Chong. *Thank heavens that'll never happen to me*, she thought.

Due to an election, and so the men would have time to vote before work, most downtown stores had opened an hour late and the streets were unusually empty. However, Louise wasn't prepared to be stopped at the studio door by a policeman. "Ma'am." He doffed his cap. "I'm here for the carding."

"Pardon me?" Louise unlocked the door, and he followed her inside.

"The carding, Ma'am, the index carding."

"I'm sorry, but I don't know what that is." When he began to look exasperated, she added, "I've been out of town and haven't seen the papers." Louise put her camera case down and removed the film to be developed. "Do you mind if I put these in the darkroom; you can stand by the door, but don't open it, and explain?"

"Oh, well, you see Ma'am," he said, raising his voice, "we, that is the police, are making an inspection and list of every store, storeroom, hotel, factory, hospital, factory, theater, and office building within the city limits. And all the information will be written down on cards and kept in alphabetical index cases at central station."

"For goodness sakes, why?"

"In case of emergencies."

"Isn't having to get all that information and keep it up to date a lot of work? Whose idea is this?"

"The police chief's." The officer removed a small notebook from his pocket. "Now, I will be responsible for this building, as well as a few others in this part of town, and I already have your address. I can see that it's a photography studio, and there is only one floor so no elevator or stairs. But how many rooms?"

"Uh, three, I guess, this one, the darkroom, and a storeroom."

"And I need the owner's name, address, and telephone number and the occupant's name, address, and telephone number." The phone rang while he was recording the information. Louise finished her conversation with the caller and the officer asked, "What happens if no one remembers to lock the door at night?"

"Uh. . ."

"Exactly. With the information readily available, all we have to do is call Central, get the proprietor's phone number, and then contact that person."

"Why doesn't someone at Central make the call?"

Looking somewhat chagrined, the officer pocketed the information. "It was the Chief's idea, and this is the way the he wants it. Ya gotta take that up with him" The phone rang again and he left while Louise took care of the call.

The day's first appointment arrived, followed by Mr. Aldrich.

"Stuff and nonsense" he said when Louise told him why the policeman was there. "He can just go to a call box, call the issue in, and Central can call the appropriate party."

Louise bit her lip to keep from laughing. "Well, he took away all the time I set aside to start developing my film," she said.

"Not to worry. There's generally a lull in early afternoon."

Late in the day, when the negatives were finally hanging up in the darkroom, Mr. Aldrich spent a long time considering each one. "You have some fine shots, here, Louise. Father de Rouge should be pleased, but there's one that's particularly fine. I think it should be enlarged and framed and put in the window, here."

"The one with sun on the listing ship? I like it, too. I was particularly lucky when the sun came out just at that moment."

"Lucky, yes, but you have a good eye." He sat at his desk and Louise knew something serious was on his mind. "Do you read the newspapers; that is, do you follow the war news?"

Louise pulled the customer's chair closer and sat. "No, I don't, I know I should but what with Nell and Annie talking about it all the time, I only just want to read the society news."

"Next time you get the paper, look at the photographs accompanying the war news. They aren't of men posing; they were taken in the moment. Candid shots with friends, pets, in the trenches, in the hospital. The days of people coming to a studio like this are fading away. And we have to be able to adapt. Now, I have a gift for you." He opened a desk drawer and handed Louise a package which, once opened, revealed a book. "It's a photo-essay book."

Louise flipped through the pages and stopped at a photograph labeled 'The Open Door.' A few pages on she saw 'The Bridge of Orleans.' "What a lovely gift," she closed the book and beamed at her boss. "Thank you so much."

"It's not just a book; among photographers, *The Pencil of Nature* is considered to be the first commercially published book with short essays accompanying pictures. It's fortunate you took so many photographs at the reservation because this is what I was thinking about when I said you could make a photo-essay book."

"Gosh." Louise opened the book again and saw that under a picture called 'The Haystack' there was a short description of the scene and the process used to capture it.

"There's a new interest in various lives and cultures about which most people know nothing. And, right now, there's a lot of interest American Indians. The government has been opening up some tribal land to white settlers; some men from the Yakima tribe were stopped—forcibly kept off their traditional salmon fishing site. Did you know some people are espousing the idea of 'Kill the Indian but save the man'? The time for a book on one of the tribes is ripe. I'll help you select the photographs and your friend, Dovie, can help with the writing."

"Right now, I think Dovie has other things on her mind."

"The baby she's expecting, yes I know."

"You do?"

Mr. Aldrich cleared his throat. "I've been a photographer for a long time, and she was at the picnic."

"Well, for goodness sakes."

Her boss laughed. "Tomorrow we'll go through the negatives and print the pictures Father de Rouge wants. Then we can choose ones for a book."

They closed the studio for the day, and Louise left with a lot to think about. She was halfway to the streetcar stop when it occurred to her that Matthew wasn't waiting, as was his want, to take her to dinner. *I wonder what his uncle is up to now,* she thought. Ahead of her, a group of men clustered around a cider vendor and caught her attention. Lately, some of the cider peddlers had taken to letting their beverage age into alcohol, and from the looks of the crowd, the purveyor ahead of her was one of them. He had set up his stand next to one where ice cream was being sold, also a common practice to make it difficult for the police to figure out who wanted a cone and who wanted a drink. Louise stopped and decided to give tutu fruitti ice cream a try. While waiting her turn, she read a poster announcing the arrival of Senior Don Alfonso Zelaya as part of the New Pantages vaudeville show.

"Looks exciting, doesn't it?" said the ice cream peddler. "There's going to be talking birds and knife throwers and all kinds of things.

Louise smiled. "My dog talks by pawing me and right now, she's telling me she needs a dollop of ice cream." He laughed and dropped a spoonful on the cement.

The weather was cool enough to make a walk home bearable but once there, both Louise and Queenie welcomed a drink of cool water. Nell had a box of used clothes on the floor beside her chair and was picking the seams apart. When she looked up, Louise gasped. "You're wearing glasses."

"I said I was going to look into them." She laughed. "Hah! A pun—purely accidental but I wish it weren't."

"I know, but, gosh. Where did you go?"

"Kachlein's."

"Golly." Louise sat at the table and looked at the clothing. Nell had an additional pair of scissors nearby, so she went to work, helping. "Do you like 'em?" she asked while picking at a seam.

"I can see."

"Huh." Louise wiggled out of her shoes. "I'm hungry. What's for dinner?"

"Dried fish chowder." Annie came in from the garden in time to hear the question, "and corn bread."

"Fish? Princess might like that."

"I'm sure my chowder will be better than the fish stuff you ate at Neah Bay and as for Princess, she needs to kill a mouse once in a while."

Louise cuddled her cat. "She doesn't like mice."

Annie added seasonings to the chowder and carried a plate of cookies over to the table.

Louise helped herself and bit into one. "These are new. What are they?"

"Dutch Moons."

"What's the filling?" She finished the first one and took a second."

"War time honey berry jam. One of the Aide ladies got the recipe from a cousin in England."

Louise stood up and gave Annie a kiss on the cheek. "You do a wonderful job, what with the war restrictions and all, of keeping us well-fed."

"Ah, go on with you." Annie turned red. "I saw your beau earlier."

"Matthew? Where?"

"Standing outside his office, talking to a young woman."

"Gosh, I wonder who."

"A pretty blonde with a pompadour."

"Sounds like Mrs. Baker's niece, Mildred, but then there are a lot of pretty young blondes in Tacoma." Looking pensive, Louise decided a cup of coffee was in order.

"Did you buy a new book?" Nell asked. She picked up another article of clothing and turned it inside out.

"Mr. Aldrich gave it to me." Louise opened it to a Paris street scene and turned it so Nell could see. "It's called a photograph-essay book, and he wants me to try my hand at creating one with some of my Neah Bay pictures."

Nell, with Annie leaning in to look, read the caption aloud before gently closing the cover and tapping it with her finger. "I think that's a wonderful idea, and along those lines, I have another. Why not offer to take some pictures for Dovie's book on Tacoma's history."

"Truth be told, I forgot she was writing one."

Nell sighed and rubbed her eyes, and Annie brought her a wet rag. "I'm afraid most of us have shown little interest in her book." She tipped her head back and put the cloth on her eyes, "but it's a worthwhile thing to do and I think she'd appreciate the offer. So many of the old things are already being torn down so something new can go on the land."

Louise sighed. "Well, I don't want to, but I'll offer."

"That's my girl. And Annie, if the chowder is done, how about just putting the pot on the table and we can help ourselves. This feels like one of those days when we shouldn't stand on formality."

It wasn't until later that evening that Louise heard from Matthew.

"Where is it you've been really wanting to go?" he asked when she answered the phone.

"The ocean?"

"Guess again."

"Well, we haven't had our picnic yet."

His warm laughter filled the phone. "I know and we will, but someplace else, someplace that's not quite so far away. Think closer to home."

"Uh?"

"Haven't you been wanting to see the internal workings of the powerhouse?"

"And take pictures?"

"What else, but that's not all. Where else have you wanted to visit?"

"I don't know. Where?"

"K Street. We're having a small dinner here today, but I have Sunday off, so how about I pick you up after church at around eleven? We can visit the power plant

240

and then drive up to K Street, have something to eat and just walk around."

"Oh, Matthew. That sounds wonderful. I can just hardly wait. I can't believe you actually remembered."

'Hah. How could I forget? Uncle Altamont thinks it's odd, but my aunt says it promises to be an interesting day, and said if she were ten years younger, she'd want to do the same thing."

They chatted for a few minutes and before hanging up, something told Louise to say, 'Tell Mildred, 'hello.'"

"I will," Matthew surprised her by saying."

Well, I didn't expect that, she thought.

When Louise returned to the kitchen, her Uncle Ike was sitting at the table eating a piece of cornbread and telling Nell and Annie about a streetcar accident. "Boys that age shouldn't be working," he said, pushing a bit of cornbread to one side of his mouth so he could talk. Louise poured herself the last of the coffee and sat next to him.

"Who? And how old was he?"

"Twelve."

"Twelve! What was he doing working?"

"Supporting his family."

Louise choked on her coffee and Nell asked about the phone call. "Matthew has arranged for me to see inside the powerhouse on A Street and then we're going for a walk on K Street."

"Why would you want to see inside the powerhouse?" Annie asked.

"Because I hear it controls the streetcars and I hear it every day and I want to see what makes the noise." She and Uncle Ike both reached for the last piece of cornbread. "I had a serious injury and need to eat to help rebuild my strength," Louise said, while her uncle explained that he worked hard to support his family and needed to stay healthy. With a sigh, Annie found a knife and cut it in half.

"I guess you and I don't count," she said to Nell.

"Well, all I can say is, I hope your young man's intentions are honorable." Ike looked at his sister. "You want I should have a talk with him?"

Louise screeched, Nell grinned, and Annie put the empty plate in the dishpan. A boy came to the door saying Ike's wife wanted him home and could he please have a ride back in the car because he'd walked.

Nell hooked her arm through that of her brother and sauntered with him and the boy out to the street, and Annie wandered down to inspect her vegetable garden. Louise, looking regretfully at the empty plate of cornbread, took her book up to her room. While wondering what so appealing about it a photograph labeled *The Ladder*, she fell asleep.

Looking forward to a day with Matthew in no way interfered with Louise's work at the photography studio. She had always been able to compartmentalize her interests.

"I am fascinated by some of the pictures in the book you gave me," she said the following morning. Negatives of the Neah Bay were spread out on the desk where both of them could see.

"Why do you think that is?" Mr. Aldrich asked.

"I don't know."

"Let's start by which photos you liked the best."

"I like *The Ladder* best."

"Not the street scenes? That surprises me."

Louise tipped her head to one side and considered his words. "Every town has street scenes but not everyone can make three men standing around a ladder seem provocative. Who are they? One doesn't seem to be a laborer but is he the boss? Could it just as easily have been three women; Nell, Annie, and someone else in the yard?"

"Making the ordinary seem extraordinary?"

"Maybe. Is that it? It's very humbling."

Mr. Aldrich laughed. "I wouldn't worry about it if I were you. You have a good eye and good ideas and will only get better. Now, what's on Father de Rouge's list?"

In between walk-in customers and appointments, they managed to find pictures to meet the Father's requirements. At the end of the day, Mr. Aldrich decided to stay in town and eat at Feeny's and Louise decided it was too hot to walk home by way of Japantown as she'd planned earlier. Instead, she and Queenie waited for the streetcar and hearing the sounds its cables made, she was glad she had a good supply of camera film.

Chapter 13

The following day, Matthew picked her up at a little after eleven and complimented her boater hat. "These feathers around the brim are called Rooster Hackles," Louise said. "Did you know that?"

"I did. Mildred Baker told me." Louise looked so surprised that he added, "The Bakers and my uncle and aunt are close friends, so I see a lot of Mildred. Now," he opened the car door, "Your chariot awaits."

He turned the car toward 11th Street and soon they were headed down the hill to the powerhouse on 11th and A Street. "I never really paid attention to this building before," Louise said as she looked at its high Victorian style. "It's old though. It was built in 1889." Matthew parked and they got out. "It's sort of medieval looking, isn't it?"

"Sam Perkins took the Bakers and us out in his yacht *El Primero* and you can just about see it from the water." Matthew took her arm and hustled her toward the building. "Sam won the yacht in a craps game; did you know that?" Without waiting or an answer, he added, "from Chester Thorne."

"Oh, poor Mr. Thorne," Louise said, adding, "but you never can tell when bad luck will turn out to be good luck, can you?"

"Wow, I'm impressed," Matthew said.

"Well, every now and then I have a deep thought." Louise grinned, but at the same time was thinking that he seemed to spend a lot of time with the Baker family. "When was this trip?"

"Um, after my uncle said I was fit enough to go boating. Sam was hosting a party, and we were invited.

It was mostly for newspaper people such as the Bakers. Frank Baker owns *The Tacoma Tribune*. Okay, here's the door. Be prepared to hear a lot of noise."

He opened the door, and the first things Louise saw were red lights created by flames behind the fireboxes' glass windows, and big, conflicting shadows on the walls of a very large room. Many times, in the morning, she'd heard a rumbling noise under the road, and she asked about it.

"What you hear is the steel cables," said a man Matthew introduced as Charles Schrum. He glanced at her but was mainly keeping an eye on the massive machinery. "They leave here and travel in ducts under the roads. There's a piece of equipment that looks like giant pliers that extends through a slot between the rails. When it grabs on to the cable, it pulls the car along." He waited while Louise took pictures of the huge drive wheels around which the thick steel cables were wrapped, and of the various pulleys. Warming to the subject, and to the interest a pretty young woman was paying, he continued. "Now, the gripman is of the most important person; he's the one who's in control. When he pulls on the rear grip handle, the grips tighten down on the cable and that starts the car moving. The harder he pulls back on the handle, the more pressure the grip puts on the cable, and he does that until the cable, and the cable car, are moving at the same speed." As Louise seemed to hang on his every word, which she, in fact, did because it was so hard to hear, he continued. "Up on the street, there's a grip lever that pokes up through a hole in the road; and each car also has a grip lever controlled by a gripman. He pulls a lever making jaws clamp onto the cable and pull it along. To stop, the gripman releases the grip and the car coasts or brakes to a stop."

Behind her, Louise felt Matthew beginning to fidget. "Thank you so much," she said. "This has been very kind of you to stop your work and show us around."

Mr. Schrum pushed his hat back. "Well, it's been my pleasure. The next time you're riding up a hill, watch the gripman." He followed them toward the door still talking. "He'll be working hard on the grip because a steep grade takes a lot more pressure, and then there's a central steam engine that makes it all run..."

He had to stop when Louise asked to take his picture. She promised to send him a copy, waved, and hurried out the door and to the car. For a minute neither she nor Matthew said a word. "Wow, that was loud," Louise eventually said, "but really worth it."

"Did you actually understand all that stuff?"

"No, he lost me on the third grip, but I love learning how things work, and I got some really interesting pictures."

Matthew leaned over and kissed her, his hand straying to her breast. "You are so beautiful when you're excited about something." His ardor grew until a car approached them and he reluctantly pulled away. With a sigh he started the car and began the arduous climb up the 11th Street hill to K Street. He found a parking place and, exiting the car, Louise was overwhelmed by the noisy sounds of the many people going in and out of the many businesses. She was looking around when a little boy in torn white shirt, and shorts held up by suspenders, and wearing a hat, ran by chasing a cat. He scared a flock of birds pecking in the grassy verge and all but knocked over three men with large black hats, and shawls over their shoulders who were walking in the opposite direction.

"They had pigtails by their faces," Louise said, turning around in time to see them turn the corner. "How very unusual.

Matthew took her arm, and they started walking, passing businesses she'd never heard of: Macksoud's Dry Goods and Notions, Ernest Niehoff's Grocery, and a shop labeled J.W. Fisher Confectionary. There were two tea shops, Gresham Tea Company, and Great American Tea Importing which had dozens of teapots on prominent display in the window. Through the open door of one small restaurant, she saw a man filling bowls with what she recognized as being Lutefisk. Further along, in the window of a confectioner's shop, a young woman was filling trays with hand-crafted chocolates. She wore a white blouse and full skirt with an apron. Her thick blonde hair hung in braids. She looked up and nodded and smiled when Louise stopped to watch and then gestured toward her camera. As she snapped away, Louise mentally crossed her fingers that taking a picture through glass wouldn't be a problem.

Faded awnings and large business signs extended from store fronts to the street. Homemade posters advertising church dinners, civic events, and concerts hung off poles from which electricity wires and telephone lines zigzagged haphazardly back and forth from each side of the road and drooped in the middle. A car covered in dirt and dust chugged past them and Matthew laughed.

"There's a dirt hill starting at Center Street," he said. "It's covered with tall grass and is pretty much impassable when it's been raining, but during summer men like to show off their cars by seeing if they can drive up it from bottom to top." He took Louise's arm, and they continued walking. "From the looks of it, that car just made it up."

"Gosh, I didn't expect so many different businesses, or to see so many foreigners. And look at all the different street peddlers," Louise paused. "For goodness sakes, what are those?"

The 'those' to which she referred were items wrapped in corn husks a street vendor was selling.

"They're tamales," Matthew said. "The Mexicans eat them."

"And the street even smells different."

"If you had a whole day to just sit and watch," Matthew said, "you'd see about every nationality there is. Italians, Swedish, Jews, Russians, and over near 15th Street is where the Japanese are settling."

"How do you know this?"

"Everyone needs a doctor sometime."

They stopped in front of a shop where a gentleman's suit was on display in a large window. And as they did, a man carrying a broom came out to sweep his doorway. "Mr. Nordi," Louise said, looking startled. "What an unexpected surprise."

"Well, my goodness, Miss Louise, what are you doing up here?" He chuckled. "Come to have me make you a dress?"

"Over Nell's dead body." Louise laughed. "We're sight-seeing." She introduced Matthew before continuing. "Nell would never let me come up here alone. The newspapers have her all het up about the Black Hand and she was afraid I might be kidnapped." She looked down the street where five old ladies, each wearing a scarf tied under her chin, made careful use of their canes. They passed several dogs sleeping undisturbed in doorways. "It's very different from downtown, isn't it?"

Mr. Nordi leaned on his broom. "Those ladies are from Ukraine. The war is bringing people from all across Europe to the United States, and many have settled here. My father brought me from Russia when I was very young. We left to escape the Czar's pogroms against the Jews."

Louise bit her lip looking puzzled. "Why doesn't he like Jews?"

"Many Europeans don't like Jews..."

Before he could go on Matthew stared at the tailor and said, "It's because they killed Jesus."

"Matthew!" Louise gasped, but Mr. Nordi merely nodded. "Yes, many people think that's the reason, however to us, he was not the Messiah." He started sweeping. "It's very complicated."

Recognizing dismissal and troubled by Matthew's remark, Louise took the time to say a pleasant goodbye and started walking, but Matthew quickly caught up with her and took her arm.

"Do you dislike Jews?" she asked.

"I used to think it was a very complicated issue," he said, "but Uncle Altamont teaches scripture classes at church, and he explained the issue. They did kill Jesus, and he was a Jew and one of their own, regardless of whether he was the actual Messiah or not. But, of course, he was. I can ask my uncle to tell you all about it I you want."

"No, I don't think so." Louise spotted a small restaurant. "Shall we have some lunch?"

Soon they were sitting at a window-front table eating potato chowder. "It's awfully warm for soup, isn't it?" Matthew tested a spoonful with his tongue.

"We can finish it and have ice cream." Louise smiled at him and then at some of the children who were sitting with their parents at a nearby table. One little boy was playing with a kitten tucked inside his shirt front. Seeing Louise looking at his pet, the boy tried to push it out of sight but relaxed when she grinned and winked. He smiled back showing the spot where two missing teeth had been, then turned his attention to an ice cream cone a waitress handed him. Louise's gaze followed the server as she returned to where more cones were lined up so people could see them. When she picked up another, Louise excused herself and walked over to see where the cones came from. Most of the kitchen was out of view but behind a low counter, next to the ice cream, a man was operating a four-iron waffle maker. While three waffles cooked, he removed the fourth and quickly rolled it into a cone. *It's certainly an exacting job*, Louise thought and later, when telling Annie and Nell all about it, explained that he had to keep batter on the hot surface and remember to flip the waffle over, all the while picking up the fourth one, rolling it and putting it in a stand to cool. "And then he had to pour more batter on the empty space," she said with something like awe in her voice.

Asking for, and receiving permission, she took several photographs of the operation. She was smiling when she returned to her table, and Matthew took her hand.

"I don't know if you remember but the government requested that each state submit a list of all licensed physicians with details about their age, experience, health, and availability to be drafted," he said. Louise nodded while at the same time trying to imagine Dr. Clarke in a uniform. "Well," Matthew continued, "I found out that the draft board can make temporary local deferments and Uncle Altamont wants me to apply."

"You mean you would still be here in Tacoma, not fighting in Europe?"

"Yes. All I have to do is make a presentation to the local draft board and tell the men there that I'm responsible for small communities in the foothills, the local dock workers, industrial workers, and lumbermen." He leaned close and half-chuckled. "I could even mention the Puyallup Indians though I haven't been on the reservation yet."

"You'd probably be given a white feather," Louise said dully and feeling stunned. Did she want him in the war, in danger on the front? Of course not, but still, did he mean to sound so happy to be able to get out of serving?

"Not if I have my medical bag with me," Matthew was saying. "And Uncle Altamont will claim economic hardship and religious scruples if I'm drafted. How lucky is it that I've been attending his scripture classes." Seeing how dumfounded Louise looked he began rubbing circles on the palm. It occurred to her that it was something he often did. "There's a hotel nearby. Oh, Louise, how much I want us to be together, really together, as in the biblical sense. Don't you?"

Still looking expressionless Louise said, "I didn't think to bring anything with me."

"What do you mean?"

"Any of my sponges and things so I don't get pregnant." Wondering if this had been his attention all along, she said, "Do you have a French letter?"

"What?"

"A *capote anglaise*?"

"I know what it is, but you know if anything happened, that I'd stand by you."

"'Stand by me?' What does that even mean?"

Matthew dodged the question, saying, "I'm amazed that you know about French letters."

"Nell told me."

Matthew's normally friendly expression changed to something Louise didn't recognize. "Of course she did."

"What do you mean?"

"I assume she didn't want you to get caught like she did."

"Caught?"

"With you. Uncle Altamont told me all about it, but I guess everyone knows."

"Knows what, exactly?"

"That she made a sudden trip to San Franciscan, supposedly to buy things for her shop, and returned four months later with a bunch of fabric and you. She told people you'd been orphaned in the big fire and that she adopted you. It was her good luck that your hair is so dark, otherwise she'd never have gotten away with the lie."

Louise was dumbstruck. "And what would you do if I did 'get caught' as you so quaintly put it?" She pushed away from the table and picked up her camera. "Would your uncle actually let you marry me? I think not, not a photographer, a working woman, not a dressmaker's daughter. I'm pretty sure he has in mind some higher class woman for you. Possibly Mildred Baker."

"Well, you can't argue the fact that she comes from wealth."

"Wealth? Is that what you want?

"Uh..."

"I think I'll walk home now, Matthew. Thank you for lunch and a very informative day."

"Wait, I'll take you," Matthew was saying as he jumped up but he had to stop and pay for the meal and the restaurant door had already closed on her back.

The business next to the restaurant had a barber pole outside, and shaking in anger and feeling ill, Louise impulsively ducked inside to hide in case he followed her. Neither the black barber cutting a black man's hair nor the three other black men waiting their turn were expecting to see her, nor was she expecting to see them.

"Uh," she began, "I'm hiding from someone, that is, there's a man I don't want to find me. Can I stay here for a bit? I promise I won't cause any trouble." She put her camera bag down and bent over. "Sorry, I'm just a little light-headed."

After a moment the barber said, "Lawd, Miss, you just sit on down back here and we'll keep you hid."

He took her arm and led her to a wooden chair at the back of the room where Louise sat down grateful for his kindness. Looking around, she saw that the barber chair itself was leather and that the waiting men faced it, sitting on a long bench along one wall. In front of the bench was a table covered with magazines, newspapers and, surprisingly, a Bible. On the opposite wall behind the barber was a large mirror in front of which was a shelf holding clippers, scissors, brushes and combs. A razor strop hung near a pile of towels. Everything was clean and tidy, even the wall-hung posters. "Please go on with your conversation," Louise said. "Don't let me stop you."

"Well, Perlie, here, was just tellin' us that his boy Titus got his papers and is headed to Camp Lewis for trainin'."

"Titis ain't but a boy."

"That's what his mama says..." Before he could finish, the door opened, and another man came in.

Seeing Louise, he gave a start and the barber explained that she was hiding from someone.

"He wanted me to go to a hotel with him," she said, and the men shook their heads and made sympathetic noises.

The barber spread lather on his clients face and sharpened a razor. "Now I'm commencin' to start shaving so you hold yourself still and, y'all on the bench, scoot on over and make room for Willie," he said. "His skinny b— er, self won't take up much room."

The conversation slowly resumed, focusing on war news, jobs for black men on the waterfront, the loggers strike, and other items of general interest giving Louise time to relax and begin enjoying herself. The barber finished and his client paid and left, and another took his place. With a sigh, she reluctantly stood.

"This has been so very kind of you all." She picked up her camera and then said, "I'm a photographer. Would you like me to take your picture? I'll develop it myself and mail it to you."

For the next few minutes, the men jostled around trying to find the best place and pushing and shoving hoping to be in front. When they finally came to an agreement, Louise took several photos from slightly different angles.

"I work at the Aldrich Studio downtown," she said. "I'll develop them there and you should have it in a couple days."

"That'll surely be somethin' to look forward to," the barber said. "Now, why don't you just go out the back door so's that fellow won't see you."

Thanking them all again, Louise took her leave, and it wasn't until she was halfway home that she realized she didn't know the barber's name or the shop's address. *I'll have to get Uncle Ike to help me*, she thought.

Reflecting on the day and particularly on Matthew brought tears to her eyes. *I've enjoyed every kiss and caress we shared,* she remembered, *and I might have gone with him if either of us had protection. But he just talked too much—about the Jewish people, about trying to get out of going to war, and especially what he had to say about Nell. Gosh, he wasn't like that when we first met. At least, I don't think he was. Maybe we just haven't spent enough time together.*

Using alleys and vacant lots where possible, she made it home without Matthew finding her. Queenie was ecstatic to no longer be left with Annie and Princess, and Louise hooked up her leash. After making sure the coast was clear, they walked across the street to the alley behind Hildy's house. Louise liked alleys. "I like looking in backyards," she told Nell and Annie. "That's where you can see how people really live. A messy backyard is like wearing a clean dress with a dirty corset cover." Nell laughed and confessed that both she and Hildy used to eavesdrop on adult conversations when they were young. "That's where we heard the best gossip," she said.

Now, ambling along, pausing frequently for Queenie to investigate overgrown foliage, Louise saw lines of laundry and vegetable gardens, swings tied to tree limbs and weedy grass crying out to be cut, children playing, and chickens running loose. "Why don't we have an alley?" she once asked John. "It's up to the developers," he told her. "When a developer buys a big piece of land and builds houses on it to sell, he can include an alley or not, it's his choice." She was thinking about that when Queenie decided cold green grass on a hot day was better than an alley's hot dirt under her feet, and they cut through Reuben's yard and crossed the street to home.

"Did you have a nice day?" asked Nell who was sitting in the kitchen with her feet in a basin of cold water.

"Um—not so much." Louise sighed and began rooting through her needlework bag. "I seemed to have done a lot of knitting since I got home from Neah Bay."

Nell took one foot out of the water and began drying it. "I just don't find it very relaxing."

"I do," said Annie, who was busy adding chopped onion to various other items in a large pie pan.

"What are you making?"

"Saturday Pie."

"What's that?"

"A way to use up left overs."

Nell laughed and started drying the other foot.

"The *Times*," Annie added, "thinks we should be using corn meal for a crust. But, honestly, we gotta draw the line sometimes and somewheres."

Louise laughed, hoping Nell would have forgotten her question, but to no avail. "Did you and Matthew have a fight?"

"No." Louise got up and went to the stove. "Coffee anyone?" The others declined and Louise added cream to hers and sat down.

"You sure drink a lot of coffee," Annie said. She put a crust over the Saturday Pie, vented it, and put it in the oven.

"It relaxes me." Looking pensive, Louise said, "He may come from money but today he was sorely lacking in breeding."

"Oh, dear."

"Do you remember Mr. Nordi?"

"The tailor?"

"Yes." Louise took a healthy swallow of her coffee. "He's Jewish. Did you know that?"

"I suppose I did but I never thought about it."

"Well, right in front of him Matthew said the reason people don't like Jews is because they killed Jesus." Annie gasped and Nell looked shocked. "Then he told me about a letter he's writing to the draft board to get out of enlisting. But that's not all, he wanted me to go to a hotel with him but was shocked that I knew about how to prevent getting caught and made a remark that if you'd 'a known, you wouldn't 'a had to go to San Francisco." Louise put her cup down and started to cry.

Annie made a choaking noise and Nell's eyes filled with tears. She put her hands on Louise's and after a minute, handed her a handkerchief. "I'm so, so sorry you had to hear that." She sighed. "I imagine he picked that up from his uncle. Dr. Altamont certainly spread around a rumor about it. Way back when, I heard his wife and Mrs. Baker whispering about me. They came into the shop saying they wanted to see what I'd brought back from my trip but I think they just wanted to see a fallen woman."

"Well, that explains why Mrs. Baker gave me short shrift at the Women's Camouflage meeting." Louise wiped her eyes and blew her nose. "Goodness, that seems a long time ago."

Nell sat back and tipped her head slightly. "May I ask you something?"

"Of course."

"When you returned from Neah Bay, your feelings seemed to have waned."

Though not a question, it nonetheless required a response. Heaving a gusty breath Louise said, "Maybe. I guess. I don't know. If he hadn't been such a beast today, I'd 'a probably just gone along as I have been."

Annie got up to check the Saturday Pie, and Ike came in the door while Nell was wiggling her toes and putting on her slippers. "You certainly know when we're about to eat," she said.

"Too many females at the house." He straddled a chair, and Annie took a fourth plate from the cupboard.

"Uncle Ike, do you know about the barber shop on K. Street?"

"I know Connex Brown who runs it, but I never been there." He turned his chair around and scooted closer to the table. "Gosh all hemlock, that smells particularly fine."

"I used some Point Defiance potatoes," Annie said.

"Potatoes is potatoes," Ike said. "Can't see hows being called Point Defiance makes any difference."

"Can you please take me there in a couple days so I can deliver some photographs? Princess, get off the table." Louise lifted the cat down.

"Where? Point Defiance?" Ike looked with pleasure at the generous helping Annie gave him.

"You tell me if you don't think these potatoes are special," Annie said.

"No, the barber shop."

"Seems a strange place to deliver pictures."

"She's doing it as a favor to me," Nell said, adding, "Annie, this looks wonderful."

When Ike was visiting, a conversation full of *non sequiturs* was often the norm. Looking suspicious, he raised an eyebrow and scowled, but otherwise kept silent on the matter, preferring to eat and knowing that sooner or later he'd find out what was going on.

And sure enough, late in the afternoon, three days after the Saturday Pie dinner, he found a parking place right in front of the barbershop and pulled his car in on the wrong side of the street, facing the wrong direction. A man behind him honked and Louise pointed out that he must have wanted the spot. However, Ike ignored that, and the fact of his incorrect parking. "He's gotta slow down and let happiness catch up," Ike said, "It don't pay to worry about the little stuff."

"You can wait here," Louise said, picking up an envelope and getting out of the car. "I won't be but a minute."

"Not on your tintype, niece. I know you been up to somethin'"

Louise sighed and opened the shop door. Taking advantage of a lull in business, Connex Brown was sitting in his barber chair reading the paper. Louise managed to put a finger to her lips before her uncle followed her in, hoping the barber would stay mum on her previous visit. "Con Brown," Ike said, "How the h— heck are ya?"

"Well, saints alive, Isaac Tanquist." Connex got off the chair and moved to shake hands. "I'm doin' alright. How 'bout you?"

"Can't complain, Con, can't complain. We ain't stoppin'. I just drove my niece, here, up so's she could deliver some pictures my sister said she's owin' you."

Connex saw Louise's intense stare and said, "And you drove in that old getabout o' yours? I don't know as how it made it up all the hills. Why it's bringin' shame to the street."

Relieved and laughing, Louise removed five photographs from her envelope and spread them out on the table. "One for each of you."

"My, my." Connex pulled a pair of glasses out of his pocket.

"You weren't wearing glasses when I was here before," Louise said.

"Men started complainin' about the quality of their cuts, so I had to do something." He looked carefully at each picture. "You didn't have to do that, but they'll be mighty pleased."

"Louise, here's a fine photographer," Ike said. The two men looked over the pictures, pointing out things that caught their attention, and made inconsequential chitchat until a client came in. "Con," Ike said, "Take care now."

"Ain't doin' nothin' but tryin', and you too, now."

Out on the street Louise said, "Come on Uncle Isaac, I'll treat you to an ice cream cone."

"None of that tryin' to put on how's you're innocent, Missy," Ike said. "There's something' you're not tellin' me but I'll get to the bottom of it. I generally do."

Chapter 14

Over the next few days Matthew called the house several times, stopped by once, and even visited the studio. However, seeing him through the window, Louise told her boss to say she was out working, and ducked into the darkroom. Queenie's presence might have given her away if Matthew'd thought to look for her. However, as August's dog days crept slowly by, he gradually stopped trying to make contact with her and Louise found plenty to keep her busy. The Carstens Plant fire, the prohibition trial of Roy Magill, the Northwest Federation of Indians attempt to have Mount Rainier's name changed back to Mount Tacoma, and the haphazard new public market set up on the Market Street curbs between 11th and 13th. There was the arrest of nine members of a Chinese secret society known as the Hop Sing Tong, and the unexpected appearance of a mountain beaver in vegetable gardens on G Street. The Annex Saloon announced it would be selling Lo-ju, a fruit juice made from Loganberries that the Olympia Brewery was manufacturing, and also a beverage called the Chocolate Soldier that the Columbia Bottling Company was making. There were so many weddings, Duenwald's on Broadway began baking wedding cakes to order. However, the event that interested Louise the most was the graduation of eight students at the Cushman Indian School.

"We've been invited to a picnic," Nell said one Friday when Louise got home from work.

"When and where? It's awfully hot for a picnic." Louise hung up her hat and stepped out of her shoes.

She picked up one of the fans Annie had purchased at a small Japanese-run store and applied it vigorously to the back of her neck. "Did I remember to thank you for buying these?"

"Several times," said Annie.

Since the kitchen was on the east side of the house, it was cooler in the afternoon and evenings than rooms on the west side, but only if Annie wasn't cooking. Louise plopped down on one chair and propped her feet on another. "I don't smell anything cooking," she said. "I don't suppose you thought to make another Saturday Pie. We could eat it cold."

"Even if I had, your uncle would hear about it some way," Annie said. "You'd think his wife didn't feed him. As to dinner, I made soybean and rice croquettes this morning. All I have to do is reheat them."

Louise leaned her head back and stared at the ceiling. "You know, Annie, while Nell and I are at work, you have to slave away over a hot stove all day long. Have I ever told you how much I appreciate it?"

"Here, here," said Nell. "You are a wonder in the kitchen."

Annie's knitting needles clicked as she added another row to her sock, but she looked up long enough to give them a gratified smile. "What food do you want me to cook for the picnic?"

"Oh, yes." Nell picked a sheet of paper. "Eight students are graduating from the Cushman Indian School and Mary and Piney are related to one of them. Since the government has put the kibosh on potlatches, there's going to be a picnic to celebrate."

"What business does the government have in telling the Indians they can't have a potlatch?" Louise began stroking Princess who'd jumped on her lap.

"As I understand it, the powers-that-be think it's wasteful because of the gift-giving."

"How is that wasteful? Are birthday gifts wasteful? And what about Christmas presents?"

"Ask the Bureau of Indian Affairs, I guess. Anyway, it's the day after tomorrow on the reservation and I haven't the faintest idea what food to take. Knowing the Puyallups, there will be clams, fish, berries, and oolichan, probably other stuff, too."

Louise sighed. "More fish. But eating something called oolichan, that sounds awful."

Nell laughed. "It is. I had it once. It's something the natives make from candlefish. Annie, do we have enough stuff to make a batch or three of cornbread."

"Cornmeal is one thing we have plenty of."

"I'd like to take a gift of some sort," Louise said. "I can take a photograph and would a jar of honey butter from Hildy's bakery be okay, do you think?"

"They would like that, probably more than the book I'm giving."

The Puyallup Reservation was near to Tacoma's east side. And though it was located on Commencement Bay, the Puyallup River was more important to the natives. Two days later, when John drove the two of them past the river, Louise saw men clearing away debris. "It was put there to protect the Lincoln Avenue bridge," John said, "but the water started backing up causing flooding."

They passed the river and drove up hill to where Louise got her first clear view: small farms that consisted of wood-framed houses, fenced in chicken yards, vegetable gardens, and a few dairy cattle tethered to whatever was handy. In some ways it was like the Makah Reservation. Only here, railroad lines and dirt roads helped create a patchwork-looking landscape. In the distance she saw the skeletal remains of a longhouse and for a brief moment memories of Peter taking her to one at Neah Bay tugged on her heart.

"I think that must be the Cushman School," Nell said pointing to a long, two-story building where a few people sat on the steps of its covered porch. "John, would you stop the car, please, so I can ask where Piney and Mary live."

Then, armed with instructions, they made a right turn and an immediate left, stopping at a house where the whitewash was mostly gone, and where a crowd of people outside milled around. "I'll pick you up in an hour or so," John said.

Louise opened her car door and welcomed the slightly breezy, briny-smelling fresh air. Nell was right behind her, and they made their way through the surprised-looking group.

"I think we're the only white people here," Louise whispered.

Nell knocked at the opened door and called a cheery, "Woo-hoo, Piney? Mary?"

Both ladies appeared, Mary stooped and wrinkled; a far cry from the day she'd helped rescue Nell from a riding accident and taken her to a potlatch, and Piney, just as she'd looked at the Better Babies Contest. *Which seems like so long ago,* Louise thought. Looking around the room, she saw a number of bright cloth wall hangings, several shelves of woven baskets, and miniature totem poles painted and adorned with feathers. One shelf held a carving that resembled a whale complete with eyes, a mouth, and covered with striations. It had both pectoral and dorsal fins and, looking closer, Louise saw three human faces on the back side. *How peculiar,* she thought. A corner table held what she later learned was a *wapaas* basket acquired in trade from the Yakima Nation. She saw beargrass earrings and cedar ornaments and arrowheads made from bone and shells, horns and antlers, metal and precious stones.

"My goodness, you have such wonderful things," she said. "Everything is just asking to be photographed." Both Piney and Mary beamed, proud of their heritage and of her approval.

Meanwhile, Nell relinquished the tray of Annie's cornbread. "Who's the graduate? When someone pushed forward a rosy-cheeked young woman wearing an apron over a red, hand-woven skirt, a yellow shirt and with yellow ribbons on the end of her braids, she said, "Well, congratulations. This is for you."

"And also, this." Louise said. They each handed over their gifts. "And our friend Annie sent the cornbread and I'm going to take your photograph."

"This is Ramona," Piney said, taking the cornbread and handing the tray to a woman behind her. "She's going to college this fall and learn to be a nurse."

"That is wonderful," Nell said.

And Louise chimed in. "I was in the hospital a while back and I know how important nurses are. They certainly took good care of me." For a minute she had a vague recollection of a Makah woman named Ramona and wondered if it was common among the tribes. She looked around. "Where do you think would be a good place to stand for a photograph?"

Ramona chose a place on the porch, and Louise had just enough time to snap some pictures before one of the boys, who'd been hanging around the kitchen, called that the soup was on. Men appeared seemingly from thin air, and people crowded a trestle table covered with food. As expected, seafood predominated: salmon, cod, clams, and abalone, but also duck, pheasant and quail. There was white fish soup, several plates of fresh vegetables, bowls of berries and the aforementioned oolichan. Louise filled her plate with sliced carrots and tomatoes, some of the baked salmon and pheasant and a piece of cornbread. She hid a grin when hearing Mary urging Nell to try the oolichan. People sat wherever they could, on the porch or the steps, on logs and tree stumps and, when necessary, on the ground. Looking around, Louise spotted a bulging tree root near Cushman Creek which ran down the property's edge and managed to beat a boy to it. The food, particularly the pheasant, was good and, after a while, she heard someone playing a drum. Soon other drummers joined in, followed by people blowing whistles and hand-made flutes. She was enjoying the music and was just about to return her empty plate to the house when she heard someone say, "Would you like me to take that?"

"Thank you." Thinking the voice sounded familiar, Louise stood and turned around to see shining varicolored hair, a dimpled cheek, and green eyes. "Peter Hay! For goodness sakes."

At the same time Peter said, "Louise Tanquist. I don't believe it. I never expected to see you here."

They stood staring at each other for a minute and then simultaneously burst out laughing. "Let me take your plate in. Save a spot for me on the root and I'll be right back."

Smiling and shaking her head, Louise sat back down. *I'd forgotten how handsome he is, and how strong he looks* she thought watching him make his way across the yard. *And he even looks good from behind.* She remembered him lifting her off the log when she'd been sick and taking her hand and their running to get out of the rain, and his taking her to wherever she wanted to go for photographs, and the bearskin from an animal he'd shot that had kept her so warm in the drafty house. And she felt her pulse quicken when she remembered the deerskin gloves and the intimate and strangely poetic note accompanying them.

When Peter returned, followed by a small boy with a cup of coffee, he carried two pieces of cake and handed her one. "The coffee is for the lady," he told the boy. "If I remember correctly, it's a particular favorite with her." Steam rose from the beverage and she smiled in appreciation. "Move over woman," Peter added with a grin. "This root is barely big enough for the two of us."

Louise shifted and he sat down so close their thighs touched. She felt his arm rub hers every time he shifted, and the warmth of him, welcome even on an August day. To distract herself, she said, "How long have you

264

been here, in Tacoma? On the reservation? And what are you doing here? And why didn't you get in touch?"

"How long? About three days. What am I doing here? It's complicated. Willie Daw and I came to enlist."

"Why? Why would you do that?"

"To get away for a while. See other places; learn how other people live."

Louise took a deep breath. Around them, the air was growing warmer, and the nearby woods earthy smell was fading, replaced by the familiar, somewhat pungent odor of salt and seaweed from a retreating tide. Distant vine maples were already mostly red and from everywhere came nature's noises: things rustling in fallen leaves, the wing-sounds of darting birds, the creek's race to the bay.

"Will you be at Camp Lewis?"

"I failed the physical, so no, the army doesn't want me."

"How could you possibly fail a physical? You're..."

Peter sighed and dry-scrubbed his face. "When I was a kid, I punctured an eardrum and hearing in that ear is bad, so the army has deemed me unfit to serve."

"Will you be going back home then? I hope not." Louise felt her face turning red.

"The Red Cross is training men to be ambulance drivers, and I was accepted."

"I didn't know you could drive."

Peter laughed. "I can now, and I know way more about motor oil than I thought possible. The first aid wasn't an issue, but engine work is a challenge." He looked at her and half-smiled. "You know what Shakespeare said: 'Cry "Havoc!" and let slip the dogs of war.'"

"Well, I think it's horrible. People will die and I hate it. And you didn't even call."

Louise burst into tears and Peter put his arm around her. "Then, let's not talk about it. Let's talk about other things. Tell me what you've been photographing."

Hearing about the photo-essay book, he made suggestions and offered to help with the essay portion. "I am an English teacher," he said.

"I didn't know that. I think Dr. Clarke said something about your being out of school for the summer."

"And about Dr. Clarke, did you know she is still at the reservation? The *Retriever* is repaired and ready to sail but some of the men aren't."

"It was good of her to stay."

Peter reached for her cup of coffee and took a sip. "It wasn't just the men who needed her. Martha lost her baby."

Without thinking, Louise put her hand on Peter's. "Oh, no. She was so excited. I am sorry."

He turned his head and gently wiped where some tears lingered. "She was so pleased to get the blanket you sent. And they'll keep trying."

"And the book and photograph you asked for?"

"I sent you a note. It was a nice gesture, thank you."

A very stiff and proper note, Louise thought.

Around them, bees came to feed on salmon berries; a dragonfly paused in mid-air before darting away. In front of them, food-scavenging crows scouted the ground; from the bay came the calls of gulls. *Gesture?* Louise had a sudden urge to find Nell and hope John would be arriving soon.

"And your lady friend," she asked. "Is she back? Will you marry before you're sent to Europe?"

"She's back but she's no longer my lady friend. She's found someone she likes better."

"Well, more fool her. Gosh, there's so much bad news, isn't there? But I am sorry."

"I'm not. I found someone I like much better, too." He took her hand and intertwined their fingers. "And how about you? I thought it better not to get in touch with you because you definitely had someone else in mind when I kissed you."

"When we kissed each other, you mean? Well, let's just say he's no longer part of my life, either."

"I'm sorry."

And Louise leaned in to kiss him. "I'm not," she said. "I also found someone I like much better."

The End

Karla Stover books published by BWL Publishing Inc.

A Line to Murder
Murder, When One is Not Enough
Wynter's Way
Parlor Girls

Karla Stover graduated from the University of Washington in 1995 with honors in history. She has been writing for more than twenty years. Locally, her credits include the *Tacoma News Tribune*, the *Tacoma Weekly*, the *Tacoma Reporter*, and the *Puget Sound Business Journal*. Nationally, she has published in *Ruralite, Chronicle of the Old West*, and *Birds and Blooms*. Internationally, she was a regular contributor to the *European Crown* and the *Imperial Russian Journal*. In addition, she writes a monthly magazine 'The Weekender" for *Country Pleasures*. In 2008, she won the Chistell Prize for a short story entitled "One Day at Appomattox." Weekly she is the host of "Local History With Karla Stover" on KLAY AM 1180, and she is the advertising voice for three local businesses. Her book, *Let's Go Walk About in Tacoma* came out in August 2009 and *Hidden History of Tacoma: Little Known Stories From the City of Destiny,* in March 2012. Catch her at karlastover.blogspot.com